A KILLING SIN

First published in Great Britain in 2019
by Urbane Publications Ltd
Suite 3, Brown Europe House, 33/34 Gleaming Wood Drive,
Chatham, Kent ME5 8RZ

A CIP catalogue record for this book is available from the British Library.

ISBN 978-1-912666-44-7
MOBI 978-1-912666-45-4

Design and Typeset by Michelle Morgan

Cover by Dominic Forbes

Printed and bound by 4edge Limited, UK

URBANE

urbanepublications.com

A KILLING SIN

K.H. IRVINE

urbanepublications.com

For David, Kathryn and Martha.
The whole squad. My whole life.
And
For Jean and Deric for everything.

'Lord, thy most pointed pleasure take
And stab my spirit broad awake.
Or, Lord, if too obdurate I,
Choose thou, before that spirit die
A piercing pain, a killing sin
And to my dead heart run them in'

Celestial Surgeon,
Robert Louis Stevenson

TODAY

Tuesday 25th May 17.24

I guess we never know what our last thought will be before we die.

I am going to die in this room. Today. A room full of terror. A room full of the stench of my blood. And worse. The smell of my burnt flesh.

They have taken everything.

But they have not taken my last thought.

I will not give them my last thought.

I close my eyes and will myself to remember a day. An ordinary day. A June day. There is cherry blossom lining The Meadows in Edinburgh. Their scent not quite enough to mask the smell of the brewery carried on the chilly wind. Chilly even in June. I picture it. Arthurs Seat and Salisbury Crag outlined against a watery sun. Standing bold and resolute for thousands of years. The university emptying of students, pouring out as finals are finally over.

The three of us together. We have a picnic of stale pizza and cheap cider. It's perfect. We have a Frisbee. I throw it to Millie. She misses. She always misses. I smile at the thought. The last thought.

I pull the burqa tighter. I can hear the jack boots. They are coming back.

Coming for me.

Tuesday 25th May 17.25

NUSAYABAH

Everything has gone to plan.
Perfect in every way.
I flick through the screens.
The clock is counting down.
Less than 35 minutes.
Meticulous planning and patience.
About to pay off.

10 DAYS BEFORE

Saturday 15h May

The Comedy Café

ELLA

The Comedy Café open mic is a bear pit. The standard is high and the punters unforgiving. I feel the adrenalin surge in my veins as the MC shouts her name.

'Amala Hackeem!'

I give Neil's hand a quick squeeze. Millie and I lock eyes. I can feel her take a breath. Part excitement and part trepidation. Amala loves it. She runs on stage, talking at the same time. Punching out jokes like a volley of Amir Khan jabs. Jab. Jab. Jab.

I hear her opening line. She's used it before and it still makes me cringe. I can't help it. I worry for her.

'I know what you are thinking. You are looking at me and thinking, she can't be a real Muslim. She's not dressed like one.'

The crowd shift in their seats. Ready to laugh but not sure yet, feeling the underlying air of anxiety in the room. Less certain of what's ok.

With a flourish that makes my heart pound, she finishes, 'She doesn't look like a bottle of Guinness.'

They laugh. They're on her side. Thank God.

In the bar afterwards, she's buzzing. She doesn't even see him coming. Neither do I. Not until I see his spit land on her face. He looks like a man possessed. 'Who do you think you are, you infidel? You think you're so special. You drag good Muslim women into your gutter.'

His mouth is twisted into a vicious sneer, his yellow teeth bared and his eyes full of hate and contempt.

'Someone is going to wipe that stupid smile off your face. One day a husband will show you what it is to be a good Muslim wife.'

In that instant I know she won't resist it. She never can. And she doesn't.

'Don't worry, mate, I don't fit the bill to be a good Muslim wife.' She lifts her chin, and with a grin that's recognised the world over, she delivers the line.

'I talk.'

I feel it before I see it. The air as he pulls back his arm to maximise the impact. Rage turns his face puce. His fist crashes into her eye before she has time to move from the full force of the blow. Before any of us can move. Stunned, she falls back. Scrambling to stay upright but failing. I rush to grab her as she falls. In my peripheral vision, I see Millie, quick as a whip, grab his hair and smash his face into the bar.

4 DAYS BEFORE

Friday 21st May 10.28

AMALA

Aafa's late. He's always late. I am waiting in the Timber Yard Coffee Shop in Seven Dials near Covent Garden. It's packed with students, shoppers and yummy mummies. The hum of conversation mixes with the swishing steam from the hipster baristas as they call the orders. 'Soya skinny latte with extra shot of turmeric.'

It is nearly 10.30 and we had agreed to meet at 10. I will be livid if he is caught up in some bloody experiment. I feel my face twitch. It throbs less than it did, but I am conscious of the surreptitious looks people are giving me, not meeting my gaze. I don't know if it's because they recognise me or they're trying to work out how I got such a shiner. I had called in a few favours and kept it out of the mainstream media, but it was still trending, picked up by the various self-styled paparazzi that had been in the bar. I put my hand to my face. It still feels tight.

I wiggle my jaw and stroke my cheek gently. Reliving last week makes my throat dry. I'm used to the abuse but there's never been violence before. That's new. I had laughed it off on Saturday night but ever since then his face keeps flashing before me.

That sneer. The viscous hatred in his eyes and the disgust in his voice. I shiver, despite the damp and cloying heat. Millie had slammed his face hard into the bar just as Neil had moved in to grab him. The guy had run off hurling threats of eternal damnation. I was more shaken than I dared admit. Neil and Millie were all for calling the police but I couldn't face the attention. I just wanted to go home. Alone. Tempted as I was by Ella who just wanted to take me home with her and Neil so she could wrap me up and force feed me hot chocolate.

I try to read the Rockeem Foundation Report on Teachers in Tents. Neil and I set up the Foundation after visiting Afghanistan. I was desperate to do something practical, not just stand up and be worthy. Our focus is giving free education to refugees. Something else we've been vilified for. I don't care what they say about immigrants and scroungers; it's making a difference. Although my heart sinks as I glance at the statistics. It's like a finger in a dyke. The more teachers we send to Syria, Lebanon and North Africa the more students desperate for an education and a better life seem to arrive. Ella had worked out in a camp in Lebanon teaching English for a bit last year. She came home wrung-out and exhausted.

God, I need to get a grip. I am tired and bad tempered. I've already had too much coffee and now I'm wired. Where the hell is Aafa?

The last week has drained me. Not just the guy at the Comedy Café but Neil and I are still cranky with each other. He's definitely too up close and cosy with the Home Office. He knows it and so do I. We need to push back. He thinks we need to build a stronger case around the misuse of Ezylocate first.

When Neil and I developed the Ezylocate software, it was for finding missing kids, then we adapted it for use by health services to respond to serious incidents. It captures biometric data and emits a GPS signal for tracking. But now it is the basis of ID cards. To pay for anything from a cup of coffee to a tube ticket, the GPS, and therefore the Ezylocate, has to be on. Being outside without an ID card is now an offence that carries a possible jail sentence. Sometimes I wonder if we have unleashed a monster.

I tut out loud. The people at the next table glance at me. I can't help it, I move my eyebrows up as if to say, 'Yeah, what?' They turn back to their macchiato and muesli.

Neil thinks we need to be careful about how we handle things with the government so they don't tie us up in legal knots. He has a point. It's also why he never lets me anywhere near the big clients, especially the ministers and mandarins. I am frustrated, though. We still keep saying we live in a democracy. We should be able to talk about the impact on civil liberties. Ezylocate was not meant to be like this. It was meant to be on the side of the good guys. Not meant to be used to pick up anyone who might be a bit suspect. It changed by stealth. This government played us. I know it and Neil knows it. We just need to agree what to do about it.

After a while I give up waiting and go to the counter to buy some water. The café is busy and there is a smell of damp clothes mingling with strong coffee. The weather has suddenly turned warm but it's wet and the street outside is shiny with drizzle. I hear a drum and turn to see four orange-robed Hare Krishna devotees chanting as they walk over the cobbles. They are oblivious to the rain and the school party running beside them. Kids no doubt heading to Covent Garden before a matinée on Shaftesbury Avenue. The forecast is for the weather to improve tomorrow but that is not helping my humour today.

The smell of muffins and pastries makes my mouth water. I give in and buy an enormous pain au chocolat. I will have to go to the gym tonight. I hate exercising by myself. I drop a quick message to Ella to see if she is up for our usual run across Hampstead Heath later. Oh for God's sake, come on Aafa.

Looking back out to Monmouth Street I see a figure stooped over with a backpack on his back. He is talking animatedly. I watch him pause as he listens to a response on the end of the call. It takes me a few seconds to realise it's Aafa. He ends the call as he pushes open the door.

I turn on him and hiss, 'Where the hell have you been? I've been here for like an hour.'

He runs his fingers through his hair, wet and sleek like a pelt from the rain.

'Look, can we sit in the corner and talk?'

One glance at him tells me something is wrong. I nod at the small wooden table tucked in the corner where I have left my coat on the chair beside my dripping brolly, not quite ready to forgive him.

Friday 21st May 10.40

ELLA

I am staring at the wall. It's covered with notes, all in different coloured paper. To the untrained eye, it's a mess. To me, it's a story. I have been working on this for months. It's starting to come together. It's a big story and now I just need to dot the 'I's' and cross the 'T's.'

I look back at the screen. The spine of the story is there and I sense that feeling in the pit of my stomach. The feeling I had dreamed of. The one when you know you're on to something. Something big.

I sip my ginger tea and start typing again. I have been at it for hours. My back and neck are cramped and I stretch out. I pull my ponytail tighter trying to stay focused. I look at my checklist. I call it my double checklist because every fact has already been checked once. I am adding all the secondary sources to the list.

I call Millie. She picks up on the first ring.

'Hey, how are you?'

I smile. I love her voice. She doesn't really like her Scottish accent, but I do. She sounds like my mum.

'Hey, Millie. Good, thanks. Any news?'

'Nah, still nothing. Grace has stopped asking so many questions about where her daddy is. I'm not sure if that's a good or a bad thing.'

I close my eyes. I picture Millie with her spiky hair and scarlet lipstick. Nothing like as tough as she looks, especially where Grace is concerned. I can hear the pain in her voice but I know she will have a lecture in fifteen minutes and won't want to get in to that now.

'Listen, hon, it'll be ok. He'll get in touch. I know he will. He just needs time to calm down.'

'Yeah, I know. But it's been four weeks and three days and feels way longer.' She blows out a long breath. She wants to move on too. Switching to practical and upbeat she says, 'Anyway, what are you up to?'

'Listen, I know you're busy so I'll be quick. I've just been pulling together some notes for a story. Do you know anyone at the university who knows anything about selling arms? Maybe the international trade guys?'

'Arms? What, like guns? Christ, Ells what kind of story are you working on? I thought you were doing the story about women and extremism?'

'I am. I've got two on the go. This is about a company that got a government contract to sell arms to ATF50.'

ATF50 is the multi-agency firearms unit set up, as part of the endless drive on counterterrorism. It was set up by the prime minister, Simon Thompson, after Brexit, but it's really the baby of the hard line home secretary, Jean Norton.

'Wow, big stuff. No, I don't off the top of my head but I'll have a think. Doesn't Neil know anyone? He's chummy enough with the government. Him and Thompson and that old boys' network that keeps clinging on by its fingertips.'

'Yeah, I've asked him. But Amala and him are really tetchy at the minute about anything to do with Thompson. She's really pissed at Neil for not going in harder with Thompson and Norton. Neil thinks they'll have more impact if they can show the data that proves they are using Ezylocate in breach of the terms of their contract. Amala wants to tell Thompson to shove it and revoke the licence. He says she's a liability. Last time they were both in the same room with Thompson, Amala called him a fascist in liberal clothing.'

I am only partly smiling. Amala, the queen of the one-liners, is bloody funny but it does get her in to trouble. I cover the smile, I don't want to get into a debate with Neil by sticking up for her again.

'Millie, I have to go. I've got a bit more digging around to do. Let me know if you come up with anyone. I'll see you Sunday. Hey, and try not to worry about Mark. He does love you, you know.'

I don't say it but I think it; maybe he just doesn't like you very much right now.

Friday 21st May 10.45
AMALA

My stomach is churning with all the coffee I had earlier, my ongoing anxiety from the last week and now the look on Aafa's face.

'Do you want anything?' I ask.

'Double espresso,' he says, shrugging off the backpack and heading to the table. I order, eying the banana bread that is Aafa's favourite. I know he would want some. My brother is constantly hungry but I don't feel like getting him any. He knows how much I hate sitting around waiting. He can get his own bloody banana bread.

I sit down and push the steaming cup to him.

'What's up?'

Aafa leans in. He looks tired.

'What's happened?' I ask again. This time more gently.

'I was picked up again, last night on my way home. That's eight times in less than a month. Eight times in the PPCs.'

I sigh. I know how much Aafa resents the PPCs. The Prevent and Protect Centres were set up at the same time as ATF50. Thompson had wanted to prove his hard-line credentials in 'dealing with immigrants and the threat they pose to our national security'. The PPCs had 'special holding and exploration suites', specifically used to hold 'persons of interest for questioning based on reasonable intelligence gathering'. In reality, they are interrogation centres run by the police and manned by ex-squaddies, with the power to stop, search and question those so called 'persons of interest'. Or in other words, every non-white, backpack-carrying young guy with a beard. They are rarely out of the press. And there is no sign of the debate going away any time soon. Far from it.

'Every time they pick me up it's the same. Am I involved in something radical? What do I know about the sharia community in Tower Hamlets? What about the Education Centre? I tell them it is a study group but they won't listen. They keep asking about you and if you give me money. Am I using your money to fund extremism? It's driving me mad.'

My heart sinks. I love my little brother. He is a good person. He didn't ask to be pulled into my public orbit. I know he's not comfortable with some of the things I say and do, especially the partying and the stuff the paparazzi love to show – usually me falling out of clubs. I hate seeing him upset and I hate the fact he's getting picked on. He's an easy target and we both know it.

Aafa hasn't finished.

'They take you into a room and they ask all sorts of questions trying to catch you out. Whether you drink alcohol or watch Hollywood films, which mosque you go to, what you think about this or that so-called atrocity, is Britain right to ally itself with the US, who am I voting for. It goes on and on. I tell them I'm just a student but they're following me to Friday prayers now.'

I know he's telling the truth. He's not wired to do anything else. He's just confirming everything Millie's been saying for years. My guts are churning. I need to check, though. Something's been bugging me for a while. Something about Aafa is different. Is it just that he's been unlucky or is there something more?

'Aafa, is there anything I should know?' I try to catch his eye. 'We hardly see you these days and you seem to be spending a lot of time at the mosque and the Education Centre.' I play my trump card, knowing how close he is to our parents and how he hates to upset them. 'Mum and Dad are worried too. Dad says you're no longer going to Friday prayers with him.' I look right into his eyes and say quietly, 'We're all worried.'

Aafa looks annoyed. 'Listen, Mals, I'm not involved in anything bad and I'm not a kid anymore. Where I pray and where I spend my time is up to me. You think the issue is that I spend too much time praying. You don't think it's a bit rich that you ask me that, but you don't ask about the bastards picking me up day in and day out. I like the Education Centre. The clue is in the title. It's about education. Educating people that Islam is a peaceful religion. I am trying to spread that message but no one is listening.' He swallows. 'Not even you.'

He is leaning across the table. Talking in a loud whisper. His indignation clear with every word.

'I don't have a record. I don't go around threatening people. I don't even go around shouting my mouth off, but the PPC guys are nothing short of racist, bully-boy vigilantes. Did you see the poor guy that died of an asthma attack last month? *Allegedly* of an asthma attack. If he had been white would it have been shoved under the carpet in quite the same way? I don't think so. Did you see the headline today?'

I shake my head.

'Beautiful seventeen-year-old girl destined for Oxford radicalised on line. I wonder if they would be quite so interested if she was an ugly hairdresser with parents on the dole or, God forbid, a nice Asian girl.'

He's right. The papers are full of it. Nice white girls are the big target.

I have real sympathy for him. He isn't the only one asking difficult questions. I am guessing that Millie would have seen the headline today and said exactly the same thing. Many of the ex-military running the PPCs have been chosen for their strong work ethic, commitment and unquestioning discipline, but a significant number of them have lost good mates in Iraq, Syria, Afghanistan and Somalia. I had seen what they had seen first-hand. It isn't simple. The enemy isn't so easy to spot. Right and wrong, black and white, good and bad are lost in a quagmire of history, politics, money and big decisions that are often based on power and expediency, rather than principle. The squaddies are sometimes ruthless, particularly around those they suspect of being involved in any extremist activity, and it is easy to understand why. They are in a no-win situation. Damned when they pick someone up just because they are brown with a beard, and damned when they don't and some monstrous act is committed by a brown person with a beard.

Aafa rubs a hand across his face, stroking his newly acquired beard back and forth. His eyes are shining and his hands are trembling. He moves to pick up his espresso then changes his mind. I go to take his hand.

He looks up, does a double take, and stares at me.

He leans across the table and in a fierce whisper asks, 'Mals, what the hell happened to your eye?'

I realise I had had my hair and hand over the bruise.

As casually as I can, I say, 'Oh, some big gob wanker threw a punch at the Comedy Café on Saturday night.' I smile. 'You should see the other guy. Millie banged his head on the bar.' Aafa doesn't smile back. I pull my hair back down. 'It's no big deal. He was just a nutter.'

I am not sure how convincing I sound. My voice catches and I gulp down some water. I feel acid rise to my throat and I swallow hard.

He grabs my hand again and gives it a squeeze. 'Amala, you know you really do need to watch out. Those comedy routines of yours – they're getting more and more outrageous. Honest to God, you think you can get away with it because you're rich and your friends are important, but you know what? That might not be enough. You have to be careful. I am not pissing about. There are mad people out there who want to do you harm. All these fatwas. It's serious stuff. You make this big point about not wearing the veil, your right to choose whatever partner you want, male or female. Have you any idea what most people think?'

I look down. I see my hands are shaking. I move them from the table and clasp them tight between my knees. I don't want to tell Aafa how much it has spooked me. I don't want to tell anyone. Not even myself.

Friday 21st May 10.50
ELLA

I click on the file. I scan the notes from the anonymous source. Whoever he is, he is well connected. This story is dynamite. I re-read the latest material and create a new sub-file with the title 'Citrussister'. I am buzzing. It's coming together and I know it's a good story. It has everything: intrigue, money, power, corruption and dirty secrets. A good story. Maybe a prizewinner?

I feel energised. This really feels like my time. I know I can write both these stories.

I look over at the collage Millie and Amala had made for me for my birthday last year. Headlines from articles I had written from student magazines, journals and some of the freelancing stories that had been picked up. Only a few had really had any impact. And here I am on the verge of breaking two huge stories.

I look at one from *The Teviot*, the Edinburgh student magazine. It was funny. I smile as I remember. I had written it as a protest letter, headed 'Bloody Lame-entable'. The idea was to have high heels classified as an instrument of torture. I had woven in part of a Wilfred Owen poem, 'I know many of you women out there have limped on blood shod, in future they will say it was a time we all went lame.'

Citrussister isn't funny though. It is deadly serious. I password protect it and close it down

Friday 21st May 10.52

AMALA

Aafa is still looking at me. 'Mals you have got to stop with this comedy stuff. At least for a while. Let things settle down for a bit. You know, I hate it when you keep shouting your mouth off. Making jokes about what it is to be Muslim. They're not funny, they're just offensive. You know this guy last week won't be the end of it. There will be other guys and next time it might not just be a fist. You're going to get seriously hurt.'

'Hey,' I say. 'Watch *your* mouth. I am not shouting my mouth off. I'm trying to be funny *and* maybe make people think a bit at the same time.' I glare at him. 'And by the way, hundreds, in fact thousands, of people come to my shows and *they* think I'm funny. They laugh and maybe, just maybe, they go away and think a bit more. Maybe they stop seeing the world as just the good guys and the bad guys.'

I'm on a roll. 'And maybe it's you who needs to stop and think. Do you ever really think about the Education Centre, or any of those so-called sharia communities, because what I see is a bunch of misogynist pricks turning them into some haven of seventh-century barbarism. I look at Tower Hamlets, and what I see is a place where women can't drive or go to school. For fuck's sake, they're wearing burqas that they can't even see through and they are getting forced into marriage to some asshole who thinks he's a jihadist. Maybe a little bit of harassment is a price worth paying if we're going to stop the spread of sharia. I've seen for myself what that does to people. Men and women.'

Aafa doesn't say anything. He knows how much I was affected by my time in Afghanistan and Syria, talking to women who had been raped at the hands of jihadists, then forced to live like a chattel.

I stare hard. I feel my anger rise and squash any fear for the moment. 'That's what comedy's for; to make people laugh *and* to make them think.'

He's twitching his knee in agitation, ready to jump in, but I don't give him the chance. I am fed up of everyone telling me to be quiet.

'You know this situation has been years in the making. Ten years back the political right just wanted to send people home or stop them coming in. They pointed the finger at Islam to say look at how badly they treat their women. Whilst the liberal left couldn't say anything for fear of being culturally insensitive. After Brexit, it just got worse. Then the xenophobia in the States just fanned the flames of racism even more. Those voters in the rust belt managed to corrode the rest of the country. Liberals were suddenly the enemy. Thompson was so focused on showing how he was controlling the borders and sucking up to the Americans to win trade deals, he missed what was right under his nose.

'We stopped looking at the rot that had already taken a grip here. We let those sharia communities take root, we let them set up schools and slowly but surely they've established their own cities within cities. They have a grip on everything. Schools can't talk about homosexuality or even sex at all. Women can't get a divorce. They go to the Sharia Council and say they are being beaten by their husbands and they are told to shut up and go back to them. You know, they're also practicing FGM in those communities? That's just another word for torture. Aafa, I know things aren't perfect. But if we can't tell people how completely hypocritical they are, then it never stops. Never.'

Aafa looks deeply uncomfortable. We have never spoken like this before. Normally we have a bit of banter, I buy him lunch and then slip him £20. He speaks carefully but forcefully. 'You are just picking on a few extremists. Violent extremists. Most people are practicing Islam as it should be, as it states in the Quran.'

'Aafa, there's nothing in the Quran that says you should mutilate a vagina. That's made-up, misogynist hatred. It's bollocks. It's barbaric. You know we got somewhere in the last decade. It was reducing and now it's back with a vengeance. You show me where it says in the Quran you should cut out a woman's clitoris and more. Not even women. Little girls. It's an affront to Islam and it is happening on our watch. Don't get me started on the fucking burqa. You know that's not in the Quran either. You're not the only one who's read it. It says both men and women should dress modestly. It says women should cover their bosom. It does not say wrap her in a fucking tent so she can't walk, she can't breathe, she can't eat or drink. She can't smell the roses and she can't fucking see.'

I sit back, drained. I realise I have raised my voice and people are looking over, clearly uncomfortable. I catch the eye of the man at the next table; I glare at him, and he looks hurriedly away. Typically English, appalled but not enough to make full eye contact or actually say anything.

'Come on, Aafa, you can't believe that stuff. Look at me, look at Mum and Farah and Leila. Do you really want us locked away so we can't speak or move? Can't even buy a pint of milk without an escort, never mind get a job.'

When I look up I can see Aafa's eyes dart all around. They are searingly bright and his pupils are like pin holes. I feel my heart thump as I look into his face for clues.

He leans further across the table so he is within inches of my face. 'You're a bad example. You don't even cover your hair. At least Farah has some modesty and acts like a good Muslim girl. But you, you are out every night in those filthy comedy clubs taking Allah's name in vain. You're a disgrace, Amala. You'll find yourself in trouble if you don't stop. Someone is going to take real offence and make an example of you. You better be warned.'

I am stunned. Aafa has never spoken to me like this before. He has never said anything like that to anyone before. There is something else too. I can smell it. Fear. He's scared. More than that. Terrified. Whether for me or himself, I can't tell.

'Amala, you are one of the richest women in the country. You are telling jokes that cause deep offence. You are funding programmes for girls that not everyone believes are right and you are always in the media. Your business partner is chief technology adviser to the prime minister, for God's sake. It doesn't get much bigger than that. I am not kidding. It's dangerous.'

'Well, I'll take my chances.'

'You are so stubborn. You are playing with fire and someone's going to get hurt.'

I am shocked to see tears in Aafa's eyes. I can't bear it. 'Hey, little bro, it's ok, I'm really not that big a deal. I think there are bigger fish.'

He starts to get his stuff together. Pulling on his backpack he gives me a quick, fierce hug. 'Look why don't you come to the Education Centre? I'm meeting a few people there on Tuesday. There's a women's study group. They would really like to talk to you and I would really like you to meet them.'

He sees my look of deep scepticism and says, 'Hey, don't. Don't look like that. Why don't you just give it a go? Meet me there. I can be there from about 9 or 9.30. They're not fanatics. They are serious people, concerned with the world. Good people trying to do the right thing. Just like you. I've talked to them about you and a lot of people want to meet you. They don't understand you, so why not give them a chance. Get to know them. Let them get to know you. You might even find you have something in common. It's a special session on Tuesday. Open to all women to foster understanding.'

I sigh. 'I'll think about it.' But I know I'll go. I never can resist Aafa. He knows it too. We both smile, albeit half-heartedly. I watch him walk away. Head bent, backpack slung over one shoulder. I feel a shiver. Why do I feel like someone has just walked over my grave?

Friday 21st May 11.15

ELLA

I close the last file and wander downstairs. I hear Neil talking. He has the phone on speaker and I hear Amala's voice.

'Listen, I've just seen Aafa and it's got me thinking about Ezylocate again. We really need to make a move. Aafa keeps getting picked up by the PPCs and he's pretty sure they're tracking him. And it's not just him. We've got enough ammunition to take it to the Home Office. We need it back on Thompson's agenda.'

When Neil and Amala invented Ezylocate a few years ago, it was their second big product and, like the first, had the same Midas touch. They are a good team. Neil has the cool, structured brain of an engineer and can schmooze the birds from the trees. But Amala is the real genius behind Rockeem. Her brain is original and unbounded by convention. Neil is always the first to admit he is not the innovator, Amala is. He lacks her pure imagination, vision and creativity. She's one of a kind.

Neil answers her. 'You know I talked to him a few weeks ago at the reunion dinner. He's pretty fired up at the minute. I think he reckons Norton's circling for his job, which usually means he feels the need to be the tough guy. I've been thinking about it, too. You're right, we do have enough evidence. Let's put our heads together next week. Work out the best plan of attack.'

A thought strikes me. 'Hey, Mals, it's me. The other option is to just bypass Thompson and talk to Norton. The Home Office owns civil liberties and she's always keen to grab the moral high ground from Thompson. She might be especially interested if it puts him on the back foot, and technically the PPCs sit with her.'

'Hey, Ells, you ok? Are you up for a run later? Yeah, good idea. What do you think, Neil?'

As usual she never waits for an answer.

She ploughs on. 'Yeah, underneath the frost, Norton's pretty good and she's less of a sound-bite master than Thompson. The whole sharia thing is really sinister too. It scares the hell out of me anyway.'

Neil and I exchange a smile. Amala on a mission is a force to reckon with. She'll have done the analysis by the weekend, ready to clobber everyone over the head with it.

'Ok, have a good day. See you later, Ells. Last one up the hill buys the beers.' She laughs and then says, 'Hey, by the way, I can't believe you're still going to those old Etonian dinners. For God's sake, Neil it must look like something out of Dickens.'

Neil snorts out a laugh and says, 'I have to go. Sure, I'm the token black guy. They love me. I give them edge. Makes them feel right on. Hey, and more than that, Mals, I was the guest speaker. Super trends in technology.'

'Edge? I hardly think so posh boy. See you Sunday.'

I put my arms around him and say, 'Come on, posh boy, what about some brunch?'

Pulling me close he mutters, 'I have got edge. I'm not posh. I am a man of the people!'

'Neil you went to MIT, which, by the way is one of the top universities in the world, and before that you went to Eton and Cambridge. You're hardly a man of the people.'

'Yeah, but look at me now messing with the Nofas.'

I give him a shove then snuggle in to his neck. He thinks he's hilarious. Twenty years ago, in our first year at Edinburgh, the film *Charlie's Angels Full Throttle*, had come out. I had been livid that in 2003 the Angels still needed Charlie. Millie, Amala and I had done a spoof version at Bedlam, the student theatre, for a bet. We called it NOFA: 'No One's Fucking Angels'. It had stuck. Ever since, we were known as the Nofas by all our mates. In our final year, we had all got a tiny tattoo of a naughty angel.

Friday 21st May 11.25

AMALA

Ella's right. Norton is a much more likely option. I look around the café, full of young people looking at various devices, reading, listening to music, and working. Oblivious to the turmoil in my head. I look at the pain au chocolat still on the plate. I have crumbled it, in my agitation talking to Aafa, and it looks totally unappetising. I realise my fingers are greasy from the pastry and also that I feel nauseous. I decide to walk around and try to get my thoughts in order. I shrug on my jacket and pull the hood up, pulling the corner over my eye.

I turn right on Monmouth Street and wander down towards the crossroads, not even glancing at the trendy boutiques on either side of me. The smells from Chinatown make my mouth water. I swallow and turn left onto Long Acre, towards the main part of Covent Garden. I wander through the market, barely seeing the stalls selling hats and jewellery, posters and ceramics. Armed police are patrolling, as they do in all major cities. A gloomy presence. An image of the Death Eaters in Harry Potter flicks across my consciousness. I stop to watch a street artist doing the usual monocycle juggling act. I wonder briefly how much less money they get now there is so little cash.

I don't know anyone that carries cash anymore. Embedding transactions into ID cards is one of the ways the government had eventually managed to make them a legal requirement for residency.

Aafa did have a point. Sometimes I wonder if we have made a serious mistake. Have we made things so much worse? Have we given what Aafa calls the bully-boy vigilantes the tools to do the job? I have jammed my Ezylocate so only individuals I have invited can track my location. Most people don't have that option.

Even Neil can't find me if I want to hide or bunk off. I can't help a little smile. It really seriously pisses him off that I can still run rings around him. Mr Big Technology Adviser!

Ella's right, we should get to Norton. And soon. With the government coming up for re-election in less than two years, it might just be the time to get civil liberties back on the agenda.

TODAY

Tuesday 25th May 06.30

MILLIE

I dunk the tea bag then add a tiny bit of milk until the colour is a deep terra cotta. Real builders' tea. Navvies' tea my gran used to call it. I take a satisfying slug and switch on the radio. A song finishes and the traffic report comes on. The usual chaos for a Tuesday morning.

'Good morning, London. If you are just waking up it's a bright morning and unseasonably warm, record highs for the time of year. We are looking at ten, five and one year ago. So, do you remember 25th May 2013? It was a big day for me. I saw the great Alistair Cook lead England out against the Kiwis at Headingly that day; a great year for English test cricket. Did a bit better than my team, Watford, who were beaten by Crystal Palace in May that year. Robbed by a penalty that stopped them moving up to the Premier League. Gutted. I cried like a baby. I'm not going to open that wound up anymore.

'It was also the day Romania made it in to the *Guinness Book of Records* for unfurling the biggest flag ever made. Bet you didn't remember that from ten years ago. The size of three football pitches apparently. Anyway, give us a call if you have your own special memories of May 2013, 2018 and 2022. And now, the traffic.'

I can't help it; my head goes straight to the murder of Lee Rigby in Woolwich in May 2013. Too many years steeped in extremist research means my head is a catalogue of hate and barbarism.

The cheery traffic reporter interrupts. 'If you are thinking of heading towards Heathrow or anywhere on the M4 near the M25 please allow extra time. Traffic already building there. Half-term holiday mayhem kicking in as usual. Tubes and trains are all running well so far on this bright Tuesday morning. Now to the news.'

I think, poor buggers, they'll be expecting the roads to be quiet for half term but it never is around Heathrow. I grab my tea and head upstairs to shower. Grace is sitting on my bed, sucking her thumb and staring intently at the giant pink rabbit hopping across the TV screen. At two years old she is utterly beautiful, still with some of her baby features, but already showing glimpses of the feisty, funny girl to come. She has my red hair with her father's big brown eyes and she looks good enough to eat.

'Hey, pumpkin, Mummy is just going to jump in the shower and then we'll get you some breakfast, ok?'

Grace nods solemnly, eyes never veering from the TV. Cuddling her own pink rabbit close.

By 7.10 I am washed, dressed and ready to go. I drop a quick message to Ella and Amala, 'Wish me luck. Big day!!'

Ella's comes back by return. 'Go for it, babe. Sorry about breakfast xx'

I send back a smiley face. A little guilty about how relieved I am to have skipped the inevitable 'big talk' over breakfast.

A few minutes later, Amala's message comes and makes me smile, 'Don't take any shit. Thompson's a dick!'

Grace holds up a bag with her crusts. 'For ducks, Mummy.'

'Mmm, does that mean no crusts for Grace?'

She nods, knowing enough to know I don't have time to insist on crusts. The nanny gives a quiet rueful smile, knowing full well that if Mark was here Grace would eat them up.

I grab my bag and run out, but not before four lots of, 'One more kiss, Mummy.'

I feel something a bit sticky by my right ear and reaching to touch it, I realise it's a blob of strawberry jam, deposited there by Grace in her enthusiastic kissing.

I smile as I give my fingers a lick and head to the Tube. It is a big day today. A meeting with the prime minister and home secretary. I hum the tune to the *Big Pink Friendly Rabbit*, swinging my bag as I walk.

Tuesday 25th May 08.10

AMALA

Moving when you are swathed in a tent with nothing but a mesh window to peer through is claustrophobic and hellish. I have trouble breathing as the cotton fills my mouth, making me feel panicked. I feel as if I am going to suffocate. The Tube is packed and I am crammed in with hundreds of other bodies as I hold on to the metal pole.

I can't drive to the East End because Tower Hamlets is a sharia-dominated community and, as a woman, I am not allowed. Also, it would likely attract abuse or worse and I want to be sure I am able to meet Aafa today, so I have to get there by Tube. I am frustrated by the heat and the fact it is so hard to move. Trust me to be doing this in the middle of a bloody heatwave. London in May and I'm sweltering. All this cloth makes me so hot. I can feel sweat under my arms and trickling down my back and legs.

I can hardly imagine what it must feel like to wear this every day.

The swaying of the Tube is hypnotic. I can still smell the cardamom from the Kulcha Shor on the burqa. I had pulled it from the back of the wardrobe this morning and was immediately engulfed by the smell of the Afghan streets folded within the harsh cotton. It had been a gift from a beautiful and tragic Afghani woman.

Her story had never left me. I had heard a hundred stories like hers but hers was the face that came to mind whenever I thought of Afghanistan.

Neil and I had met Leila along with her mother and daughter in their home, a few kilometres from the centre of Kabul. We were there to set up a teaching centre for girls as part of the Rockeem Foundation. They were, as is ever the case with Afghans, proud and welcoming and incredibly hospitable. We drank tea and ate Kulcha Shor, the traditional Afghan salty cookies. Leila was adept at lifting the tea pot and the cup using her left hand and the four fingers of her right. Leila had no right thumb. A soldier had cut it off when he saw her wearing nail varnish, and then the same soldier had shot her twelve-year-old brother when he tried to rescue her. It was truly heartbreaking. But more than that, it was just so wrong. It made me furious.

I pull the burqa closer and stare at my reflection in the window. Me, the big show off, now the invisible woman.

I can feel hostility all around me. In equal measure, I am frustrated by the imprisoning of this shroud and also intimidated by the hatred and prejudice it conjures. Eyes burning into me with animosity. People moving away from me, sometimes discreetly and sometimes with exaggerated deliberation. I feel, strangely, both conspicuous and invisible. I am nervous too. I am taking a risk going to Tower Hamlets alone. Aafa had offered to meet me but I said no. The two of us together might lead to even more malice and I didn't want to risk a scene.

Changing at Canning Town onto the Docklands Light Railway is an Olympian challenge. I can neither see to the left nor right, or even my own feet. As I stand on the platform a woman, holding the hand of a small boy, passes me and says, 'Bloody terrorist, go back to your own country.'

I sigh. I know my sister, Farah, faces this every day. She is kind, generous and peace-loving but only judged by what she wears. Judged by ignorant and ill-informed people who think they have the right to tar every law-abiding, peaceful Muslim with the same brush as a few violent extremists. I am now wishing I had worn my normal clothes and changed nearer Tower Hamlets but that was risky too. The SMT, the self-styled vigilantes calling themselves the Sharia Morality Team, circle the sharia communities and pounce on anyone not complying. I hadn't wanted to risk not being able to meet Aafa.

I had checked his Ezylocate before leaving home. I know he will be seriously pissed if he knows I am checking up. I have been checking on him all the time lately. I feel a bit ashamed but I figure the end justifies the means. I know he was at the Education Centre a lot over the weekend. I had even tracked some of the people he had been with. The Education Centre is attached to the mosque in the heart of the Tower Hamlets Sharia Community.

Leaving the DLR I walk the short distance to the checkpoint at the Mulberry Estate in Tower Hamlets. I feel weary already but I promised. And a promise is a promise.

I see it ahead. It is officially called the Welcome and Hospitality Centre but it is neither welcoming nor hospitable. With a quick flash of wicked glee, I vow to use that line in my next show.

Tuesday 25th May 09.04

AMALA

I pass my Ezylocate ID through the window of the Welcome and Hospitality Centre. It has my photograph on it but, as it's impossible to see me under the burqa, it's not much use. Resisting the temptation to be a smart arse, as a whole routine plays out in my head, I wait whilst the young man manning the desk runs a biometric scan.

'What is your business here in Tower Hamlets Centre today?'

I speak through the cloth, keeping my voice quiet and respectful. Not looking to cause a scene by being a woman alone.

'I am here to see my brother, Aafa Hackeem, he is at the Education Centre. I have some family news to share with him and I am due to meet some of his friends and be part of the Women's Group.'

The receptionist looks at me and then back at the information that has clearly come up on the screen.

'Are you Amala Hackeem?'

I lick my dry lips, 'Yes. I am.'

I was already feeling apprehensive and the hostility in his stare makes me even more anxious. He has my bag and my ID and I have no way of contacting anyone without it.

He says, 'This is a sharia community governed by the laws of Islam. You may only enter with your brother's permission. Wait here.'

After a few minutes, he returns. 'Your brother is busy but he will be here soon. You may wait in the women's section until he arrives. You can have your bag but we will hold your ID until you leave the community.' He drops my Ezylocate in a drawer. I can see it is a scrambler unit designed to bounce the signal and send out false locations. Meaning it would be impossible for anyone to find me.

I make my way into the women's waiting area. A small dingy room with several orange plastic chairs. I look in my bag for a bottle of water and realise I have left it on the Tube. I am exhausted and parched.

I sigh with relief when a woman comes into the waiting room and says, 'Your brother will be with you in just a minute. He asked me to provide you with some refreshment.' She hands me a bottle of water. It is icy cold. I can feel the condensation cool my hand. I lift it to my dry lips, holding the veil of the burqa out slightly so I can drink.

Still there is no sign of Aafa. I am becoming restless. I feel under scrutiny and my apprehension is turning into something stronger. Just then the door opens and three women dressed in black burqas come in. All three are armed with semi-automatic rifles.

'Get up,' barks the one in front, pointing the rifle at my head.

I stand. Then everything swims before my eyes and I begin to fall.

Tuesday 25th May 09.06

MILLIE

I try not to smirk. It's like a nervous tic. I bite down hard on my back teeth. Clenching my jaw to keep it at bay. I am nervous. I am facing Simon Thompson, the British prime minister, and the mood in the room is sombre. There are a few grey men in grey suits around the table but I am not introduced. Apart from Thompson and Norton there are six others. I don't know any of them but would lay money that, to a grey man, they are all civil servants.

Thompson is ready to start. He is a suave-looking guy with a thick head of hair, just tinged with steely silver, and piercing blue eyes. His old-fashioned charm and impeccable manners are not quite enough to mask the air of pomposity that, despite no end of PR and spin, he has not been able to shake off. He has aged in the years he has been PM. The tennis tan of his first election year seven years ago, now replaced with the tired pallor of too many late nights and not enough vitamin D. He has not been shy in saying how keen he is to equal Tony Blair's record of three consecutive election wins. He pushes back his hair, slides his glasses down from his forehead, and looks straight at me.

It is the first time I have been inside Number 10. The long room is wood-panelled and would feel stuffy but the traditional furniture of old has been replaced by a beautiful oval, cherry-wood table. Thompson's mark is all over the room. The cosy sofa in the corner next to the low-level coffee tables. The perfect setting for his famous fireside chats with the great and the good. And, of course, with his great chums in the media.

I have met Norton before but that had been in the Home Office administrative building in Marsham Street – the monstrous glass and slatted wood building close to Parliament Square. The security just to get through the door this morning was intense. Over the years most people have grown accustomed to the bag searches and body scanners in most public buildings. Today I had been told to bring my Ezylocate and passport, as well as the letter inviting me to the meeting. Each document had been scanned and almost pulled apart through three different checkpoints, whilst an armed police officer stood just a few feet away, looking me up and down.

The room is warm. The air conditioning seems to be just creating noise rather than having any other impact. Jean Norton kicks off. She is early fifties and what the media likes to describe as 'polished'. She is ferociously bright, outspoken and, in public, takes a harder line than her boss. She is ever referred to in the press as the first MP to breastfeed in the House. Something of which, I think, she may be disproportionately proud. Today she is in a navy suit with a startlingly white shirt, made a little less severe by a massive topaz necklace.

Her voice is clipped and business-like. As ever, no time is wasted in any warm-up or small talk. Turning to me she says, 'Dr Stephenson, thank you for joining us today. You were recommended to us by Neil Rochester as someone who can provide insight into what sits behind the accelerating recent trends of young girls joining the so called caliphettes and all-female jihadist groups. We are already grateful for your support to this government in helping with profiling in recent months. It has been significant in infiltrating a number of hitherto impenetrable networks.'

Although my day job is Professor of Psychology, I am increasingly asked to work with government departments to profile radical groups and their recruitment methods.

Norton gives what I take to be a nod of approval but it is so fleeting it barely registers. In a glance, she takes in my hair, which at the moment is a deep purple, and the rings in my nose and eyebrows. I am wearing a pale pink pinafore dress to which I have added huge tartan pockets. Carrying on at a clip she says, 'Today we are particularly keen to gain a better and deeper understanding of the terrorist cell Umm Umarah and its workings. We are especially interested in your research into the notion of radicalisation and the ideological desire to fight and participate in jihad amongst young, not necessarily Muslim, girls. Perhaps you could, for the benefit of the wider group, explain your credentials in this area and then share some of your key findings.'

I catch Thompson's eye and feel a surge of adrenalin. I clear my throat and glance at my notes. I don't need them but I'm looking for a security blanket. As I begin to speak I am, as ever, excruciatingly aware of my accent. It has softened over the years but it remains strong and I know that the accent, combined with my 'unconventional' looks, can detract from people taking me seriously. But I like the double take people do when I start to talk and I know I have been underestimated.

Amala had warned me not to try and do my 'posh Edinburgh voice', saying, 'It makes you sound like you're sucking a lemon whilst having a hedgehog stuffed up your ass.' To which Ella had added, 'And don't drone on. It's not a lecture. You don't have to hold court.' I smile to myself. Nailed.

I look across at Thompson. He must feel under some pressure. He has won two elections; one by a landslide and one by a whisker. He faces another election in two years and is tanking in the polls. He nods in encouragement, ready for me to start.

I am now regretting my breakfast of Grace's left over toast and jam, scoffed at high speed this morning. It has lingered and I can't get my tongue off the roof of my mouth. I am glad Ella cancelled the Cinnamon Club breakfast; having the full monty this morning would have left me feeling worse. All that food on top of my nerves for today, and the month-long anxiety over Mark leaving, would have tipped me over the edge.

The whole room is watching me. Waiting. My mind is a complete blank. Unsticking my tongue I begin at a croak, 'I am Dr Millie Stephenson and I am currently at the LSE where I am a

Professor of Psychology in the Gender Institute.' I stop. 'Um, eh, that's the London School of Economics.'

Norton looks irritated and with some exasperation says, 'Yes Dr Stephenson, we know.'

Thompson blushes slightly. Only last week he had faced a slow hand clap and booing when he had been guest speaker at a debate at the LSE. A group calling themselves 'Nous Sommes Voltaire' had challenged him for his lack of integrity and weakness in dealing with the Sharia councils. The group fashioned themselves around Voltaire's famous line, 'I disapprove of what you say, but I will defend to the death your right to say it.' Thompson had not handled it well, managing to sound both defensive and deeply patronising at the same time. Claiming 'much was happening for the good behind the scenes.'

The pressure has been growing on Thompson and Norton in recent months to stem what the media called 'the Islamist ghettos'. There are now about sixty Sharia-led communities across England. In theory, they have no legislative jurisdiction, but in reality they are a law unto themselves.

No wonder he has lost his shiny tennis tan. Last year had been the worst for attacks including the horrific suicide bombers who had wreaked havoc at Glastonbury. It had been the highest casualty rate on British soil since the long war on terror began.

Last summer had been plagued by violent riots and what the press labelled the 'toxic soup' of immigration, integration and freedom *from* speech.

Despite all the talk of border control, there was still an endless focus on the influx of genuine refugees from war-torn Middle Eastern and North African countries into communities that are less and less integrated into the mainstream. Added to that was the fear of causing offence, or provoking anger, which meant any kind of sensible narrative was nigh on impossible.

I carry on, ignoring Norton's scowl. 'After my doctorate, I received a scholarship to the Global Think Tank, Pax, based in New York. The whole caliphette issue was really starting to take off when I began my research into the radicalisation of young women to become so-called jihadi brides, and the formation of all-female jihadist groups. My particular focus was the US and UK. Most recently I have focused on the psychological profiling of those susceptible to radicalisation, particularly those targeted by, or attracted to, Umm Umarah, the women-only fighting arm of British-based Islamic State groups which form part of Har majiddoon.'

Norton shifts in her seat. Har majiddoon is the most effective and well-disciplined of the Islamic state fighting groups. Norton had been involved in wiping out a key leader just before Christmas but had lost a police officer in the raid and an innocent bystander had been seriously injured. It is a name that conjures the deepest fears of most people in the West. That is, of course, its intention. Har majiddoon is the Arabic transliteration for Armageddon and that seems to be their sole focus. To wipe out anyone and anything that comes into their path. Glastonbury was a prime examples. All designed to target everything and nothing.

I glance at Norton. She is an impressive operator. Seen by many as a bit aloof and rarely found in the bars of Westminster, her barrister brain misses very little. A committed Christian she had attended the funeral of the police officer killed in the Christmas raid. She had read a prayer that was both powerful and deeply moving in its sincerity. She may not be quite as charismatic as her boss, but you could probably trust her more with your wallet and your secrets. I wonder if there is any truth in the rumour she is after Thompson's job.

I carry on. 'In the past Umm Umarah have typically focused on high-profile targets. They are well equipped, trained in hand-to-hand combat and guerrilla warfare and to a woman are willing to die for the cause. Many have had past experience in Women's Islamic Enforcement Units, the internal police force dedicated to enforcing Sharia law on other women. They are ruthless, cold-hearted thugs. Their role now is seeking to convert influential Western women to the ways of radical Islam. They have a strong East London base, mainly around the Mulberry Estate in Tower Hamlets. They use sophisticated psychological techniques to find and convert individuals. Educated and wealthy girls are their key target.'

Never able to resist an audience I am beginning to enjoy the impact. You could hear a pin drop.

'In the early years, they favoured kidnapping, but recent conversions of some high-profile celebrities have fuelled an incredibly effective recruitment drive. The singer MX Jax is a prime example. She was seen as the epitome of Western liberalism and has now taken the name Khadijah, the first wife of the Prophet, and joined Umm Umarah. That has had more news headlines than any number of academic papers pointing out the risks.'

I say this with the frustration of being the author of such papers and only ever being asked for a view when it is much too late.

'Their need to kidnap and take hostages has fallen as their targeting and conversion techniques have improved. Although, of course, they still ensure they have a steady supply of willing, or not so willing, suicide bombers. What was unheard of a few years ago is becoming the norm. We are seeing more and more women running terrorist cells. The whole thing has snowballed out of all recognition.'

I am now in full flow, forgetting Ella's advice that this is not an undergraduate lecture but supposed to be a conversation, when there is a knock on the door and a young woman beckons to one of the grey suits. I pause as we watch him follow her out.

Tuesday 25th May 09.12

I come to with a jolt. Someone is beside me. They're pulling at my burqa. I try to grab it. Clutching it hard, grasping for any kind of protection.

She reaches under my veil and pushes her hand around my throat. My head whips back. I feel a searing pain as it cracks against the wall. Tears sting my eyes but I can't cry out. She has slapped a piece of thick tape across my mouth. The glue sticky on my lips and cheek. The smell and taste of cheap rubber is acrid and intense. I can taste the iron viscose of blood in my mouth where I have bitten my tongue. She pulls the veil back in place.

She is dressed completely in black, I can feel the sweat on her. I can smell it. Even her eyes are hidden; tiny slits behind the cloth.

Then a different smell. Gas and paraffin fill my nostrils as I gasp for air, breathing like a race horse, full of panic. And then I see it. A blow torch. She casually grabs my hand and runs the flame across the tips of my fingers.

She hisses, 'That's just a taster.'

Tuesday 25th May 09.15

NUSAYABAH

I can see her trying to work out where she is. Trying to work out how it has all gone so wrong so quickly. She freaked out when she saw the blow torch. She has no idea just how bad this day is going to get.

I close my eyes. I pull off my veil and run my fingers through my hair, trying to release the tension at my temples. I see my face in the cracked mirror. Eyes staring back at me. Eyes older than time, etched with loss.

Meticulous planning and preparation. We have lived that mantra for so long. I think back to the day all the pieces fell into place for me. I had lost everything. I feel how I was then. Like a husk. A half person. I see it clearly.

I clicked into the chat room. Faiza was online.

I typed, 'Hey, how are you?'

Rebelgirl: 'Bad day. Sad day, babe. You?'

'Why sad?'

Rebelgirl: 'Take a look.'

I followed the link.

Drones were flying across what I took to be Iraq. There was a huge explosion then dust and fire everywhere.'

I typed, 'What's going on?'

Rebelgirl; 'It's a kid's school. Twelve dead. Hey, take a look at Kardax if you wanna know more.'

I clicked on Kardax.

The first report was an investigation into sweat shops and child labour in Sierra Leone. The second report was an investigation into an arms sale.

That was the beginning.

Tuesday 25th May 09.16

MILLIE

Norton ignores the disruption and says, 'Please carry on, Dr Stephenson.'

I clear my throat and try not to sound like I am lecturing. 'Radicalisation is best compared to joining a cult. To understand how someone is recruited we need to ask ourselves three questions. First, what explains the initial interest? Then, how is an individual persuaded that a particular idea is the truth? And finally, what persuades them to engage in risky, illegal or dangerous activity?'

Norton asks, 'Isn't it the case that a lot of these people are just unstable? You know, struggling with day-to-day life; a bit lost and falling through the usual safety nets?'

From the corner of my eye I see Thompson look up from doodling on an electronic pad. There is an arrogance in him, a smugness, that despite the smile, the crinkly eyes and the charming manners make him hard to like. It's a dig and he knows it. Thompson was much maligned for presiding over cut after cut to mental health budgets. His emphasis always being trade over everything else.

I turn to Norton, 'No, in fact it's the opposite. Recruitment is now so good that it weeds out most people we might consider unstable or with mental health issues. It might seem counter-intuitive but if you look at the research, it shows us there is a far higher incidence of people with mental health issues in the general population than in these groups.'

She nods. 'Thank you.'

I glance down at my notes and carry on. 'Turning to initial interest first. This is typically sparked by what we call a cognitive opening. By that we mean where something happens to shake previously held beliefs, even those we had felt quite certain about. This can happen in many ways. It may be an experience of discrimination, or some sort of crisis. It is often deeply personal. Something that leaves an emotional scar. It may be a series of small openings. Not always one single event.'

'How come all of this happens under the nose of friends and family?' Norton asks.

'That's a good question. It is often the case that friends and family are involved in the radicalisation process, but you are right, there are many cases where the opposite is true. Often, as individuals begin to question their views and warm to an alternative set of ideas and beliefs, they become increasingly adept at hiding their involvement. They will keep their views to themselves but slowly start to alter their behaviour, eschewing Western ways, perhaps avoiding places they no longer see as appropriate or might be deemed frivolous. They sacrifice friends and family. They will no longer see themselves as able to have friends of the opposite sex. Sometimes those closest to them are slowest to spot the shifts or simply fail to see the pattern at all.'

Before I can go any further, the grey-suited, harried-looking aide comes back in and walks straight towards Thompson.

'Please excuse me, prime minister, I am sorry to interrupt but this couldn't wait.'

He bends down to talk to Thompson and Norton leans in. He is whispering urgently, gesticulating towards the door. Both are clearly shocked. The blood seems to have leeched from the prime minister's face. He stands and Norton follows.

Polite, but without his normal display of excessive courtesy, he says, 'Excuse us, we will have to cut this meeting short. Dr Stephenson, please accept my sincere apologies. We will be in touch to reconvene. We appreciate your time and we will seek to reschedule as soon as possible.'

Norton leans over to him and says something so quietly it is clear she does not want anyone else to hear. The prime minister nods and looks back at me.

'Dr Stephenson, there may be a matter where we would appreciate your advice. Please could you wait here for a few minutes and we will be back.

Tuesday 25th May 09.25

The pain is excruciating. I look around, trying to work out where I am. I hear people move in the next room. Are they coming back? I need to stay alert. Focused. I will myself to find a memory. A memory that will be mine…

15 YEARS EARLIER

Boston

'Who the fuck goes to the aquarium twice in a week?' Amala wailed, dragging Millie by the arm towards the bar. 'Tom Petty and the Heartbreakers are playing the Super Bowl half-time show. Come on, I wanna watch it.'

Millie dug in. 'You know I love aquariums and you made us rush around yesterday. I didn't see everything.' Millie looked about six, apart from the green hair and the sleeve tattoo. 'They've got loggerhead sea turtles.'

Ella started to laugh, then couldn't stop. That started Amala off and then Millie. They were holding onto each other, doubled over. 'For fuck's sake, let's get a drink. The fish will still be there tomorrow.'

It was a good decision. They found an old-fashioned bar tucked away from the main drag. Still laughing, Amala said, 'Excuse me, is this seat taken?'

'No, help yourself.' Sitting down, Amala looked at the good-looking guy in the baseball cap who was staring intently at the game. She glanced around to see the screen then did a double take back to the guy.

'Fuck me, Ben Affleck.'

'Well, that's quite an offer. Do you want to wait until the end of the game?'

Amala dined out on that for ever more.

TODAY

Tuesday 25th May 09.27

MILLIE

I am puzzled. What do Thompson and Norton want with me? I am also a bit agitated. I was only meant to be here for an hour, so I could be back at my desk by lunchtime. I have a supervisory meeting with a student but I had planned to be finished by three and home in time to let the nanny off. Hopefully banking a few hours, and brownie points, by turning up early. She has worked so many hours this last month it's the least I owe her. Apart from Ella and Amala, she is the only one who knows Mark has left. I haven't even told my mum. I can't face all the questions about why. I push the hideous feeling of shame to the back of my mind and switch on my phone.

There are a few messages from students about deadlines and references. I scroll through. Still nothing from Mark and nothing from the nanny. I quickly message Neil to ask if he is around and if he knows what is going on.

I wonder how Ella is getting on. She's meeting her contact today. Lunch on Sunday had got pretty heated. Aafa is sure he is being followed and he thinks Neil and Amala should do more. He's probably right.

I picture him around Ella's kitchen table.

2 DAYS BEFORE

Sunday 23rd May

MILLIE

I can see Ella stick the little goat cheese tarts on the plates and start taking the dishes to the table. I stand to help her, getting a whiff of something odd. I look at Ella, she shrugs, 'I followed the recipe.' I look down and see a wizened and slightly charred tart, smelling vaguely of sweaty socks.

I sit back down beside Aafa, he looks deeply uncomfortable. His voice is quiet but determined. 'You don't know what it's like in the PPCs. They take your clothes, your stuff and put you in those paper jump suits. They leave you in a holding cell with nothing but a hard bench and toilet pan. Half the time they switch off the lights and leave you in total darkness. It's impossible to know how long you've been there or how long they'll keep you. I hear them talking and joking about me, about my beard, and how am I going to find Mecca in the dark. They take your phone and they read your private messages. How would you like it if every text you sent, every picture you kept had some ignorant squaddie leering at it, laughing at it?'

Amala says, 'Christ, if they looked at mine they would round me up for debauchery.'

I chip in, 'And if they looked at mine they would send me a sympathy card for being so boring.'

Amala says, 'Hardly Mills, all those testosterone-fuelled students, eh?'

But I would hate it and so would they.

Aafa bites his lip. His face an equal mix of anger and sadness.

Ella is full of sympathy. 'I know, Aafa. I know it's an outrage. I'm still working on this story about young girls being radicalised. I know it's your subject, Millie, but I want to make it a human story. Until the public get to hear real people telling real stories, like Aafa, they are never going to see past the stereotypes and the statistics.'

I look over at Aafa. He's such a good kid. I give his hand a squeeze. 'I know it must feel crap. It's deeply unfair. The PPCs *are* profiling. They're under the cosh every which way they turn. All their stats tell them that the likelihood is the person stopping you being safe in your bed, or on the Tube or at a concert is probably brown, probably Muslim and probably a young man. That doesn't make it right. But people are scared. They want easy answers, easy solutions. They can't get their heads around the fact that it's just as likely to be the nice, middle-class white girl blowing things up, as it is the bearded brown guy.'

We all seem to have been talking about Ezylocate for weeks. Amala's right. So is Aafa. It's a nightmare that is keeping us all awake at night more and more. Not just me. Ella, Neil and Amala too.

Ella says, 'Something's got to change soon. It's not just Britain. It's the rest of Europe, the US and Australia. They are all grappling with assuring the public they're safe while still protecting their civil liberties. There are no easy answers, despite Thompson's rhetoric.'

We go quiet and eat our food. The only sounds are from the speakers above us quietly playing *Carmen*, and the chipping noise of cutlery trying to chisel through the pastry. Neil gives up, cranks up the music and sticks a rose in his mouth. He begins to dance around the kitchen table. Singing with exaggerated passion, 'Habanera', his favourite aria.

He shouts to Amala, 'Come on you wonderfully debauched creature,' and throws a flower at her. She sticks it between her teeth and they start to dance. Badly. Very badly.

TODAY

Tuesday 25th May 09.30

MILLIE

Aafa's right. I don't really know what it's like to be targeted and followed, but I keep hearing the same story over and over again.

I feel sick to the stomach. I have felt this way for weeks. I have my own shopping list of shame swirling around along with my worries about Aafa. And my worries for Amala. The guy hitting her last week had really shocked me. She was all swagger but it was just that. Swagger. I know underneath she must be scared.

To distract myself I flick through my notes. They make pretty grim reading. I don't get very far when the same harried-looking aide is suddenly in front of me. 'Dr Stephenson, the prime minister and the home secretary would like a few minutes of your time. Please can you follow me?'

I follow him into a small, airless and windowless room, very different to the meeting room of earlier. There are no cosy sofas and coffee tables here. This one is all business. The tension is palpable. The prime minister is perched at a desk with several telephones and open devices on it. He has a stack of papers in his hand and is ignoring the three large screens on the wall, all on mute, each showing a different news channel. He stares at me as I walk in.

He is distracted and looks flustered. Something in his look makes my stomach churn even more. The Home Secretary is talking on her phone pacing back and forth. Her hands are gesticulating and whoever is on the other end of the call is clearly not giving her what she wants. In the small space, she is giving off what feels like barely contained rage.

She raises her voice and says, 'I don't care. Just do it and do it now.'

There are three other people in the room. Two men and one woman. I recognise both men but not the woman. One is James Mitford, the head of the Met's anti-terrorist squad, generally viewed as a hardliner and a big advocate of the Prevent and Protect Centres. He is on secondment from West Yorkshire Police, where he had successfully handled a number of major political scandals. He is in London to gain more experience in anti-terrorism, and clearly sees himself as a shoo-in for the top job. A media darling and rarely one to share the credit, his naked ambition is clear to see.

The other man is Rehan Ali, the leader of the British Integration Party, sitting in a winged back chair, legs outstretched, as if he has all the time in the world. Of all the people in the room, he looks the most in control. He and I have worked together in the past and he is a good friend of Amala's father. I like him a lot. He is ferociously bright, provocative and well-connected across the Muslim community. He has brokered a number of negotiations to liberate women from abusive marriages with the Sharia councils, combining a deep knowledge of his faith with a sound dose of pragmatism.

He uncrosses his legs and stands up to shake my hand. 'Dr Stephenson, Millie, it is a pleasure to meet you again. Albeit in rather tricky circumstances.'

I shake his hand. 'Dr Ali, it's good to see you too. I have to say I still have no idea of what the circumstances are.'

He smiles and pats my hand. 'I think we are all about to be briefed.'

At that moment, Jean Norton hangs up the phone and turns to us. Again with no warm-up, she speaks at breakneck speed. 'We have a serious situation. The terrorist group Umm Umarah has made contact. They say they have taken a high-value hostage and want to talk. We believe they are looking for some sort of trade. The message is that they will make contact again at 10 am through a secure link.' She glances at her watch. 'That's in just under thirty minutes.'

She looks at me. 'Dr Stephenson, we are hoping you will be able to help us. As you know we have had few direct dealings with Umm Umarah but we believe this is a credible threat. The contact is from someone calling herself Nusayabah. Is that a name known to you in your work with us?'

I shake my head, but add, 'No, not specifically, but Nusayabah is an important name in Islam. She is the first woman to have fought in battle beside Mohammed. It likely signifies someone in a senior position.'

Norton nods and turns to Rehan Ali. 'Dr Ali, thank you for getting here so quickly. We are hopeful that you and Dr Stephenson can help us. We would appreciate your experience in reviewing some recent material linked to this group. Could you remain here for the duration?' Peering over her glasses, she adds, 'If you would both be prepared to help, I am sure I do not need to remind you of the need for the utmost secrecy.'

I nod. More than a little thrown to find myself in the midst of a live situation. A high-value hostage? I wonder if this Nusayabah will tell us who it is.

Rehan Ali says, 'I hope I can be of some assistance and, as you know, discretion is guaranteed.'

Norton continues, 'So, Dr Stephenson you know Dr Ali and this is James Mitford and Alex Dalgleish.'

Clearly I am not to be told the role of Alex Dalgleish. I presume she's from MI5, but if she is, I have never heard her name in any of my dealings with them. She has brown, almost translucent skin and high cheekbones. Her accent is clipped but neutral. English with no trace of a dialect, region or class. There is no telling her heritage. She could have been Indian or even South American. Her hand is cool and light, her smile as contained as the rest of her. She seems to move with grace and poise without expending any energy. She is the polar opposite of Norton who is like a coiled spring. I turn to Mitford. I only know him from the media and by reputation. He shakes my hand with some vigour. A man unable to meet any situation without feeling the need to assert his own importance. As I turn to look at Thompson, I flex my fingers from his crushing grip.

The prime minister speaks for the first time. He has the air of someone used to being in charge.

'Ok, as Jean has just said, Umm Umarah claim to have a high-value asset. We have people pulling together everything we have that might be helpful. We only have around twenty minutes to get a grip on who and what we are dealing with. At this stage, we are taking them seriously but we have no indication of who the asset may be. GSOC are on it.'

GSOC. The emergency rapid response team at GCHQ, who gather intelligence through the interception of signals. I know a few people at the Government Communications Headquarters in Cheltenham. They are amongst the best in the world. I wonder vaguely who the hostage is. They must be terrified. I can't help myself. I feel a rush of excitement. This must be big.

Thompson looks directly at me. I swallow hard, feeling a mix of anticipation and dread.

'So far we have found a blogger using the same name. Nusayabah. She seems to be pretty active and has increased her online presence lately. Dr Stephenson, we would like you to look at a dossier. It's still being complied but there are a few things we would like your thoughts on. We need you to pull out whatever you can to help us understand who and what we are dealing with.'

He turns to look at Rehan Ali. 'As ever, Dr Ali we appreciate any help you can offer through your contacts on the ground as well as reviewing the materials.' Ali nods.

Rehan Ali and I are each handed a smart block containing the dossier. It looks to run to about eight pages.

Norton says, 'Everything we have so far is on there.'

I am about to start reading when Norton asks a question. 'Dr Stephenson, what can you tell us about Nusayabah? You said it is a significant name?'

'Nusayabah bint Ka'ab is also known as Umm Umarah. The same name as the group we have been investigating. It may either be a splinter group or just another way of broadening reach through a different name. It may be the same group just optimising search engine hits. Or it may be that Nusayabah is a key leader within the group, or part of a breakaway. Sorry, it's hard to be specific without any more background.'

I look at Rehan Ali, who is nodding. 'If I was to take an educated guess it would be that we are dealing with a splinter group. As you know, the Modus Operandi is always to limit knowledge and communications through the creation of a complex network of cells.'

I add, 'What we know already is Umm Umarah is likely to be East London based and they have been very successful recently in recruiting wealthy white girls, many of whom have brought significant money with them. Sometimes their own funds or, as often as not, stolen from family.'

Rehan Ali nods again in agreement and says, 'As things stand at the moment, I understand they have been very hard to locate beyond the general East London area so they are clearly sophisticated enough to avoid even our best surveillance.'

Simon Thompson is also looking at the dossier. 'Dr Stephenson, you have often said Umm Umarah is the most effective of the all-female mujahedeen cells, and likely to make a significant impact on the war on terror. What do you think might be going on if their presence has increased?'

'I believe they're shifting from recruitment to direct action in some way. It would explain the high number of white girls being radicalised. The shift, in general, amongst jihadists is to focus on high-profile people, events or institutions where a strategic attack instils a disproportionate level of fear. Everything we know so far says that, in addition to being well-funded, they are well-organised, focused and committed to the cause. My guess is they now have a sufficient army to move to the next stage. But what that might be is anyone's guess.'

Tuesday 25th May 09.38

MILLIE

Rehan Ali is making calls. I start to look at the dossier. I see the BSU, the Behavioural Science Unit – part of MI5 – have been involved as well as GCHQ. The BSU are responsible for tracking changes in an individual or group's behaviour that might suggest they are planning an attack or have been radicalised. They have some great people, most of whom have paranoid as a middle name. But that's what makes them so good.

I covertly stare at Alex Dalgleish; she must be a spook. She looks so calm and so freaking cool. I could never pull that off in a million years. I run my fingers through my hair, conscious that it looks like it is a stranger to a brush. I tug at it but it makes not a jot of difference. I wonder what she has to do with Umm Umarah. She gives nothing away. I pull my glasses out from my hair, click the smart block and start to read.

The first piece is a link dated 29th November last year. It is a demonstration outside the Freedom Tower in New York. A woman, from the US Umm Umarah cell, had tried to erect the Black Standard, the flag originally carried by Mohammed, but now the symbol of all radical Islamic groups across the world. The flag has been associated with extremists since it was used by the Taliban in Afghanistan in the 1990s.

Loud music plays and then is quietened as the woman points at the flag. Her voice is angry and obviously British. She says, 'The white writing at the top of the flag is the first half of an Islamic phrase called the *shahada*, or declaration of faith, and it reads: "There is no God but God. Muhammad is the messenger of God."' The camera pans in close so even through the burqa, the rage in her eyes is clear. She spews out the last point with bitter resentment, 'Allah Akbar. This is the truth and there can be no debate.'

I recognise her. She had been protesting about the decision by the State of New York to ban burqas, following in the footsteps of a number of European countries over the last few years. The same woman had turned up more recently and made the same call from the steps of St Paul's Cathedral. She is a known Umm Umarah activist in London.

I glance down until I see the first entry by the group, or person, calling themselves Nusayabah. I try to block out everything else and concentrate. I am too jumpy. I bite down on my back teeth and force myself to pay attention to the words in front of me:

Nusayabah
9th December

Sisters, the infidels think that the way to worship their god is at the shrine of consumerism. Gaudy trifles, indecent clothes and lights across the streets. That is no way to worship.

I say this to you:

How are you attracted to the jewels of this world when there are hidden diamonds in Allah's Mercy (Paradise)? You have not died o Martyr! But it is us who have died through shame! I pray to Allah SWT

Shaykh Abdur-Rahman al Ashmawe

The compiler has added two notes. One to explain that the quote is from a well-known radical, and the second to explain that SWT is often placed in blogs and online to show respect, meaning Glory to Him, the exalted i.e. *Subhanahu wia Ta'ala.*

Rehan Ali is off the phone. I show him the first entry.

'Ah yes, Millie, everyone is a scholar these days. They pick and choose from the Quran and make it fit wonderfully into their interpretation. Skipping the bits that don't fit quite so neatly.'

He sighs slightly then continues, 'Do you think things are getting worse?'

I say, 'It's hard to see it any other way. There's fault on both sides. The PPCs are making enemies out of good people, but the attacks by extremists are also on the up. It's hard not to be pessimistic.' Then I add, 'And paranoid.'

'Yes, maybe we should pay more attention to our good friend, Voltaire.' I raise an eyebrow. Not quite sure this is really the time for a lecture. Unfazed, he quotes, '"What is tolerance? It is the consequence of humanity. We are all formed of frailty and error; let us pardon reciprocally each other's folly – that is the first law of nature."'

I recognise the quote as one I use in many of my lectures. I smile ruefully, 'Although I don't see Thompson seeing it quite that way if today's hostage hits the press and hits his ratings.'

Ali nods in agreement. 'Indeed, our PM certainly likes to "manage the message" as I constantly hear him say.'

Tuesday 25th May 09.43

MILLIE

Norton has the air of the Commander-in -Chief. The room already feels overheated and stuffy. Someone has brought coffee in and the table is looking cluttered with cups and crumbs from the stale, dry biscuits. I can't help it. I reach over and start munching on a biscuit, hoping it will settle the coffee swishing around in my belly. Norton is brusque, 'We have less than twenty minutes before the first contact. I have Neil Rochester outside. I am hoping he can help us figure out a location whenever the contact is made. He has hooked up with GSOC and I know the guys at Fort Meade will be interested.'

I try to swallow the biscuit, now stuck in my throat, as I feel the heat rise in my face. Fort Meade in Maryland is home to America's cyber spooks. Neil has a good mate there, Spike Callaghan. They met when he and Amala were at MIT. Spike's a Boston Southie with a dollop of inherited irresistible Irish charm. I feel my face flush scarlet as I remember a particularly sexy one-night-stand with him. It wasn't even one night. It had been a drunken and fantastic, quickie up against a toilet wall in Shay's Bar. Not classy, but hot. I was so embarrassed I couldn't look at him the next day. Amala, knowing how excruciatingly embarrassed I was, had sung:

'Millie has a super Spike inside her knickers and it feels so scrumptious and totally delicious

If you say it loud enough
It's something quite atrocious,
Even though the sound of it
Is Millie-bonking-ishis
Um diddle diddle diddle um diddle ay,
Um diddle diddle diddle um diddle ay'

All to the tune of *Mary Poppins*' 'Supercalifragilisticexpialidocious'.

Norton looks at me with the disapproval of a stern headmistress. I blush even harder as if she could read my thoughts. Pulling myself together, I cough and try to surreptitiously wipe the crumbs off my dress.

I look to the door. Neil walks in looking as dishevelled as ever, talking as he walks. He smiles at me and I stand and give his arm a squeeze. He nods at my mouth. I put my hand up and feel the last bit of digestive dislodge and fall on the floor. Whatever happens, it feels good to have someone I know and trust here with me today.

Amala and Neil formed their fledging tech business, All Talk – a simultaneous translation tool that understands thousands of regional accents – after they got back from Boston. The idea was conceived one drunken night in good old Shay's Bar again. Amala had been imitating her mum's Pakistani accent trying to book cinema tickets on a voice recognition system. She still has the framed beer mats in her downstairs loo showing some indecipherable algorithm. She claims it was the best night of her life. A few years later it had made them both as rich as Croesus.

Neil and Ella had met at one of Amala's parties. Until then I didn't think anyone believed in love at first sight but those two were besotted with each other from the first instant and still are. He fits into our little group in a way Mark never quite does. Or maybe that's did. I give myself a mental slap. Christ, I need to focus.

Neil is at ease in the corridors of power. Thompson trusts him. He was at Eton with Thompson's younger brother. Although both are brushed with the fairy dust of noblesse oblige the similarity stops there. Under the geekiness, Neil is all hopeless romantic, whereas I suspect underneath the charming façade, Thompson has the heart of a swinging brick.

Neil smiles at the room in general and turns to Thompson and says, 'Morning, Simon. I hear you might need some help. What's going on?'

Thompson quickly brings him up to speed as Neil pulls out his mobile integrated computer. Over his shoulder, I see him create a live link to his team at Rockeem. Confident, and fitting in quickly with the rest of the room, he is on familiar turf. He leans back in his chair with his hands behind his head, ready to try and intercept the contact as soon as it is made.

I sit next to him and whisper, 'Who's the good-looking woman? Alex Dalgleish? Is she a spy?'

Neil smiles and says, 'If I told you I'd have to kill you. But since it's you. Yeah, she's pretty hard core. MI5. Serious undercover stuff. Pretty cool to do this together, eh? Ella's on a story but I bet this must be bigger, right? She'll be totally miffed when we tell her we were in the middle of all the action.'

I smile and say, 'I'd better do my prep. We can't all loll about because we're chums with the PM. Some of us are still trying to impress with wisdom and expertise.'

I start browsing the notes again. Someone has given a description of Nusayabah, or rather her namesake. Copied from some academic text. I skim read it.

'Nusayabah was originally a teacher in Medina. She attended the Battle of Uhud, initially, like other women, to bring water to the soldiers while her husband and two sons fought. At the point she believed the battle was about to be lost, she took up a sword and fought alongside the Prophet Mohammed. When a horse-mounted Quraysh attacked her, she pulled on the horse's bridle and plunged her sword into its neck, toppling the horse on top of its rider. She is said to have fought viciously and valiantly. By all accounts, Mohammed said that wherever and whenever he looked he saw her protect him. In the battle, she sustained twelve major wounds, which took a year to heal. She had no concern for herself only the Prophet. She then fought by his side in many battles. Both her sons were martyred.'

I sigh. It is the sort of story teenage girls can relate to. It feels romantic and adventurous. If those girls look beyond the story, they will also see something that will appeal to feminists. I read on until Norton calls us all to attention.

Tuesday 25th May 09.59

MILLIE

The clock ticks alarmingly slowly towards ten. Seven of us sit at the long, dark, wooden table, highly polished and now littered with papers and integrated mobile devices as well as coffee cups. Norton, Thompson, Mitford, Dalgleish, Ali plus Neil and me. No one says a word. Each of us is focused on what is to come and the need to pay attention to every detail. We are about to hear who the asset is and what is to be demanded in a trade. I am excited. This is massive.

Neil is sitting at the table behind a series of large screens that have been rolled in in the last few minutes. He is staring intently at them and tapping furiously, both on the screen and at a keyboard. He has a phone tucked under his ear and is talking to several people at once. Some of the conversations are to his own tech team at Rockeem, many of whom are serious hackers. He and Amala had recruited the best creative and leading edge technical thinkers on the planet. Some orthodox and legal and some a little less so. He is coolly giving multiple instructions to his team, and to GCHQ, about live feeds and the need for them to hook into the secure link that was about to come into the prime minister's office.

I hear him ask one of his guys to track down Amala because her Ezylocate is off and Neil wants her help. They are better as a team in a crisis. It is also clear that other messages are being relayed to the Ezylocate team embedded in the Home Office. In theory, they can track every man, woman and child in the country through their ID card or any device with a GPS component, which means pretty much everyone.

I am not naïve, and more than most, I know the threats we face every single day but I am pretty sceptical of this government's motives and underlying desire to get rid of 'immigrants'. Or maybe the more prosaic and truthful, 'People not like us'.

I am so nervous, I physically jerk when the phone on the desk buzzes and a voice says, 'The feed is live, sir.'

The screen on the wall crackles and a woman dressed in a niqab appears. Her face is invisible. Her eyes are veiled by black mesh.

Behind her is a large screen, it's got what looks like the geometric patterns you see in a mosque but they're opaque or pixelated, to the side of it is the black standard. She speaks slowly and clearly.

'Prime Minister Thompson. We have a high-level strategic asset in our control. The asset is of extreme value to you and your government.'

At that point, the scene shifts. Another woman in a burqa is in full shot. It is impossible to identify any features. She is on the floor and her hands are tied, her legs are straight out in front of her. She is slumped with her back to a wall. It is hard to see if she is even conscious. Then I hear a pitiful whimpering.

The seven of us collectively hold our breath. The woman is in some sort of cell or small dim room. There are no visible clues as to where she might be. The camera pans back and beside her, holding a knife with a serrated six-inch blade, is a figure wearing a black balaclava and black combat gear. For some reason, I am profoundly shocked when I realise it is a woman. Without uttering a sound, she grabs the hands of the cowering figure and slices through the cheap plastic tape binding them together.

The woman, still whimpering tries to scramble out of the way. Her feet scrabbling at the floor, trying to get a grip to push herself backwards. Frantic but with nowhere to go, she pins herself to the wall moaning incoherently. Something else is about to happen. We can't see what.

Then we do.

The hostage -taker has a blow torch. The blue flame vivid in the dim room. She is holding it aloft in front of the terrified woman.

Jesus Christ. I can't look. I bite hard on my lip. What the hell is she doing?

She grabs the woman's hand and holds the torch to her right index finger. I can almost smell burning flesh. I swallow as nausea rises into my throat. The woman bucks and howls. The screams are intolerable and eventually give way to an excruciating, panicked gasping as she slumps to the floor.

Horrified, I watch as the convulsing woman is dragged upright. She lets out a low moan as the jihadist then grabs her right hand and slams it on a wooden table. She has the knife again. Within a second the shining, serrated blade is raised and with one swift movement it slices off her charred index finger. The screams are inhuman and go on and on.

Oh my God, this is really happening. I can't believe I am seeing this. I have read a thousand papers and heard countless stories, but none of it has prepared me for the real thing. It doesn't feel quite so exciting anymore. Just sick.

I turn to look at Neil, his face is deathly pale and his hand is over his mouth. He winces as the woman pulls back her hand and clutches it to her chest. Blood is soaking the front of the burqa and dropping on the floor. After what seems an eternity, but may have only been a few seconds, she gives a pitiful and pathetic sob. She drops and lies, foetus-like, on the floor.

I hear a piercing shriek in the room. I grab Neil's hand and squeeze it in a vice-like grip. My heart is racing and I can feel adrenalin shoot through my system. I realise the noise is coming from me and I try to control it. Gulping it down, I force my eyes back to the screen.

The black clad woman with the knife is holding up a screenshot of this morning's BBC online news and I recognise the photograph of the holiday traffic on the M25 earlier this morning. Proving that what we had just witnessed was live.

The screen returns to the woman in the niqab. As if reading from a script, and with no hint of emotion, she says, 'Prime Minister Thompson and Home Secretary Norton, you have much innocent blood on your hands. You have brutally murdered many of our brothers and sisters. Innocents and children. Your deliberate intervention in Muslim countries, along with the Americans, the Germans and the French has caused war after war. You have brought that war to your own streets. The war will continue until we win. Until the black standard flies above Downing Street. Today we have two simple demands, well within your gift to deliver. First, we demand the immediate closure of the Prevent and Protect Centres that harass and beat our brothers and sisters. This must be announced by 6pm today. Second, we demand £100 million to be sent securely to us today. We will contact you through this link at 1pm to check everything is on track. At that time, we will provide bank details. Payment must be made by 3pm. Our intent is very clear. Fail to comply and she dies at 6.01.'

Looking straight into the camera, she spits out every word.

'I am sure you are wondering who we have that might be worth £100 million to you. I presume you have Mr Rochester there trying to track us. Mr Rochester, let me tell you directly who is worth £100 million to you.'

She pauses, well aware of the impact of her words. Neil jerks in his seat, looking up from his screens and stares straight ahead. His grip on my hand tightens and I instinctively move closer to him.

'We have your partner.'

I feel as if a thousand volts have shot through my body. My brain has frozen. My mouth is dry and my heart feels as if it will pound right out of my chest.

Her considered delivery makes every word seem even more chilling.

'I presume we can rely on you to pay for her release? The details we send for payment will be to your office at Rockeem. I am sure you are well able to convince your colleagues of her importance, not just to you but to them. All the dirty little secrets the two of you share about what this Kaffir government will do next. Know this…'

She pauses and the silence is deafening. 'We will be without mercy. We will make sure she tells us everything. In case of any doubt, proof of identity will arrive within the hour.' At that point the screen goes black and all hell breaks loose.

Tuesday 25th May 10.06

I must have passed out. I can taste blood. I cannot get my thoughts to work properly. I can't work out where I am and what has happened. I still can't make the thoughts fit together to make a picture of the last few hours. Everything feels dislocated. Has it even been hours? More? Less? I can't tell.

I can feel that woman, not Nusayabah, the other one with the stale breath, pull at me. She refastens my hands with more cheap plastic tape, pulling them hard in front of me. The pain of my burnt and severed finger is beyond belief. A smell of burning flesh is choking me. She grabs both feet and fastens tape around my ankles, pulling it tight. Cutting the flesh.

She looks down at me and kicks my feet, 'Let's see if your powerful friends can get to you now, bitch.' She bangs the door and leaves me alone.

I am leaning against the wall tied up. My chest is heaving and I can feel the sweat slide down my back. I can no longer feel the cuts and bruises. My fingers, where she had casually grazed them with the blow torch before making her sick video, are blistered and raw. I was completely wired a few minutes ago and now it feels as if every bit of fight and energy has slipped out of my body. All I feel is utter exhaustion. I had watched her take the blow torch to my severed finger before dropping it into a box. Nausea and bile rise in my mouth. I try to see in the semi dark, straining and blinking. I feel like I am being sucked into a swamp.

I still can't work out where I am. There is the sound of traffic outside and somewhere a radio is playing some sort of news channel. I have a feeling that I heard a call to prayer so there must be a mosque nearby. I am pretty sure I am still in London but I could be anywhere. I close my eyes and try to just slip away.

Grasping a memory. A good memory.

11 YEARS EARLIER

The Polo Bar, London

'Fuck. I mean fuck, really fuck. Mals, what have we done? Fuck.'

We were all giggling. It's too bizarre. We're rich. Like really rich. Gobsmackingly rich.

'Yeah, fuck.'

Millie said with deep irony and caustic wit, 'Well, it would seem the main impact of a billion quid is to render the pair of you incoherent.'

That made us laugh all the more. Neil pulled Ella towards him and kissed her deeply. He sighed happily and said, 'Millie, one point two billion if you please… ah fuck what's two million between mates?'

Ella looked at him, deadpan. 'Neil, point two of a billion is two hundred million not two million, even amongst friends that's quite a lot. Hang on, or is it two thousand million?'

Completely pissed she looked confused and trailed off.

'Two hundred thousand million million. Ah fuck it. A lot.'

Mark, ever the numbers man, rolled his eyes.

That set us all laughing again. Millie laughed so hard she snorted mojito through her heavily pierced nose.

TODAY

Tuesday 25th May 10.07

MILLIE

Seven minutes and a lifetime have passed. I feel acid rise in my throat and I am certain I am going to throw up. I look at Neil and his face is ashen. There is a lot of noise in the room but I can't make out any words. It feels as if they are swimming around in a frenetic Tower of Babel. A hundred different languages that I can't understand.

Neil and I lock eyes. A thousand images are in my head. I am devastated and so is he. I grab his hands again, we are both shaking violently. Neither of us able to comprehend what has just happened.

I hear myself saying over and over, 'I can't believe it. I can't. It can't be Amala in there. It just can't.'

Over the rabble I hear Alex Dalgleish tell everyone to sit down so we can assess the situation. Norton and Thompson are both on the phone doing God knows what. James Mitford seems to be tapping away at a hand-held device. Only Rehan Ali is sitting calmly looking at the scene around him. Taking everything in, waiting for order to be restored.

Dalgleish bangs the table and the noise swirls to a stop. Neil picks up his smart block to bring up Ezylocate so he can try to pinpoint Amala. He is tapping furiously and swiping the screen.

'What the fuck has she done? I can't find her on the main site and I can't find her on the company one. She can't have an ID card with her. She must have something – a phone or a smart block… Christ, where is she? Why the fuck has she switched it off. She knows if she does that, no one else can ever break her codes.'

He looks frantic. His eyes darting around the room. Looking for answers. Finding none. Dalgleish looks to Thompson, Norton and Mitford.

'Do we have a complete media lockdown?'

Norton nods. She has lost some of her polish and is emanating enough raw energy to fire up a small power station.

Thompson suddenly seems to realise he should take control and says, 'Ok, we have a serious situation. Neil and Dr Stephenson, I am aware that Amala Hackeem is not just a colleague but a close personal friend, but I need everyone to stay calm, and I would like both of you to help us navigate this situation to a safe and satisfactory conclusion, if you feel able?'

My heart is hammering so hard I assume everyone can hear it. I am struggling to follow the most basic of sentences and I can feel my whole body shaking. Tears start to fall down my cheeks.

I look at Neil. I know both of us are picturing Amala. I keep seeing her. I keep seeing Amala's hand hacked and burnt to a black crisp and I feel sick to the stomach. How could my ballsy mate be cowering in a corner with some maniac torturing her? It can't be real. It just can't be.

'Dr Stephenson, would you like to take a few moments?' asks Thompson.

'No, thank you,' I whisper. 'I would like to help. I need to help.'

Tuesday 25th May 10.20

MILLIE

Neil stands up. Blinking away tears, he speaks with a terrible conviction borne out of love and terror. 'Look, I have the money. I can pay it. I am not going to sit around here and let them hurt her anymore. No one outside this room need ever know. We can transfer the money in secret. Millie's husband will know how. All you have to say is that you are going to close the PPCs, they can't expect you to really see it through. You can just say it.'

He runs out of steam. He looks hopeless. He is chewing his lip with such an intensity he is oblivious to the fact he has drawn blood. He is desperate. He loves Amala.

So do I. I try to stand up but I can't. My legs are like jelly. I hold on to the table. I close my eyes and try to think what to do. I feel a tiny glimmer of hope. Maybe we can get her back before things get any worse. Maybe we can work out a way to get these people to believe we will do what they want. Neil will be able to find her and he can pay the money.

Norton looks at us both. I can see a look of pity fleetingly cross her face but almost immediately it is replaced with an implacable hardness. I don't trust her and I certainly don't trust Thompson. My whole adult life has been about understanding why humans do what they do. There is no way Thompson will do anything that doesn't suit his own dirty ambition. And no way Norton will do a deal.

I look at Thompson through new eyes. Wary eyes. Suspicious eyes. He tries, and fails, to sound compassionate. 'Neil, Millie, I know you are devastated. I really do understand. But you know as well as I do, we cannot and we will not negotiate. You especially, Neil. You've been here before.'

Neil is suddenly roaring. 'I know I've been here before and I've helped you before. But every time before it was a stranger. Not Amala. That woman is like a sister to me. And to Millie. If you think I am going to tell Ella she's dead, and she died on my watch, you must be insane. She has done more for your fucking government than anyone else on the planet. Are you going to let her die? Are you? You're more concerned with your own skin than hers!'

Thompson says with little conviction, 'Look, we'll work something out. We have our best people on this. I promise it will be ok. Jean and I have to brief GCHQ. I suggest we meet back here in thirty minutes. In the meantime, our Ezylocate team is at your disposal. Let them know what help you need.'

I watch him walk away with Norton. Amala is right; he's a dick.

Tuesday 25th May 10.22

I can't focus. It's so dark in here. I can hear them in the next room. Laughing. I need to stay awake. Think.

Think about the good times.

The party trick.

18 YEARS EARLIER

Edinburgh

'My party trick,' said Millie, pushing out her chest and wriggling like a worm. 'Ta dah!'

She whipped her bra out from inside her sleeve. It was a dingy grey that may have been pink at one time but had seen better days. She waved it above her head like a lasso.

'Come on.'

She leaned over the balcony of the ornate wooden staircase and with the perfect shot of the truly drunk, hooked the bra straight onto the antlers of the moose head adorning the wall.

She took a bow as thirty rowdy students gave her a round of applause. 'Go NOFAs! Let's see the rest.'

The barman told us off. Back in the corner of the Library Bar, Millie said, 'Ella Russell, world famous journalist and published author. We propose a toast to world domination of all things writerly and raise our glass.'

Amala is on the table reading from the article published in *The Teviot*, the student newspaper. Ella's article.

'The new adaptation of the truly wonderful *Pride and Prejudice* is a joy.

'Keira Knightly plays Elizabeth as she should be played, sparky, funny and her own woman. The opening line of the novel tells us it is about marriage and class but it is also so much more. It is two fingers to the patriarchy. Austen shows us that woman have strengths and wisdom often too readily dismissed by the gullible men around them, and that they may be more calculating in their ability to outwit than the credit given to them.

'What the film shows, as with the book, is men's minds are raised to the level of the women with whom they associate.' Amala looked up. 'Hey, Ells, that's a good line. I like it.'

'Yeah, so do I. I wish I had said it first. It's actually Alexander Dumas.'

Amala snorted, 'Ells, babe you can't just nick stuff!'

'It's going to be my signature – sneaking in bits of poetry and seeing if people can spot it. I'm going to find ways to kind of just fold it into the article.'

Millie said, 'Yeah, but not obvious. Make it hard so only us special friends can see them.'

'A deal. Come on let's get some pizza. I'm starving.'

Millie suddenly looked forlorn. 'How am I going to get my bra back?'

TODAY

Tuesday 25th May 10.27

MILLIE

Rehan Ali and I are alone. Everyone else is off working on their piece of the puzzle. Neil is talking to his number two at Rockeem about tracing the link.

I am staring into space. I can hear that woman's voice chilling me to the bone.

Ali is gentle. 'Millie, do you know if anyone has a grudge against Amala?'

I shiver. It would be quicker to list the people she hadn't offended. 'There must be thousands of people. Have you seen her stuff? She always has about six fatwas on her head.'

Ali's phone rings. 'Excuse me, I need to take this.' He turns his back to me but I can see from his stance he is listening intently. I don't know quite what to do first. I had better call Ella. She will want to know what's going on. Before I make the call, I hear Ali finish. He is speaking quietly, 'Shukraan. Inshallah.'

He turns to me. 'It seems there is a lot of activity in The Bush today. Young men are congregating more than usual. May just be the half-term holiday. Maybe not. We should keep an eye on it, though.'

The Mulberry Estate, known as The Bush, is smack bang in the middle of the Tower Hamlets Sharia Community, notorious for having housed various terrorist groups. A large number of suicide bombers have spent their last hours on this earth there. It is a no-go area for most people – often including the police. I knew of it from my research but had never been granted permission to visit. Getting in and getting Amala out would be a job for ATF50's specialist firearms unit.

Just then Neil comes back in. 'Thompson's briefing his people.' He nods at Ali then says in a hush to me, 'Millie, we have to get the money. I can work on Thompson about the PPCs. We need to show willing. Thompson and Norton will take a hard line on negotiating. They can't be shown to give in. We need to find a way to transfer the money. It's easy to get it but it's not so easy to make it both invisible and traceable. We'll need Mark to help us. You know he can hide it, despite what he always says.'

I nod. Mark always said that in the days of electronic global transfers, money can always be traced, unless it's hidden the old-fashioned way. In his words, 'up an ass'.

I explain to Rehan Ali, 'Mark, my husband, is a banker. He specialises in Sukok bonds.'

I say this knowing Ali probably has heard of them, given they are the bonds that comply with Islamic law. He says, 'Yes, I saw him give a presentation once. Very impressive he was too.'

I am sure he was. Everything about him screams accomplishment and money. His father was an old-style workaholic, rags-to-riches industrialist with fingers in pies that ranged from diamond mines to steel to manufacturing to high tech and big time media companies. Born in Tennessee, Mark hadn't relied on a silver spoon, preferring to make his own money on Wall Street. Enough to buy an $80m apartment in the Puck building in Manhattan and a five-bedroom house on Hampstead Heath. More than enough for most of us mere mortals. Never quite enough to please his father, though. But there never would be enough for that, I think bitterly. I never really did pass muster for Mr Carter senior.

However, the rich, accomplished and beautiful Mark is no longer living in our house in Hampstead Heath. I don't know where he is. He left me exactly four weeks and three days ago. But Neil doesn't know that.

'Let me call him. I'll try and see where he is.'

'What do you mean, where he is? Isn't he at work?'

'Yeah, yeah. I'm sure he is.'

Neil looks at me, clearly perplexed but assuming I am just stunned by what has happened. I am, and now I have to factor in finding Mark. I'm not even sure if he is still in London. He said he was going to spend some time with his folks. He is talking to Grace every day. But not me. We have not spoken. Not for four weeks and three days. A lifetime in a marriage.

I scroll through my phone. It's 5.30 in New York but only 4.30 in the morning in Memphis. Either way he would probably be up.

I hit 'call'. It goes straight to message.

'Hey, it's me. It's really important you call me when you get this. It's urgent.'

I'm not sure what else to say, then I realise he will assume it's about Grace.

'It's not Grace. She's ok, but it is urgent. Please call.'

I choke then. I can't say anymore. It is urgent. It is life or death.

An aide knocks on the door.

'There is something on the internet from Nusayabah. She is posting something about Amala Hackeem.'

Neil switches to a live screen on his computer. Ali and I lean in. It is Amala at Jongleurs Comedy Club a couple of weeks ago. She had called the act 'Muslim Mascara: brown eyes, green eyes or radical eyes.' The clip shows her being heckled.

Tuesday 25th May 10.35

NUSAYABAH

There is a tiny glimmer of sunlight fighting its way through the threadbare curtains. I feel the warmth. I close my eyes. I can smell the desert heat. Feel it through the cloth. Warming me.

Another beginning.

The first time I saw him.

I saw him before he saw me.

I felt a change in the group when he walked in. A slight tension; a standing to attention. He was covered in dust and wore his AK47 lightly. A piece of him. A part of him for so many years of struggle. He had the look of exhaustion that comes from months of fighting. His eyes hollow and his whole body weary.

One of the women brought food. He hardly had the strength to eat it.

I kept watching, hidden under the cloth. Glad to watch without anyone knowing.

I pull myself back. Rage and hate sear through me. It's time.

Time to send a message. I am doing this for him. Everything I do today is for him.

Tuesday 25th May 10.36

NUSAYABAH

It has taken months to pull the footage together. The camera pans back. I watch with disgust as it starts to play across the globe.

The purple neon sign behind her reads 'Jongleurs'. She is grinning at the camera.

An infidel in the crowd shouts, 'What about a blow job?'

At lightning speed Hackeem shouts back, 'Sorry, love, I don't eat pork.'

My voice comes over the clip. 'This woman is an abomination. She takes Allah's name in vain. She is godless. Her head carries a fatwa and she will be judged by God.'

Another clip starts. One when she was still a student. She squints in the spotlight. She is holding a bottle of beer, swigging from it. Swaggering on stage. She is an arrogant fool.

My voice again. 'For over twenty years, this woman has taken Allah's name in vain. She has been corrupt and filthy and disrespectful. She commits the Hadd crimes of adultery and consumption of alcohol.'

The picture switches again. It is Hackeem on a chat show. She is wearing a short black dress and has no self-respect.

The sycophantic presenter says, 'Amala, welcome. So the question on everyone's lips, since you were seen at the premier of the Kate Adams film two weeks ago is; are you and Kate an item?'

The screen behind shows the two women, drunk, practically having sex in the back of a taxi. A tattoo of an angel on Hackeem's shoulder is in full view.

I speak the quote slowly and clearly. 'May Allah curse the women who do tattoos and those for whom tattoos are done, those who pluck their eyebrows and those who file their teeth for the purpose of beautification and alter the creation of Allah. Peace be upon him.'

I continue, 'This is the history of Amala Hackeem in the last twenty years. Filth, debauchery and alcohol. Ignorant and flaunting the laws of Islam. Ignorant of Sharia. Her punishment is coming. She will be judged by Sharia; she will be sentenced by Sharia. Inshallah.'

I raise my forefinger, in the universal sign to show jihad is coming to you, and flick the switch. The clip changes and shows that it is moving to live footage. The rainbow-painted headquarters of Faith to Faithless comes into focus. Right on cue, a man clad in black, covered by a balaclava, raises an arm and throws a petrol bomb through the window. He runs to a car nearby and they drive off.

I watch as six young people run out of the building. I am calm as I hear their screams and see that one girl is clearly badly burnt. The sirens start up.

The screen goes black.

I sit back. So far so good.

Tuesday 25th May 10.45

MILLIE

Neil and I are transfixed. Despite the horror, I am thrown back almost twenty years. The clip when Amala was a student was her first solo spot. She was electrifying. At the time, she thought it might be the pinnacle of her 'career'. It was a show at the Edinburgh Fringe in a tiny venue in the Cowgate.

I can almost smell that damp church. The stage was tiny and the whole place held about forty people. It got pretty good reviews and was described by one reviewer as 'Edgy. Hackeem has a caustic wit and the best heckle response on the Fringe.' She still has that review. She framed it and put it up on every toilet wall. Along with the algorithm. She always jokes that the best bits of her life are in the loo.

I swallow and try to blink back tears. I need to focus. I put my hands to my stomach to try and quell the churning. I watch in horror as the scene moves to the young people running from the building, screaming. A man pulls off his sweatshirt and tries to wrap it around the burning girl. She falls to the floor as he uses his bare hands to try and beat out the flames.

Neil, Rehan and I stare at the image. I say, 'My God, those are just kids.'

At the same time, Neil says, 'Good God, those people are burning. Look at that girl, she's on fire. Jesus, what's that building?'

Rehan Ali says, 'Oh no, I know that girl. She's only a teenager. Please don't let her be too badly hurt, Inshallah. These people, these people… when will they stop hurting us?'

Seeing Neil's face he adds, 'That is the London Faith to Faithless office. It is an umbrella group for anyone who has left a faith and is feeling ostracised or scared. The bulk of members are young people leaving Islam. Good people. Good people being hurt.'

I say, 'Amala gives them the money to run their annual conference.'

We watch until the screen goes black.

Neil swings into action and starts rerunning the clip, desperate to find something that can help locate Nusayabah. Anything. He is slowing it down, zooming in. He is also calling Sean Menzies, his main guy back at the Rockeem office. Second only to Amala in his technical prowess.

Neil turns back to the screen, forcing himself to sound calm, talking to Sean he says, 'Hey, can you look at a clip that has just gone out? It's someone talking about Amala. We think someone might be threatening her and I want to try and find the source. I need to know where it's coming from. Can you do anything on the voice? Anything that can get us more of a picture of who she is? Anything on the accent. Any clues?'

'Will do, mate. I'm just getting it up now. Is it some fanatic saying she's got another fatwa on her head?'

'Yeah, I think so but let's just check it out. Call me back.'

Neil and I look at each other. We each see fear and dread in the face of the other.

Neil says, 'Any luck getting hold of Mark?' I shake my head and he says, 'I've messaged Ella, she needs to know what's going on.'

Neil turns back to the clip. Trying to find the server, knowing it will have bounced halfway round the world. But knowing if anyone can trace it, it's his guys.

A few minutes later, I hear Sean's voice over Neil's computer.

'We're trying to locate the server but so far no luck. Whoever put this stuff together you should hire them, mate. We did better on the accent though. We know it's British and likely born British. It's not London, more North. Maybe Yorkshire or Lancashire, but quite mild. We're working on it.'

'Thanks, Sean.'

I look at Neil, 'Chances are she will have been radicalised here. Likelihood is she's got funds if she's well-educated.'

'Anything in the stuff you've read so far giving any clues?' he asks.

'No, not yet but I'm going to take another look. I'll try Mark again first.'

Tuesday 25th May 10.53

MILLIE

Like us, Thompson and Norton have watched the footage over and over again. The horror of it not diminishing one iota with repetition. Thompson looks drawn, anxiety etched deep on his face. 'We've already had a bombardment of calls to Elliot Mitchell.' Mitchell is Thompson's Head of Communications. An old-school spin doctor, usually found in the bars and restaurants around Westminster dishing out titbits to a salacious and insatiable media; laconic and a bit too ready to believe his own spin as the power behind the throne.

Thompson's obsession with image and the media was seriously pissing me off.

Rehan Ali says, 'I know some of the people working at Faith to Faithless. They're good people. I have put out some calls to ask about the person throwing the petrol bomb. A colleague has already been in touch to say he recognised the car. It belongs to a young activist who is heavily involved at the Tower Hamlets mosque. Closely aligned to Abdul Izz al-Din, the Imam there.'

My heart skips a beat. I know him. It can only be bad news if he is involved.

Norton says, 'I know Izz al-Din. He is someone very much of interest to us.'

Norton is well known for her ferocious memory. She is able to hold incredibly complex relationship webs in her head. Vital for dealing with the likes of Har majiddoon. She is widely considered to be one of the best home secretaries Britain has ever had, which is probably one of the reasons she unnerves her boss so much. She, too, knows if al-Din is involved it does not bode well.

Rehan Ali nods and says, 'He's trouble. He refused to condemn the atrocity at Glastonbury last year. Strikes me that he carries a lot of sway. Way too much. If Amala is in The Bush my guess is Izz al-Din knows where. Trust me, I am doing everything I can. I'm asking all my contacts. I promise I will keep everyone abreast of anything I hear.'

He looks at me. He can see my lip trembling. I can't stop it. My hands are shaking too. He says 'I have put out quite a few feelers. I'll hear something soon. She can't stay hidden for long. Try not to worry.'

Thompson says, 'Thank you, Dr Ali, I know we can rely on you to be discreet. We need to try and keep a lid on this. We don't need some intrepid media hack asking tricky questions about Nusayabah until we have this totally under control.'

I think, 'Asshole, he just wants to save his own skin.'

Norton turns to Neil, 'I presume your guys are trying to trace the server. Any luck?'

'Not yet. They are using some pretty sophisticated technology. Our guys confirmed the accent, though. It's probably born British, Northern but a mild middle-class accent. A young woman, somewhere in her twenties. We are also trying to trace Amala's last movements before she cut her Ezylocate.'

Norton says, 'We are looking too but nothing yet from this morning. We are pulling together CCTV footage. GSOC is working with Sean Menzies at your office. Although if she is in that part of London, spotting a woman in a burqa is no easy task. We have face and body recognition working on it.'

Before she can say any more, a knock on the door makes us all jump. Every fibre of my being is on hyper alert. We turn as one to look. A man in his mid-fifties, dressed in an ill-fitting navy suit appears. He is wearing gloves and holding a box away from him at arm's-length. It is about the size of a shoe box. I feel a wave of nausea wash over me.

This is the 'proof.' He hands the box to Thompson without a word.

Mitford asks him, 'Anything from the swabs?'

'No, sir, it's clean. We can't get anything from it.' He turns to Thompson. 'It was brought by a commercial courier who said he picked it up at an office block in Tower Hill. The security guard who gave it to him said it had been left there a few minutes before, but he had no description. Whoever left it was in motorcycle leathers and a helmet. We have someone on their way there now. We are checking the cameras for every possible route. The security guard is being debriefed by Commander Mitford's team.'

Mitford pulls thin blue gloves from his bag and looks at Thompson. 'Let me open it, sir. I want to be sure we don't destroy anything that might be important. We'll give it back to the analysts once we're done.'

Thompson looks ashen as he hands the box over to Mitford. Mitford takes it carefully and gingerly starts to peel at the edges. It has been securely taped with what appears to be strong gaffa tape. A light powder is still evident on the box from the swabs.

Mitford slowly but deftly lifts the tape. Peeling it from the box with a steady hand. It is immediately evident what is inside. The metallic stench of blood is in the air. I can taste it in my mouth. Something worse fills the room, seeming to suck out every bit of oxygen; the smell of burnt flesh. I gag. I hadn't realised I had been holding my breath until then and it comes out as a loud retch. Neil has his arm on my shoulder and I can feel him shaking. Even Mitford's hand is trembling a bit as he uses forensic tongs to inspect the bloodied and burnt finger. Burnt almost black.

I feel the room spin around me and I slump forward, my head on the table, trying to take in air, gulping convulsively and feeling the nausea rise in my throat. I can hardly believe only a few hours have passed since I kissed Grace goodbye. I can still feel the remnants of the jam behind my ear, sticking to my hair.

Mitford turns the severed finger around, peering closely, looking for God knows what.

Stating the bleeding obvious he says, 'I think we can pretty safely conclude it's a finger, and from the looks of it, it is recently severed and burnt. The charred flesh suggests it has also been burnt after it was severed. Presumably to make it more difficult to identify without DNA testing. Whether it belongs to Amala Hackeem is impossible to tell at this stage.'

He turns to the man who has brought it in.

'Get it checked out.'

But then he stops. He looks inside and using a pen he pulls out a pendant, holding it by its fine chain. He holds it up. Dangling, twirling and glinting in the overhead light.

I hear Neil groan. It has three leaves in bronze and silver. I recognise it immediately and my stomach turns a somersault. I bought it for Amala when we graduated.

'Oh my God, that's Amala's. I gave it to her. She never took it off.'

It is highly unusual. I had bought three of them in a tiny silversmith in the Grassmarket in Edinburgh, one for me, one for Amala and one for Ella.

Amala wore hers all the time.

'Are you sure this belongs to Amala Hackeem?' Thompson asks.

I swallow hard. 'Yes, I bought it for her. They were made to order in a small shop in Edinburgh a long time ago. The shop closed down shortly after.'

Neil speaks directly to Thompson. 'Simon, we need to work out how to get her back. We might just have to do what this woman wants.'

Thompson speaks gently, his palms up. 'Neil, you know we don't negotiate. We can't. Not even for our friends. We can't. I am really sorry but I can't let you do that. We all need to focus everything we have on finding her.'

In my head I hear the unsaid, 'before it's too late.'

Neil looks aghast. 'So, what? You are going to let them hack her to bits? After everything she has done for your government. I can't believe you'll gamble on us getting to her in time.' His voice rises and he bangs the table. 'What are you? A complete monster? Are you some sort of fucking animal?'

He is shouting across the table at Thompson. Alex Dalgleish moves to intervene, Thompson waves her away.

'Neil, you know our policy. You know we can't negotiate. If we did they would just keep killing us. Every time we gave in there would be a hundred more.'

'But they wouldn't be Amala,' he roars.

'No, but they would be someone else's brother or sister, son or daughter, husband or wife.'

I move beside Neil. 'Please,' I beg. 'Please do something. Please don't let them kill her.'

Suddenly, it hits me like a thunderbolt. 'Aafa. We need to find Aafa. Amala was worried about him. She said she was going to see him in Tower Hamlets today. He wanted her to meet his friends and for her to go to the Education Centre. If we find Aafa, we might find Amala. He must know something. I can't believe I forgot that.'

My hopes soar; surely that will be enough to have a fighting chance of finding her and to get her out. Any hope is better than no hope.

Before I finish speaking, Neil is already back at the screen, trying to locate Aafa.

Thompson, mopping his brow with a large white handkerchief, turns his attention to Mitford and Dalgleish. 'Do we have any more on tracing those feeds? Have we any idea where these people are? Is it Tower Hamlets?'

Dalgleish and Mitford both shake their heads.

Dalgleish speaks first. 'We have people scouring the clip for anything that will give us the whereabouts, as well as anything about the people involved, including voice and body recognition. We are working with Neil's people and we know she's playing her class and education down. We have our best people working on it. So far no absolute confirmation on the location and no other clues on the woman. Rockeem can probably track Aafa faster than any of us.'

Mitford says, 'We have all units on alert and we have all potential informants being located for anything that will enable us to work out who is behind this and where they might be holding her. As Alex says, we are fairly confident, but not conclusive, that it's Tower Hamlets. There has been a higher than usual level of internet chatter on the dark web in the last few weeks and we know from a pretty reliable source that a safe house has been prepared with some heavy security in the Mulberry Estate.'

Dalgleish adds, 'And we can confirm that the safe house belongs to Abdul Izz al-Din.'

I turn to Dalgleish. 'Has the BSU come up with anyone?'

Dalgleish nods. 'They are on it but they have over seventy individuals in Tower Hamlets currently on the radar. Do you know Toni Roberts'?

I nod. Toni and I had worked on some policy papers together. She is an astute observer of human behaviour. Much understated with a wicked sense of humour. On her desk she has a framed copy of the Oscar Wilde quote, 'Every saint has a past and every sinner has a future.'

Dalgleish says, 'Hook up with her, she is in the loop. Best talk to her about Aafa. She has a file.'

I hadn't expected that. I didn't think Aafa would be on their radar. How had that happened?

'Ok,' Thompson says. 'Keep on it, everyone. Back here in one hour.'

Looking at Norton, he barks, 'Let's find Aafa Hackeem. Pick him up and bring him in. No mistakes. This is still a total media lockdown. The clip she has put out about Amala is already attracting a lot of interest. Keep it tight. Got it?'

There is always a hint of a Messiah complex in Thompson's behaviour – a sense of being so special that the normal rules don't apply. He strides out without another word to the rest of us.

Norton nods and moves like an army drill sergeant, all the while shouting into her phone.

Bloody hell, I had only seen Aafa the day before yesterday at Ella's. I make myself replay the lunch again. Had I missed something? He had seemed pretty normal. Bit het up maybe. He had wanted to talk about profiling and the PPCs, but after a while we had talked more about the increase in women being radicalised. I wish I could get Ella's view on it. He talked to her more than me. They often walked KK, her ugly pug schnauzer, together.

What would she see that I had missed?

TWO DAYS BEFORE

Sunday 23rd May

Ella

Neil and Amala have given up dancing. Aafa is having a go at her. I hear him from the kitchen. It sounds like they are picking up from an argument they had already started somewhere else.

'Lots of people think you're helping the government spy on Muslims. Ezylocate means a lot of innocent Muslims are followed and tracked. The police and security services are tracking thousands of people and then they feed the information to the PPCs. Most of the time they add two and two and get ten. It means people like me – people with nothing to hide – get stopped day after day.'

This whole weekend seems to have been about the PPCs and Ezylocate. I pour the lumpy gravy through a sieve. Well, not the whole weekend. Looking at the burnt pot I smile. I was making the gravy earlier when Neil had come in from his run, hot and smelling of the outdoors. I relive his hands on me as I stir the pot. As soon as I had thrust my hips in to his I knew I was a goner. He had kissed my neck just how I like it and ten minutes later the pot was burnt. I add a hefty drop of red wine to mask the taste.

I head in with the roast lamb and smile at the table. I see their anxiety that I might have created some monstrous concoction, and then the relief as I place the dish down.

'It's ok. It is all very staid. Proper roast lunch, although I have added a few interesting items to the cous cous.'

They groan as one as I dish up the cous cous, which seems to have congealed into a nasty lump. Then they get back to arguing.

Aafa's frustration is crystal clear. I decide to dig a bit further. I want to know more for my story.

'Hey, Aafa, why do you think it's getting worse? Why do you think the PPCs are helping turn more people towards extremist groups?'

He leans back. 'Because no one is talking about profiling. Ask Millie. The government is refusing to say the PPCs use profiling but Jean Norton's a liar. She knows as well as I do that you are eighteen times more likely to be picked up if you are brown and have a beard. God help you if you're carrying a rucksack. No one thinks I might be a student and it might be my research in there.'

I turn to Millie. 'I get that but it still doesn't answer why more women are turning into extremists? Are they as likely to be picked up by the PPCs?'

Millie puts her glass down. She has her lecturing look about her.

Amala shouts, 'Short version, Mill, or we'll never get whatever dangerous pud Ella has made.'

I do my mock cross face. 'I bought it myself so you're safe. It's an apple pie.'

Amala sticks out her tongue and then does a wrap it up signal with her fingers to Millie. 'Ok, thank God. Nothing that might kill us. Hurry up, Mills, make it the quick version.'

Millie puts on her pseudo lecture voice. We are all trying to diffuse the tension. Aafa looks fit to explode.

'Well, there is an increase in women being picked up. Still less than men, though, but they are being converted at a higher rate. Especially white girls. I have seen hundreds of websites aimed at drawing girls and young women in. Often by linking to their insecurities and offering them a bigger cause and purpose.'

She grabs her glasses from somewhere in the bird's nest of her hair, and looks over them, going for the scholarly professor look. 'They start by playing to real vulnerabilities and then create a tempting offer of a family who doesn't judge you on how slim you are, how popular, or what grades you get. For them, it's like joining a sorority. The stuff out there is really sophisticated. But it's not just white girls. It is Muslim girls too. They feel oppressed and harassed and also disrespected.'

I think about my story. Everything she says rings true, but it's not the theory that gets people to see the world in a different way. It's story or a drama. Something that grabs their imagination and gets them to wonder, what if that was me…

Millie looks more serious for a moment and, glancing at Aafa then me, says, 'The PPCs are adept at stripping Muslim men of their dignity and respect. Aafa's right. With women, though, they force them to take off their veils. They say it's to identify them but then they don't give them back. It's brutal and degrading. And it feels deliberate.'

She shifts, sensing the high charge in the room. 'Anyway, that's the short version.' She sticks her tongue out at Amala then turns to me. 'So, what's your story Ella? I thought it was trying to give a human face to radicalisation? Is it about the PPCs too?'

'Sort of. Well, not really. It's about women, though. About giving a taste of how things feel from the inside.'

I don't get to finish because Aafa jumps back in. 'It's not right, though, is it, Millie? Thompson and Norton shout from the rooftops about our security and that some intrusion is a small price to pay. The Prevent and Protect Centres are supposed to be about keeping us safe. In reality, they are state-sponsored harassment for men and women, but only if they are obviously Muslim.'

Looking directly at Amala, he says, 'And you and Neil have helped make that happen.'

I squirm a bit in my seat. I hate conflict. He does have a point. Maybe he's right. That's why it's important for people to know the whole truth.

TODAY

Tuesday 25th May 10.58

MILLIE

Still thinking about Ella and what she might know about Aafa's plans, I see Norton close her phone with a snap. She turns to Ali. 'Dr Ali, is there anything else you can do discreetly?'

It is evident Ali has already shared something that is not going to be divulged to the rest of us.

He nods. 'I will see what I can do.'

She thanks him and asks that he return at 12.15 with everyone else to pull together whatever findings we have before the next contact at one when we would be given bank details.

I realise something is tugging at my thoughts, through all the horror and confusion. Not just Aafa but something is bugging me about the blogs and chatter. Something important. Something I've missed.

I turn to Norton and ask if I can look through all the materials not just the edited highlights. My thinking is, if I can work out what makes Nusayabah tick and where any recent recruits may have been taken, then we might have a chance of working out where Amala is being held and why. It seems more and more likely Nusayabah is the woman in the clip rather than the name of a group. I am pretty certain she is a leader of something. She has a lot of authority. She acts as if she has real power.

Norton nods. 'Of course, we will have everything uploaded and you can take a look.' With that she marches out the room with a brisk order. 'Get Dr Stephenson everything and get it now.'

Is this about Faith to Faithless? Amala gives them a lot of money. Is that it? Or something else? There is a reference in the correspondence between Nusayabah and someone calling themselves Ackwaat, which talks about a meeting at a women's group today. Was that just coincidence? Has Amala ever mentioned Nusayabah before and I can't remember? Something in her stand-up routine maybe? Has she said something to offend Umm Umarah? Oh, Amala what have you done?

I have known her my whole adult life. I love her like a sister. I can't imagine what my life would be like without her in it. She is the most stubborn and the cleverest person I know. But she is also one of the kindest. It's unbearable.

I wonder if Neil has heard from Ella yet. I check my phone. Nothing from her and nothing from Mark. I had messaged her this morning when she cancelled breakfast. I was glad then. I hadn't been able to face a debrief of the whole Mark thing before getting my game face on to come here. I know I am being a coward. I had avoided all her sympathetic looks on Sunday too.

I can't get the picture of Amala out of my head. For a moment, I give into tears. Trying not to hear Amala's screams, to stare down my worst fears. I ring Mark again. It goes straight to message. Again.

'Mark, it's me. I know you don't want to talk to me but I really need you to ring. I can't say more on a message but please believe me it's urgent. Please, please give me a ring.'

I hang up. I force myself to concentrate. I am going back to the beginning.

Tuesday 25th May 11.05

NUSAYABAH

I hardly ever think about *before* but there is a smell of cut grass in the air. So sweet and fresh. So English.

For a moment my mind wanders. I can see our garden right on the edge of the woods. I was wearing a pink dress. It's my party and Mum had made a huge chocolate cake. Everyone was singing 'Happy Birthday'.

'Make a wish. Make a wish.'

I blew out the candles. I squeezed my eyes tightly closed and tried to think what to wish for. I peeped through one eye and Daddy winked. I knew then what to wish for. He picked me up and twirled me around in circles. I inhaled the fresh smell of the grass and the slight sickly smell of cakes and lemonade.

Tuesday 25th May 11.06

MILLIE

Everything has been downloaded to my smart block. I begin to read. The blogs start from eight months earlier. I scan to the ones headed 'Nusayabah'. Someone has made notes and added events that may be relevant around the dates, and translated words that may not be well known. It is a good piece of work in a short period of time. The text follows the usual turgid pattern.

In December, a series of posts stand out for their sheer viciousness. The big news at that time had been the discovery of a high-level cell in East London. Jean Norton had been all over the press hailing it as a victory in the long war against terrorism, and used it as an opportunity to affirm the necessity of effective surveillance, making the point that it was a small price to pay if a few people lost their privacy.

The ring leader was the Strategic Commander of Har majiddoon. The analyst has even given the phonetic pronunciation (Ha –ram–gee–dawn).

The blueprint for Har majiddoon could be traced back eighteen years to the embittered soldiers in Camp Bucca. That history is a core part of my teaching. The American controlled internment camp was seen by many as a world-class training ground for jihadists. Hundreds of thousands of men had passed through. A hundred thousand prisoners; disciplined soldiers from the secular Baathists in Saddam's army as well as any man the Americans thought might be a terrorist just by how he looked. Many were imprisoned with no evidence against them. Regardless of their beliefs when they were interned, 90 per cent of those who were released left as ruthless jihadists.

Har majiddoon had formed from the various factions that had split and reformed from Al-Qaeda. It was perfected through the bloodbaths of ISIS who meticulously combined their passion with a cold calculated discipline and a forensic and deliberate long war. The off-shoots that came after built an incomparable army. Every soldier willing to give his life. Her life. To give it freely. To give it in a heartbeat.

Oh yes, we all know the legacy of Camp Bucca only too well. We are still paying for it in Britain, France and the USA.

I click on the report in *Newswatch* from that time reporting on the ATF50 raid.

Top Terrorist Killed in Dawn Raid
14th December

In the early hours of yesterday morning ATF50, the multi-agency Anti-Terrorist Force which combines intelligence, technology, surveillance and Special Forces, intercepted a high-level Har majiddoon cell in East London. The cell involved at least six men and was headed by Abu Bakr (37), the long-time strategic commander.

Bakr was in the top 10 of most wanted global terrorists. Wanted by both US and British authorities for atrocities committed both here and in Washington, DC. It is widely believed Bakr was the mastermind behind the coordinated suicide bombers in the Tysons Galleria Shopping Mall in Washington which killed 28 and injured hundreds two years ago.

I remember the raid that killed Abu Bakr. The day after he was killed Amala, Ella and I were shopping in Oxford Street when the Christmas lights had all gone off and a massive black standard was projected on to the front of Selfridges alongside the face of Abu Bakr. Ella and I were horrified but Amala kept ranting on about how difficult it would be to work the switches remotely. She was more than a little impressed by their technical prowess. Ella and I less so. We had hurried back to Ella's and comforted ourselves with hob nobs and hot chocolate. The Christmas spirit momentarily gone.

Thinking of it now, I realise despite everything I am hungry. I scramble in my bag for the ginger biscuits I've been carrying around. They are right at the bottom, already crushed. Greedily, I tip them into my mouth.

Regan Ali comes in as I wipe the crumbs from my dress.

'Listen, Millie, have you seen the parts in the dossier about something called Touchstone?'

I shake my head. 'Why? Does it look important?'

'I'm not sure yet, but it seems to come up a lot.'

He brings up a page further on. The word Touchstone appears a few times in block capitals but with no explanation. I can see that the blogs are becoming increasingly sickening as they shift to being more personal than political. More threatening.

I say, 'I hadn't really clocked it but it might be important. I think it's worth asking.'

'Yes, I did, but I got nothing back from Thompson or Norton. Hard to tell what they know.'

I scroll down and go back to the conversation between Nusayabah and a girl called Emily, who part way through changes her name to Ackwaat. An interesting choice of name, Arabic for sister. More interestingly it says that there is to be a special meeting for Ackwaat today. Ali was right, Touchstone comes up more and more. In fact, I see now there are several mentions of it. Always next to Thompson's name and always capitalised. I note it down again, assuming it's relevant but not recognising it.

Whoever she is, Nusayabah is clever. She knows the best way to reel vulnerable people in and then hook them. The thing about effective recruitment is not just to find the opening but to fine-tune the argument, create an alternative set of beliefs so that vulnerable individuals come to the conclusion themselves. Pull, not push, selling. As in all behavioural change it requires not only logic but passion and emotion.

I look down. A missed call. Mark.

Shit, I had it on silent and missed it.

Shit. Shit. Shit.

Tuesday 25th May 11.20

MILLIE

I am dreading talking to Mark. My throat is dry at the thought. I hold myself still for a moment, trying to focus. I turn back to the transcripts. I need to get some answers then I will try Mark again. I had taken a course on psycholinguistics at Edinburgh and tried to stay up-to-date with the latest developments but it isn't really my area of expertise.

I'm not sure what else I can pull from the dossier. I want an old friend of mine to take a look. Daisy Woo is a brilliant professor at Edinburgh University. We have worked together a number of times looking at the language used in recruiting for extremists but never on something like this in real time. I am pretty certain if I ask Norton whether I can talk to her she will say no so I decide not to ask. I would rather face Norton's wrath than not act.

I tap into my smart block:

Hey Daisy, how are you? Still enjoying the freezing winds of George Square?

I need a favour and it's pretty urgent. Like right now. Sorry! Please can you take a look at the attached and tell me what you think about the two authors – Nusayabah and Ackwaat. I really need something back within the hour, quicker if you can. I am in a meeting for the next 30 minutes so even some initial thoughts would be fab– sorry to ask. The tequilas are on me next time I'm up. xx

I hit send and make my next call. It is to Toni Roberts. She answers on the first ring.

'Hi Millie.'

'I'm thinking maybe you were expecting me?'

'Yep, Alex gave me the heads up. We are looking at everything we've got on Aafa Hackeem. I know this must be an absolute nightmare for you, Millie, but I have to say everything is pointing to Aafa being turned. We are checking out his computer, Ezylocate and his university attendance. Doesn't look like he's been to too many lectures lately. Izz al-Din looks like the translator.'

I let that sink in. She's talking fast and I am struggling to keep up. I'm reeling from the fact they are watching Aafa. They clearly think he must be in deep if they are talking about a translator.

Toni knows the impact of what she's said. Translators are critical to radicalisation. They are typically the Imam or a serious and respected figure in the community. They provide a clever counter-argument, finely tuned to that individual. Framed in such a way it will resonate at the deepest and most basic human level. They need to be well-informed, not just on the Quran but on modern-day living. They must understand and appeal to how it feels to be a young person in modern Britain. Izz al-Din would fit the bill. Worrying if Aafa is spending a lot of time with him.

She says, 'Aafa has been seen with Izz al-Din and a number of his trusted foot soldiers at various events over the last few months. Through analysis of CCTV, biometric data and a cross reference of his calls and visits to the area, we know they have all been active recently in the Ealing and Tower Hamlets Education Centres amongst other places.'

Toni carries on, her voice slower as she senses my anxiety. 'Aafa has been picked up over twenty times since Christmas, eight in the last month. There is a lot on his phone and chat about PPC profiling and harassment. I'll send over what we have.'

'Toni, I know everything must point that way but honestly I've known Aafa since he was a kid. I just can't believe he would do anything that would end up with Amala being hurt. He's like the perfect student. Straight As. The perfect son. Christ, I can't believe you guys have been watching him.'

Toni's voice is quieter still. 'I know, Millie, but you know as well as I do that it can happen under our noses. We can't always see the signs when it is the people closest to us. I am still on it, still looking, so let's not get ahead of ourselves, there may be a perfectly reasonable explanation. We're pulling his bank records at the minute.'

'Really? He's always skint. He's just a student.'

'I know, Millie, but it's our job to check.'

My heart sinks. She's right.

'Thanks, Toni, I appreciate it. Keep me posted.'

I can't believe he's on their radar. He has been getting so angry these last few months. I don't know what to think. The PPCs are really divisive and they are mushrooming, not just in London but all over. I know Toni's team are stretched to the limit, so if they have Aafa in their sights, they must think it's worth it.

It feels like we have hit a tipping point where more and more people are prepared to see refugees and immigrants pulled out and discriminated against, without really thinking about the cost. It's something Aafa has been talking about more and more. For him the personal and the political injustices will have fused together.

I can see it through his eyes. Something that Izz al-Din would no doubt have seen too and will have known exactly how to exploit.

Tuesday 25th May 11.22

NUSAYABAH

They will be looking everywhere. Looking to find me. Analysing my voice, working out my history, poring over the VT clips. Working out how I was 'turned'. Working out who did it. Trying to piece it all together. Faiza will be somewhere on their radar. Faiza was a strong and important voice for me. She is part of my story. But she is not the whole story. There were many others who helped me see things clearly. One voice more important than the rest. His was the best voice.

I think of him. My husband was the bravest man I ever knew. I picture him when we were together. The him no one else saw. That will never be part of their story. Behind their analysis and behind the headlines are the real people with a real purpose. People with beliefs and hopes for a better world. A world lived according to Allah. They'll never tell that story.

I breathe in, I can smell him if I hold my breath, feel him and taste him.

My heart is ripped asunder. A physical pain I have channelled into hatred.

Tuesday 25th May 11.23

MILLIE

I see Neil walk in. I have been so absorbed I didn't see him leave. He sits beside me and leans in close. 'Listen, Millie, I have got our best guys at Rockeem working on tracing Amala and Aafa.

There's no way I'm leaving it to those fucking baboons working for Mitford. Look, it's urgent we get hold of Mark. We really need him to transfer the money. We need him to make sure we can keep it quiet but know it can be traced.'

Neil is so focused. I usually see him with Ella where he is all loved-up, but there is no way you can build and sell a £1.2 billion company, create another one from the ashes, and operate at the highest levels of government without being pretty steely. I realise at that moment I have more faith in the pair of us getting Amala back than in the guys supposedly in the driving seat with a long history of public non-negotiation on hostages and just as long a history of dirty backroom deals.

'I've left messages for Mark. I am going to try him again now. I contacted Daisy Woo and sent her the blogs to try and pick up some clues on Nusayabah and also someone calling herself Ackwaat – her latest recruit. If we can work out where the latest recruit has gone, we might be able to work out where they have taken Amala. The blogs and emails talk about a special meeting of a women's group for Ackwaat today. That can't just be coincidence, can it?'

'No, must be the same group Aafa wanted Amala to go to. Good idea to send it to Daisy. If anyone can crack the pattern you and Daisy can. It would be a pretty big coincidence if it's separate to this, don't you think? Do you think that this Ackwaat might have something to do with burning the Faith to Faithless building? To test her? See if she has really been turned? Could the meeting be to give her a job like that?'

'Yeah, it could be linked.'

I quickly tell him about the call with Toni. 'I can't believe Aafa's on their radar. That's hard core. Shit. I know he's pissed off but he loves Amala. As much as he hates her doing stand-up he wouldn't want her hurt. Amala said he was appalled when he saw her black eye.'

Neil pulls on his bottom lip.

I glance down at my notes. 'There's something else. Rehan Ali spotted it first. Every time Nusayabah mentions Thompson she has the word Touchstone next to his name always in capitals. It's really bugging me. I am sure it's relevant but I can't work out why. Neither can Rehan. Is it something Amala or the two of you were working on?'

'No, never heard of it. If Mals was on something big she would have talked about it.'

I type in 'Touchstone'. We read it together. Various items come up. The first is the dictionary definition: 'An established standard or principle by which something is judged.' Then various things about a 'stone that's used to identify precious metals by testing their purity'.

I keep looking. 'Is it something to do with mining? Did Thompson have a dodgy deal somewhere?' I'm thinking out loud.

Neil says, 'If it's judgement, maybe it's something to do with the final reckoning? The day of judgement? Armageddon? That could point to Har majiddoon.'

I try 'Touchstone + Simon Thompson.'

Nothing.

There are various companies called Touchstone but nothing linking them to Thompson.

'I'll ask Sean to get some guys on it. It must be relevant but I don't think it's linked to Rockeem.'

Neil passes the message to Sean who promises to do some digging.

'Quick as you can. Make this and the tape the top priority.'

Sean's answer is quick and business-like, 'You got it, boss.'

'Our guys are going through everything too, looking for traces. Whoever Nusayabah is she is good at hiding. The encryption is high-quality stuff and the messages are bouncing all around the world. We'll get it, though.'

He sighs and blows out a long breath. I look straight at him. Not wanting to voice my deepest fear. Avoiding the one question I am too scared to ask. Neil is silent.

I can't help myself. I ask it.

'Do you think they will let Amala die?'

Neil looks at the floor. He has been involved in some seriously high-level discussions about surveillance and I am sure some of it was pretty dark. He has seen the inner workings of government and the security services in a way that few people have.

'Yes,' he says, and walks out.

Tuesday 25th May 11.45

MILLIE

3D maps of East London are on the wall screens. Along with Aafa and Amala's last Ezylocate movements. They now have tracking from two nights ago through to this morning when both had gone black. At which point the conclusion is that they are both, as suspected, now in Tower Hamlets Sharia Community Estate.

Copies of the BSU report are on the desk headed, 'Aafa Hackeem'. It confirms that Aafa has stopped attending university and that he is classed as a known associate of Izz al-Din.

Norton turns to Neil, 'Anything on the whereabouts of either Aafa or Amala since they went black?'

'Nope, not yet.' Neil is swiping through layers of code still trying to track either of them.

Thompson speaks to the whole room, 'The media lockdown

is holding. We have calmed down the queries about the clip Nusayabah sent out about Amala. Very few people outside this room know what has happened and for now let's keep it that way. I am afraid to say we have riots breaking out all over the Mulberry Estate. They could be random but we don't think so. There are a number of serious burns as a result of the Faith to Faithless fire and one woman remains critical. Police have cordoned off the area.'

Norton points to the large screen showing the map of The Bush. She clicks on a residential street. A camera zooms in. There is a crowd of mainly young people. A lot are wearing the *kufiyah*. The chequered scarves tied around their heads, hiding their mouths and noses and rendering them unidentifiable. On the right-hand side of the screen are the constantly updating results of face and body recognition scanning. The camera zooming in, with a name appearing above a person when a hit is made. The crowd is mainly men but some female names are appearing too. So far, no name of major significance has shown up.

I watch as the young men, and a few women, line up against the police. The long line of police, some in riot gear but some ordinary coppers from neighbouring areas obviously hauled in to support, are struggling to maintain control as the crowd starts throwing anything they can lay their hands on. Bricks, stones and bottles are flying through the air. Mostly hitting the shields holding the police front line. Norton clicks again. Another street. Another riot. And again. It doesn't look random to me. It smacks of a well-ordered army.

Norton turns to Ali and asks, 'Anything else, Dr Ali?'

'Only what I have told you. It's hard to know quite where all this activity is leading to at the moment.'

Norton replies, 'The whole estate is in uproar. Fights seem to have broken out all over. It's hard to pinpoint a trigger. Our guess is this is orchestrated. They look choreographed.'

I look at her. No one in the room believes this is coincidence.

'We have more police heading in to try and contain things.' Norton uses her pointer to highlight a terraced house and continues, 'We believe this is the home of Abdul Izz al-Din.' Tapping the screen a picture of Izz al-Din appears. He could be anything from forty-five to sixty. His face is rugged and weather-beaten underneath the long black beard. He wears black robes and a turban – an outfit meant to evoke the last caliph. Norton starts a clip playing of Izz al-Din at a recent rally.

I am drawn to a figure behind him. Clear in the background is Aafa. The voice from the clip is biting. 'The banner for jihad has risen in the UK. The war will continue until the caliph is secure. Our brothers did not start this war. I praise our brothers who last year made history in the den of iniquity – Glastonbury…' He raises his forefinger and continues, 'I am asked to denounce those brothers. I will not denounce them. I say it is magnificent that our brave soldiers attack these symbols of greed and debauchery. Forwards to the caliphate. Raise the banner, brothers. The banner for jihad. Allah Ackbar.'

Aafa is holding a flag. The black standard. Waving. Supporting. I look away. Not wanting to see. Not wanting to believe my own eyes.

Tuesday 25th May 11.55

I hear loud noises outside. Shouting and glass smashing. It sounds like a march or a protest. I strain to listen. I can't focus very well. The pain is excruciating.

I must be somewhere with lots of people. People shouting. I start to drift. To another time. Another march.

20 YEARS EARLIER

Edinburgh

'No blood for oil!'

'Say no to war.'

'No war in Iraq.'

For once the sun was shining as we shuffled past St Giles Cathedral, along The Royal Mile, passing the medieval alleyways on either side. Dark passages full of ghosts and grizzly stories, past the Scottish parliament keeping Arthurs Seat straight ahead and in to Holyrood Park, arms linked as we repeat the megaphone chants.

Everyone was shouting at the top of their voices. Ella had made placards and we held them aloft, joining the calls to avoid a bloody war. We sat on the grass in Holyrood Park listening to the speakers.

Ella said, 'I can't believe this. We're going to send soldiers to fight, to die, and all for oil.'

Amala grinned. 'You know if you Google the word oxymoron it comes up with The George Bush Centre for Intelligence.'

Laughing, Ella opened the wine and offered up a picnic. She passed a plastic box that contained a weird greenish mush.

'What the fuck is that? Is it dead?' Millie exclaimed.

Miffed, Ella replied 'It's avocado and some stuff I found in the fridge.'

As she tucked in with gusto, Amala grimaced. 'Ella Russell, one day you'll kill me.'

TODAY

Tuesday 25th May 12.03

MILLIE

Norton has drawn a ring with her pointer around Aafa, forcing us to face the inevitable. Forcing us to believe Aafa has been radicalised. I have known him since he was a toddler obsessed with Lego and building bridges from coloured blocks. An only son with three older sisters, he is the heart of a whole family who dote on him.

Neil lets out a groan. He is chewing hard on his bottom lip. I hear him mutter under his breath, 'Shit.'

I look at the screen. I can't stop staring at Aafa. Now just another maniac with a flag and a beard that I hardly recognise.

Norton says, 'The clip is from two weeks ago. On Saturday 8th. It's outside Cubbitt Hall on the Isle of Dogs. Aafa Hackeem was manning a dawah stall. After the rally he went back to the Tower Hamlets Education Centre with Izz al-Din.'

I wince. I have never seen him at a dawah stall. If I had, I might have talked to him about it. Dawah stalls have sprung up everywhere. It's impossible to walk past most major stations in London now without seeing them.

Neil looks quizzical. I quickly explain. 'They're set up as propagation channels. Dawah is a key Islamic principle where good Muslims invite others to join. It's more than just spreading the word of Allah, though, it's a conscious effort to link thoughts, attitudes and behaviours to a particular interpretation.'

'You mean those guys that are always trying to stop you to talk about the Quran? Like the guys on the Corner of Oxford Street and Regent Street I see every weekend?'

I nod. 'Yeah.'

Rehan Ali adds, 'It's the same principle as in most religions – spreading the gospel. Mostly they're benign or, in fact, more likely positive.'

I cut across him. 'In extremis, though, it's a manipulative technique; brainwashing if you like.'

Ali nods, a little irritated. 'Yes Millie, in extremis.'

Norton moves us along. 'Our assumption is he convinced his sister to visit the Sharia community today in a pre-planned hostage-take. Dr Ali has told us that Aafa has been increasingly speaking out against his sister, saying he was embarrassed and humiliated by her stand-up routines and her controversial stance on sexuality and other issues.'

Rehan Ali sits up in his chair again and looks over at Neil and me. 'I heard this morning that, apparently, Aafa asked the women's group at the Tower Hamlets Education Centre to pray for Amala. I have spoken to a number of friends close to that community and they confirm what I told you this morning, Mr Thompson. There has been a lot of activity involving key members of the Council. It appears that there is a safe house deep within the The Bush which seems to be heavily guarded. Other than that, there is nothing exceptional showing up in the usual places.'

Ali continues, 'A number of my sources say that Aafa Hackeem has been in The Bush a lot. He appears not just to be heavily involved on the dawah stalls but also at the mosque and the

Education Centre. There are no reports of any radical activities as such, but he is described as fervent and devout. He has instigated a lot of discussion about the PPCs and has engaged a number of scholars and the Imam in discussions about peaceful protest and taking up cases of racial profiling and harassment. He is a very passionate young man.'

Rehan Ali is picking his words very carefully. He looks uneasy. Ali knows the whole Hackeem family and would know just how painful it would be when they found out about Aafa.

Looking at Thompson, Dr Ali finishes, 'I suspect he is exactly the sort of man we want on our side, showing the positive face of our faith, but I can imagine that becomes difficult when you are picked up time and time again and left in a holding cell with little respect for your commitment to prayer.'

I can see a slight flush appear on Thompson's neck as he shuffles his papers. He does not catch Norton's eye but I see her jaw tighten.

Alex Dalgleish sees it too. In fact, there's very little she doesn't see.

Thompson clears his throat and says, 'Ok, let's all use this next fifteen minutes productively. We reconvene at 12.50.'

Tuesday 25th May 12.04

NUSAYABAH

I am almost ready for the next contact. I feel calm and liberated. All the preparation is done. I catch sight of myself in the cracked mirror. I stare through the gauze. I realise then I feel invincible. I am ready.

Faiza taught me that striking at the head of the snake is the only way to destroy it. I will strike at the head and also the heart. The very heart of everything that matters to them. So they can know what it is to have everything destroyed.

It is time for them to feel the pain.

Time for revenge.

I am prepared for anything. Even to die. They never understand this.

That a life is such a small price to pay.

Tuesday 25th May 12.07

MILLIE

Rehan Ali, Neil and I are together. Neil is checking in with Sean again. I say to Rehan, 'What do you really think? You know Aafa. You know the whole family. Do you think it's even possible he could have been turned?'

He pauses then quietly says, 'You know he no longer attends the mosque with his father?'

Until his move to Oxford a couple of years ago, Amala's father had attended the same mosque every Friday in Luton. He had gone since he arrived from Pakistan as a small boy in 1974. He now attends the Central Oxford Mosque and until recently Aafa had attended with him.

I nod. 'I did know. Amala kind of mentioned it on Sunday at lunch. They thought the whole family was seeing less and less of Aafa but thought maybe he was attending the London mosque, more for convenience than anything else.'

Ali looks pensive. 'Yes, maybe. You know Amala's not the only one who's been threatened? So has their father.'

I didn't know that. I feel shaken.

'Why? Why on earth would he be threatened? Mr Hackeem is anything but outrageous. He hates being in the spotlight.'

'Indeed, that's true. He is a quiet and thoughtful scholar.'

A picture of him flashes before me. A reserved, considerate man of huge integrity. He is now based in the Oxford School of Islamic and Cultural Relations. A key moderate and well-respected by most of the Islamic community.

'He has received hate mail. He is seen as too liberal. He is a strong and articulate advocate for Tajdid. As am I.' Ali is speaking carefully.

I nod. Tajdid. The notion of renewal; that Islam must be constantly reformed to keep it in its purest form.

'But he is seen as weak for his refusal to condemn Amala. Also, he is seen as a traitor by the hardliners who, as you well know, are now running many of the schools and councils in the Confederation of Sharia Council strongholds. When he controversially spoke out about Hadd recently, Amala very publicly applauded him.'

Hadd are the punishments meted out at a Sharia judge's discretion. The punishments have become increasingly brutal and covert over the years.

I remember now. Mr Hackeem had spoken out about a couple found having an affair who had been flogged near to death. They had been living in Tower Hamlets and were part of the East End community attached to the Education Centre and mosque there. They were smuggled out by family members and taken to a local hospital. The smugglers had been locked in two separate rooms and kept in solitary confinement for over a week. The charges were hard to prove and those living in the community remained silent. Whether through fear, belief or compliance – or a combination of all three – it was hard to tell. Amala had blitzed social media calling her dad a hero.

I wonder now if this is about hurting their father. To prove him wrong?

Neil is half listening and suddenly says, 'Bloody hell, there's something else here. We've looked at Aafa's bank account. He's been making payments to an unknown account. We're still tracking it. But it looks like quite a lot of money. More money than a student has to fling around. Holy shit! Over the last four months he has sent over £10,000 to an account he's called Dawah.'

'I am sure the BSU guys will have seen it too. Let me ask Toni if they know any more.'

I call. Again she answers on the first ring. I ask her if she has seen the accounts.

'Yeah, we're still checking them through, but you're right. It looks as if he has been using his university fees to pay into that account. There's a bunch of other stuff that looks a bit odd too, but we are still looking at those. There are a couple of other accounts. I'll let you know once we have some more.'

I tell Neil and Rehan. Neil is furious. 'What does she mean odd? What else have they got? Christ, Millie, we need Mark on this. He'll be able to tell us. We need to see what else Aafa's been doing. Do you think they are telling us everything?'

'I don't know but I am guessing not.'

I press redial for Mark again.

Tuesday 25th May 12.17

MILLIE

Ali has gone to make some calls. Neil and I are alone. Sean has worked fast. Neil pulls up a set of bank accounts. 'Aafa has taken the money his dad gave him for university fees and given a chunk of it to the dawah account and some to this account here. See?'

'What the hell is Education and Light Ltd.?'

Neil clicks on the website.

I read aloud. 'Our mission is to give young Muslims the confidence and tools to spread the word of Allah.'

I scan down. 'We run seminars and education evenings for those of all faiths to share in our discussions and to learn the teachings of the Quran.'

Lower down I read, 'To do our work we need your support. We need to raise funds to continue with our programmes. If you believe it is important to share the voice and teachings of the Quran and to preserve this for future generations in Britain, then click here to find out how to help with our critical work today.

'Those who spend their wealth in the cause of Allah and do not follow up their gifts with reminders of their generosity or with injury, their reward is with their Lord. On them shall be no fear, nor shall they grieve. Quran 2:261–62.'

Things are clicking into place. It's classic stuff. Aafa will have been persuaded that education and spreading the word of Islam is key. That will shift to the need to use jihad. The end justifying the means. Aafa must be a long way down the road if he is sending this sort of money.

Neil says, 'This is all new to me. I've never heard him talk about this programme. Have you?'

'No, never.'

Aafa had wanted to be an engineer since he was a little boy. Mostly he seemed to look at books and websites about building bridges.

I look at Neil. 'From the bank records, it looks like he's used this term's money to give to this Education and Light Programme. He can't have been to uni since January. He should be sitting exams now.'

I sit back in the chair, trying to take it all in. My mind working overtime to find a way to Amala.

'Bloody hell, how did this happen? How can he have hidden so much? He must have been going into London every day but going to Tower Hamlets. His mum and dad can't have had any idea. Jeez, no one in his family could have had any clue what was happening. Right under their noses.'

I think about Norton's question to me this morning. When she asked about friends and family not knowing. Had it been a pointed question?

'Neil, I am pretty sure they know something we don't. Mitford brought in a note and gave it to Thompson and Norton. Whatever it said, it either shocked them… or maybe confirmed their fears. What do you think they're not telling us?'

Neil is biting hard on his lip. 'Do you think Amala's already dead?'

I can hear the shakiness in my voice. 'I don't know.'

I have to believe she is still alive. I have to believe we can find her. I need to think hard. I need to work at this. I need to work out what Aafa has done.

I voice my fears. 'Abdul Izz al-Din is an incredibly charismatic speaker. He is good at getting under the skin of kids like Aafa. I guess if you think about it, Aafa has grown up in a pretty liberal household. He has three sisters, all of them well-educated. Only Farah is devout. Amala and Leila are totally Westernised. Amala's out there on every level. Izz al-Din will know how to twist that. To show that good Muslims, faithful Muslims who have not turned to Western ways are being persecuted. And then you couple that with getting picked on for the colour of your skin, the faith you have. Add in a dose of racism and harassment and there you are. Ripe for the picking.

'If you are surrounded by clever, articulate and passionate people telling you that the world is flat, or black is white, then eventually you believe it. Once that is in your head it's a tiny step to believe that anything that gets in the way needs to be destroyed.

Neil has been listening intently. 'Yeah, I guess you need to know how it feels to be between two worlds and possibly rejected by both. Too Muslim for the cool kids and too Western for the radicals.'

'That's what Izz al-Din will be banking on.'

Tuesday 25th May 12.27

MILLIE

Back in the room. The air feels fetid and stale with our lack of progress. Frustration and anger simmering, ready to erupt. Everyone on edge as the clock ticks mercilessly on.

I have spent the last few minutes immersed in the blogs. Neil has been trying to pin down the server. Neither of us is feeling like we are any further forward.

Norton takes control again. 'Ok, let's pool what we've got. We can assume Aafa is with Amala and we can confirm it's not in the Izz al-Din safe house we saw this morning. We have drones there now and there are no signs of activity in the house. We are still looking.'

She turns her attention to me. 'Dr Stephenson, anything else you can tell us from the blogs?'

I summarise the main points around Nusayabah and the new recruit called Emily, who changes her name to Ackwaat, and the mention of today's date for a special meeting of the women's group.

'There is something else, though, something I can't quite put my finger on and I am going to keep checking. I'm pretty certain something called Touchstone is somehow significant.'

When I mention Touchstone, I make sure to look at Thompson, but he has his head down and is intent on his geometric doodles. I circle it on my notepad.

'Thank you, Dr Stephenson. I appreciate that for you, and Neil, this is very personal and I am grateful to both of you.' Norton continues, 'OK, let's get everyone on the same page. Dr Ali, anything else you can you tell us?'

'The women's group is meeting today so that probably confirms Amala was heading there. Whether she made it to the group, I don't know. Given the mention of this group is also in Nusayabah's correspondence with this new recruit, Ackwaat, we have to assume some significance.'

Rehan Ali then looks directly at Dalgleish. 'There is talk of someone having infiltrated the women's group at the Education Centre. Someone calling herself Wasiba Hammoud. The talk is that she has been asking a lot of questions, too many questions, and now seems to have gone missing. A number of very committed people would like to find her. It's making everyone nervous. I am struggling to get anyone to really tell me very much.'

Norton looks pensive and makes a note.

I gape at Rehan Ali. He continues to stare at Alex Dalgleish. She gives absolutely nothing away. Alex Dalgleish, the beautiful and composed olive-skinned woman who had not introduced herself this morning. Definitely not an MI5 pen pusher or an average spook. Neil said she was hard core. Hearing Rehan Ali now, I suspect that until recently, she was deeply embedded in the women's group and she is Wasiba Hammoud. Clearly Rehan Ali suspects this too. And for some reason she had to get out in a hurry. I wonder why.

Dalgliesh ignores him and instead says, 'We have strong reason to believe that Umm Umarah have been planning a high-profile hostage-take for some time. We believe the woman calling herself Nusayabah is part of the high command and has set up a splinter group. The equivalent of a Special Forces team. We also believe, based on our own intelligence, that they are in Tower Hamlets. She is good and she is careful. No one from our side has been able to get near her.

'The noise leading up to today from some significant members of Umm Umarah has increased significantly. As Dr Stephenson said this morning, and I can confirm, they are devout women who see themselves as part of the jihad. Umm Umarah's strategic commander is Faiza Siddiqui. Iraqi born and widowed about five years ago. She is fiercely intelligent, charismatic and has a loyal following. Her father was a General in Saddam's army and was placed in Camp Bucca.'

She didn't have to explain the significance of that.

Dalgleish continues, 'He died when she was eight. She came to the UK twelve years ago with a specific remit to recruit British women. She lived here for more than six years. She has been incredibly effective. I am guessing she recruited Nusayabah. We still don't know enough about Nusayabah but what we can tell is she runs a very tight ship. She is technically savvy and likely to be utterly, utterly ruthless. If she has set up a splinter group it will be for a special mission. Not your run-of-the-mill suicide bomber. I have reassigned Toni Roberts to this. She is pulling together everything she can along with GSOC.'

She pauses for a moment, looking over to Neil and me. 'We should believe if she has Amala Hackeem she will carry out her threats.'

The room is silent for a moment as we take in what she has just said.

Mitford looks at Thompson. 'Will you excuse me, prime minister, I believe we have some intel coming in and it may be important?'

Thompson nods and Mitford quickly leaves the room, pressing his phone to his ear as he goes. Listening but not speaking.

Thompson says, 'Ok. Five minutes.'

I feel sick. Everything Dalgleish said fits. A group well-planned, fanatical and willing to die for the cause.

Tuesday 25th May 12.35

MILLIE

Still no word from Mark. I have even tried his office but they have said he is not reachable. Maybe he's told her to say that. I can't bear the thought of him talking to that prissy PA about me. Telling her not to let my calls through.

I start reading again. I only have a few minutes. Neil is looking too. Trying to gobble up key facts and patterns. Focusing on every word, looking for anything that might open up something about Nusayabah. Trying to see more about Touchstone.

I scan through quickly. It is the usual dense diatribe full of hatred and twisted logic and endless calls to arms and quotes from the Quran. The analyst was good, though. The chronology, context and translations are helpful but I am struggling to get to the real nub.

What is clear is that the intensity has been increasing over the months. The blogs were getting more and more frequent. Quite a few responding to the likes of the ultra-right wing groups that had sprung up after Brexit like the 'England for English League'. I glance quickly through the rest. There is the typical nonsense including far right responses from the NBNP (the New British National Party). It looks pretty much like the old one to me. The same old fascists with pit bulls but with better technology and as usual failing to see the difference between Islam and Islamist and freedom of thought and terrorist intent.

It is hard not to question how we got here. When I was a kid things weren't perfect but we didn't have these deep divides. The extremism on both sides and the hate and intolerance is everywhere. Brexit and then the clamp down on liberal ideals in the US had spawned a web of fear and hate, intolerance and ignorance. I am terrified for the world Grace will grow up in.

I think about some of the mistakes made. Centuries of mistakes really. More recently Iraq. A war built on lies. For a moment I picture Ella making us go on that march. Was it all for nothing?

Mistake after mistake. Camp Bucca was a mistake. It was like Robben Island or the Maze in Belfast. All the best hearts and brains put together in one place with all the time in the world to plot a new global order. The prisoners freed from Bucca went on to fight. But to fight better, to fight harder. And to fight smarter. There was no better university to plan the caliphate. A band of brothers was formed, united by a cause and trained for revenge.

And it spread. Faiza Siddiqui is the bastard child of Camp Bucca, as are all those that follow her. Nusayabah too, likely.

So many mistakes. The PPCs, Ezylocate… a losing battle, fuelling the divisions.

I need to focus on what's in front of me. There is something going on about women too. This special meeting of the women's group. I would have loved Ella's take on these messages.

I turn to Neil and say, 'I wonder what else Daisy's seeing? The women's group seems to be a thing in all of this. It would have been good to get Ella's take too. She's used to looking at the way people write.'

'Yep. It's like wading through treacle reading this stuff. What the fuck are these people on?'

I nod. I read it day in and day out.

Alongside the chat the compiler has again given a bit of context by showing what had been happening on that day.

10th April

Reported bombings by US and British troops in Syria, Egypt, Turkey and Morocco. Many dead.

Nusayabah

Sisters we are the carers of the mujahedeen (warriors/ engaged in jihad). We are also the builders of the caliphate (an Islamic state). Our role is to care for our men and to build the future mujahedeen. Look at your life and ask – is it full and true or is it empty and full of Western hate and waste.

There are a few more like this interspersed with offers of joy and paradise in the afterlife. Also offers of clothes and food, friendship and family. Then, about three weeks ago, the new voice emerges. Emily, who had caught my eye earlier. The one with a meeting today. I flick through the remaining pages. I look again at the chat between her and Nusayabah; their contact had become more and more frequent.

It looks quite intense. I concentrate on trying to decipher the two main voices. There are a whole host dating back to September last year but it looks like it has heated up in the last month or so. I read again the key exchange between Nusayabah and Emily who changes her name to Ackwaat part way through.

I check to see if Daisy's come back to me. There's a message. I press on the picture and Daisy Woo appears. She has left me a video message. Neil and I both look.

'Hey, Millie, sounds like you are up to your usual tricks. Look, I've had a quick scan because you said it was urgent so these are just my real quick initial thoughts. As you know, psychological profiling is like codebreaking. Key words and phrases are like conversational tics that give real insight into the personality of the author so I've looked at these as a priority for you. I've picked a few of the main ones out. You can also tell a lot from the way a person uses words and grammar. What I can tell from the word structure here is that both of them are likely well educated. If it's helpful, I can also dig into how they likely acquired language. That can give us clues to perception and memory too. Let me know. I've started with Nusayabah. She is a serious nut job. I've no idea what you are involved in, Millie, but this woman is a sick bitch. I'm going to keep looking for traces and will get back to you, but take a look at the attached. I am going to get on to Emily now. Will be quick. Love ya, babes.'

I open the document. Typical Daisy. It is a well-constructed, well-ordered set of bullet points.

1. The references to sisters and rising up is consistent with a lot of the writings we saw emerge in the post-Iraq war refugees.
2. She mentions '*The Kaffirs in Iraq tried to kill us but they put all our brothers together under one roof so they could fan the flames of our war*.'

It would appear that she is referring to Camp Bucca. Her style is similar to that of the early jihadi brides that we saw flee to Syria in 2014/15 and Nigeria, Morocco and Turkey after that. She might be an older woman trained around that time or she might be a younger bride of someone who has that history.

3. She is educated and smart and I think English is her first language. There are places where she gives herself away with quite sophisticated grammar. Her writing is trying to be less educated than she is.
4. I have done a crosscheck but I can't find any matches to the usual bloggers. I think you are looking for someone who is not yet likely to have come to the attention of the authorities. But that was just a quick initial scan. Presume you could ask the BSU guys?
5. Is it worth trying to find out what Touchstone is?
6. If I was going to take a punt, I would say that Nusayabah has some connection with the four guys that were killed by ATF50 just before Christmas. Remember? It's the only major event from around that time but it marks a real shift from something passive to something personal. Of course, something else might have happened around that time that didn't make the news.

In summary – British, intelligent and now on a personal crusade. Find Touchstone and you will likely find her.

Neil and I look at each other. I swallow hard. 'I think it might be worth looking at the most recent ones, where she is talking directly to Emily.'

We look together. There are some gaps in the flow where clearly the authorities had had some difficulty in tracing the later sets of exchanges. The trail is picked up on Monday 10th May, two weeks ago. There is a dramatic shift in the conversation and Emily/Ackwaat seems to be making arrangements to join Nusayabah.

The exchanges are more practical, mainly explaining how to meet and what to bring, as well as the great opportunity to serve Allah. They are also more littered with quotes from the Quran.

Monday 10th May
Ackwaat

I am ready. I have everything. Warm clothes, blankets and I have bandages and the medicines you asked for. I will bring the moisturisers and also cotton wool. I have Tampax and deodorant. I have your instructions to disable my Ezylocate and I will be dressed as we agreed.

I know I have sinned. My head was turned by the decadence around me but I am ready to serve. What mad pursuit. What struggle to Escape.

As it says in the Quran, 'And whoever his sins are plenty, then his greatest remedy is jihad.' I am ready sister. I believe what lies behind us and what lies before us are tiny matters compared to what lies within us.

Inshah Allah (If Allah wishes)

Thursday 13th May
Nusayabah

Sister

Masha Allah (As Allah has willed)

The time is near and we have a special job for you. You have been chosen in the jihad to serve Allah, we will have everything ready for you. The day is 25th May and it will be seared in the memory just like our joyous 9/11. They will speak your name with fear in their hearts and death in their soul.

Aameen (May it be so)

Ackwaat

I am ready. I am ready to fulfil your wishes. That is my dream. The dreamers of the day are dangerous people for they dream their dreams with their eyes open and make them come true. I will make it so.

I stare at the last few lines. I try to focus and look back through the language. One thing is sure, I am fairly clear they are both really women. Few men would think of something like asking for Tampax even when adopting a female persona. I try to think. My brain is mush. I am going to have to look again.

I realise I have had nothing to eat since breakfast apart from the bashed-up biscuits and now all the coffee I've drunk is actually making me less focused. The burning acid in my stomach is still there and I seem to have a permanent film of sweat all over. My whole body is cold despite the warm room and I can't stop shaking.

I flick through the pages, viewing them side by side. What is the pattern? What else could I see? Or not see at the moment? I try to close my eyes and visualise something else to let my brain work subconsciously.

Neil is reading the notes again. 'Touchstone is definitely not a work thing. Sean's guys have been through everything on her work computers.'

He whispers, 'We are going to have to do something. There's no way they will let her go without us meeting the demands.'

I nod. I don't say it out loud but everything I know about this group says the chances are they won't let her go anyway.

But we have to try. We just have to convince Thompson. And we have to find Touchstone.

Tuesday 25th May 12.58

MILLIE

Coming back into this room sets my heart palpitating. The tension is suffocating. The air conditioning is belting out lukewarm air making us all even more hot and uncomfortable. Thompson has his jacket off and tie loosened and keeps wiping perspiration from his top lip.

James Mitford strides in and passes another note to Thompson, who opens it and clearly blanches. He passes the note to Norton, she reads it and then looks at me. She peers over her glasses, thoughts clearly flicking through her brain. She is staring hard. Calculating. But what? What do they know that I don't?

It's time. The woman in the niqab appears. Calm and unhurried. She speaks with precision.

'Mr Rochester, we have sent the money transfer details to your finance director at Rockeem. Mr Thompson, at 5.30 you will release a statement to Tim Ellis at *Newsbreaker*. He knows he is to expect a major story from you at that time, and that he can break it publicly at 6pm, that all PPCs will be closed. I have already told you that you should not doubt our intent. We will contact you again in two hours. At 3pm. At that point, you will confirm that we are on track, the money has been transferred and you are not going to do anything foolish.

'Perhaps you feel you have less to lose, Mr Thompson, than Mr Rochester. Let me leave you with something that may help you revise that opinion.'

She pauses and then with venom says one word.

'Touchstone.'

At that point the screen turns blank.

Neil jumps up from the table shouting, 'What the fuck?'

Thompson is stock still. Norton is staring at him, not quite sure what just happened.

The rest of us begin to move, rising from our chairs, not sure what to do next but feeling the need to be active. To do something. Before we get any further the screen lights up again. Nusayabah is holding the knife. The blade glimmers in the dim light as she twirls it like a baton round and round.

The camera pans back and there is Amala, cradling her hand. Hoping to protect it. Incoherent with fear and pain. At that point, all three TV screens in the meeting room flicker and the same image appears on all of them.

Thompson roars, 'What the fuck is going on? Is this being broadcast? Is this on the TV networks? Get this shut down. Someone shut this down now. I mean right now.'

He is frantic and impotent, pulling at his hair and banging the table. James Mitford and Alex Dalgleish stare.

'People of the UK. Listen. My name is Nusayabah and this is the day of reckoning. We are at war. This infidel is a prisoner of war and we have told your Prime Minister Thompson she will die in less than five hours if he does not close down every Prevent and Protect Centre.'

The camera switches and pans in close to Amala. She is trapped.

'She will pay the ultimate price and her reward is not paradise but years of burning in an eternal hell.'

With the quickest of flicks she takes her knife, pushes back the veil at Amala's face and slices off part of her ear. The screen turns black. For a few seconds, there is the complete silence that comes with the aftermath of total shock. For a moment, I am catatonic. My brain will not shift into any kind of thought. Then there is noise all around me. Thompson is shouting into the spider phone on his desk.

'Someone find out if that image has gone out. Who the fuck are these people? How did they breach the broadcasting networks? Someone find out now. Get this shut down.'

I look at Neil. He is biting his lip again, hard. Moving closer he says in a low voice, 'I've got to get out of here. I need to get to the office and I need you to get hold of Mark. Like right now. Where the fuck is Mark? We need him. He's never out of touch like this. What the hell is he doing? Can you try him again? We need him. Now.'

I nod and whisper back, my throat dry and raw, 'How are you going to get out? Thompson will never let you.'

'I'll tell him he can send some chump from Mitford's team to come with me, but that I need the technology at Rockeem to be able to work out where they are and how they breached the networks.'

Thompson is practically screaming into the phone. I glance at the screens; the networks are trying to make sense of what just happened. I see the BBC news flash up and hear them say, 'We are investigating the breach that appears to have taken over all major networks and internet sites. It would appear that a jihadist group, a terrorist group, has taken a hostage and is demanding closure of the Prevent and Protect Centres…'

My whole body is shaking. I feel sheer and utter terror like a cancer through my veins. I am still staring at the screens but only one image is seared on my brain. The knife. The knife slicing her ear. What next? What will she do to Amala now?

It is only a matter of time before the media works out who has been taken. They will connect the clips that have gone out about Amala this morning and the hostage being held.

Dalgleish and Mitford are talking quietly to each other, their backs turned to Neil and me. Deep in conversation and looking at the block in Mitford's hand.

Something about their stance makes me more scared, on alert. It says there is something important that they are keeping from the rest of us and that does not bode well for getting Amala out alive.

Tuesday 25th May 13.15

NUSAYABAH

I stare at her as she holds the side of her head. She is bleeding like a butchered dog. I watch the blood pour down the side of her face, soaking the veil. I have no pity for her. She is trying to hang on. Keep control. Now she knows what it's like to have someone else control you.

I smile.

I am good with a knife. Faiza taught me well. When I first arrived in Syria she taught me. She could cut a man's throat in one slice. Moving like a cat, stealthy and silent. She knew I was nervous at first but she was patient and I learned fast. I think back to those cold winter nights lying beside her, sharing a blanket to keep warm. Sharing our dreams. Giggling together and sharing the chocolate bars smuggled in from home. I can taste the creamy chocolate melt in my mouth.

I look back at her. She is whimpering holding her ear.

She's trying to go somewhere else. She is trying to conjure a dream of a better place. We all have dreams. Hers don't matter anymore.

20 YEARS EARLIER

Edinburgh University

I dream of the first night. It was a good night.

'I'm doing it for me mam, she had me when she was twelve and she's given up everything for me to live me dream.'

Ella switched voices from Geordie to husky south London and said, 'This really is the Last Chance Saloon for our Katie, she has spent fourteen years playing every grotty bar and club through the North East and tonight is her chance, her last chance, here in The Saloon. Is this it? Her big night? Is this the new beginning...? Over to the judges... Andrea?'

Amala walked into the kitchen and immediately joined in, jumping onto a chair and simpering, 'Well, Shaz, I feel Katie's passion. I feel her pain of the last fourteen years.'

Ella picked up without missing a beat. 'Andrea, darling, I am surprised you can feel anything after all that botox and pouring yourself into that frock... Ha ha. Just joking, my darling, you look ravishing as ever.'

'Well, Shaz, as I was saying... Katie really is a little star but I think we all know she's going nowhere, she's not going to win...' Amala said, pausing for dramatic effect. '... Because she looks like a bag of spanners and the ugly ones never win.'

We had all fallen about laughing at the perfect take-off of The

Saloon reality show. And so it began.

'Hi, I'm Amala. I couldn't resist joining in.'

'You're hilarious,' Ella had replied.

Several hours and three bottles of her three-for-a-tenner wine later, Millie hiccoughed. 'I'm starving.'

Ella, waving her hands wildly in the air, said, 'And now my new dear friends, how about a surprise and a treat. The world famous Russello.'

In unison, 'What?'

'Russello, a dish created by my good self to fulfil the needs of even the finest palate with my culinary delight of anything in the fridge that can be added to a tin of baked beans or tomatoes to make a feast.'

In the kitchen, Ella set to making some weird concoction involving tuna, beans and cheese with the mould chopped off and plopped on toast. She was like a dervish, shaking in salt and pepper with a flourish, flinging in squashy looking tomatoes with a 'ta dah'.

Ella laughed as she presented three plates of soggy, mushy mess with a flourish. 'Russello a la fromage.'

Sniffing gingerly, Amala looked like she might throw up before she fearlessly dug in.

After a few mouthfuls, Millie said, 'Ok, confession time. How and where did you lose your virginity?'

Ella grinned, 'Oh I love a confession. Amala, you first. You must have been the most beautiful girl in school so were they queuing up?'

'Ah well, not quite. But my first time was with my chemistry partner, Tom Hollander. How geeky does that sound? He was seriously hot, though. A real babe. My parents were so obsessed with my grades that they thought nothing of Tom coming round to look at bonding.' She leered, her fingers giving quotation marks to bonding.

Millie laughed. 'Did you really just say that and lick your lips?'

'Oh, Tom and I did a lot of bonding. One night, my mum knocked on the door with tea and barfi. We only just got our jeans on in time, but even then Tom had a lovely honey glaze all over his chops. She never noticed a thing. I bet Tom's never had another piece of barfi quite like it.'

Millie said, 'At least it wasn't in the back of a car. Mike Monahan was six foot three and had borrowed his sister's Fiat 500. His arse left a perfect moon print on the window. He was so desperate he lasted about twenty seconds and actually shouted "Hallelujah" when he came. His sister went mental when she couldn't get the arse print off the window.'

Tuesday 25th May 13.20

MILLIE

The media is going berserk. I flick through the different news sites. The pictures show the burning Faith to Faithless building.

'We have been reporting all morning on the terrible fire bombing at the Faith to Faithless building in central London. One woman is badly burnt and three other men are being treated for minor injuries.'

They are piecing it together. A reporter outside the Faith to Faithless building says in a breathless rush, 'The woman calling herself Nusayabah and demanding the closure of the controversial Prevent and Protect Centres also released a threatening film this morning of the well-known technology innovator and entrepreneur, Amala Hackeem. Hackeem is perhaps even better known for her controversial stand-up comedy.

'Amala Hackeem is believed to be the woman taken hostage and being brutally savaged. Experts and police are currently looking at the links between Nusayabah, Hackeem and the burning of the building behind me this morning, which resulted in four people being treated in hospital. One is said to have third degree burns.'

Pictures of Amala are all over the media. Clips from her stand-up, her interviews on faith and sexuality are running in loops. There are pictures of her in Afghanistan with Neil.

'Hackeem and her business partner, Neil Rochester, set up the Rockeem Foundation several years ago to help girls and women in countries ravaged by war and where women are at a disadvantage.'

It moves to the voice-over clip of Nusayabah. Her voice gets no less chilling, no matter how many times I hear it. I switch channels. It is showing a clip of Amala at the Lebanese and Syrian border. She is in t-shirt and jeans, holding a small girl in her arms.

'Teachers in Tents is a programme for all young people. Without education, the world of guns and fighting is the only one open to them. It is our only way to compete and beat the likes of Har majiddoon.'

I switch again. 'Hackeem and her business partner, Neil Rochester, are the brains behind Ezylocate. Rochester is now the special adviser to Simon Thompson on technology and surveillance. Hackeem and Rochester met at MIT in Boston, Massachusetts. They made their fortune when they sold their first business, AllTalk, for £1.2bn to Gogglebits.'

Another channel. 'Ms Hackeem has always been a controversial figure. Her work with Faith to Faithless is believed to be the reason for the attack today.'

My phone rings. Mark.

Tuesday 25th May 13.24

MILLIE

I pick up but I can't speak. The four weeks since I have seen him feels like a lifetime. I try to make the words. I can hear my breath, fast and ragged. No words come. Images of him leaving, silent and stony-faced, dart across my mind. Images of me completely drunk after the argument at the restaurant, calling him 'fucking boring', with all his colleagues watching.

A cold film of shame washes over me as I replay the horror. How could I have been so stupid? But even then he forgave me yet again. The images from a few days later are different. A cold, angry Mark. One that might never come back.

I clutch my stomach tight with one hand and cradle the phone with the other.

Mark waits. I imagine him gripping the phone. His brain going at a hundred miles an hour. Terrified something has happened to Grace.

Then I hear his voice 'Millie, are you there? Is it Gracie? Is she ok? Is she hurt? What is it? Millie you're freaking me out! I was in a client pitch all morning, my phones were off most of the time. What's happened?'

I can't help it. I hold myself even tighter, the phone still at my ear, tears wetting my arm and the pages in front of me.

'Hey, Millie. Talk to me. Tell me. What's happened?' A gentler voice, one full of concern. His beautiful voice.

'Mark, I'm at 10 Downing Street. I've been here all day.' I cup my hand around my mouth and speak in a quiet whisper. 'It's not Grace. Have you seen the news? Amala has been taken hostage by some women jihadi group. They're threatening to kill her if they don't get £100m and Thompson doesn't say he will close the PPCs. Mark, they cut off her finger and burnt her with a blow torch and sent it here in a box. They just cut off her ear on live TV.'

I can't say anymore. I weep. I weep like a baby. I can't hold it together. The tension of the last three hours has just found a release valve and his voice triggers so much of the emotion I have been denying myself this last month.

Mark is silent, desperately trying to make sense of the incomprehensible.

I hear him switch on the news. He is watching. I hear him breathing. His breathing changes as he watches.

'Jesus, I can't believe it. Oh my God. Who is this Nusayabah? Is it someone Amala knows? Oh my God, Millie, there is a picture of her in a burqa. Jesus. Oh my God, Oh my God, they're cutting off her ear. Fuck. Oh my God.'

He takes a deep breath.

'Hey, listen. Where are you? I'm coming to get you.'

I can't help it. A tiny flicker of hope flutters in the pit of my gut. I put my hand back to my belly for the tiniest of moments.

'Mills, I can come. Let me come.'

That breaks me more. I am inconsolable and incoherent. Mark's voice like warm treacle has unhinged me. The history of our marriage is in that voice, those honeyed tones.

A rocky marriage that probably won't survive. I can't think about that now. That good things might just be possible. I need him to help me.

'No, no. I'm trying to help. We are trying to profile the group. I need to stay here. I need to do what I can.'

I carry on, gaining strength as I think about the practicalities. I speak in a rush, trying to get over as much as I can as quickly as I can. Knowing his banker's logical brain will be kicking into action.

'Listen, I need your help. Neil wants to pay the money. It's a 100 million quid. He is at his office. He's trying everything to get a fix on where she might be. He's trying to locate Amala himself. Thompson is adamant he won't negotiate. We think Amala's with Aafa, probably in Tower Hamlets. Neil wants to make a secret deal without Thompson. More money or something. Mark, he needs to know how he can transfer the money then try to trace it without Thompson knowing. Can you help him?'

To his credit, Mark doesn't hesitate. His fiercely structured mind immediately working out the options.

'Leave it with me. Let me see what details he has and what I can do. I'm near his office. I'll be at Rockeem in twenty.'

I start to thank him but the words won't come. I think about the fact he is still in London. I don't even know where he's staying. He only took a few shirts with him.

'Thanks, Mark,' I croak.

'Hey, that's what we are, eh? A team: good and bad, thick and thin.' His voice is thick with emotion. More than anything I want to feel him in my arms. I want to see the way he used to look at me before I ripped us apart and he became cold and angry, hardly able to look at me.

I start to cry again. It was what he used to say when anything bad happened. When I still thought we might make it as a team.

He hangs up. I whisper, 'I am so sorry' down the empty line. He still doesn't know how bad I feel. How ashamed I am. He has no idea what it feels like to lose control like that.

Mark will know how to fix the money. He would know how to trace it too. An old moneyed Memphis boy used to operating across the globe. Doing what he does best, doing deals and making money.

Ella and Amala never quite warmed to him. They first met him when I was at Pax. They came to visit in November 2016, we were drowning our sorrows, over Chinese in Ruby Foos in Times Square.

6 YEARS EARLIER

New York

MILLIE

Ella was like a broken record, 'Trump, for fuck's sake. Trump? What the fuck is going on? Who the fuck voted for Trump. The man's a fuckwit.'

Amala's latest obsession was the New York comedian, Michael Che. She was now working her way through the entire 'Black Jeopardy' clip that had been on *Saturday Night Live*, with Tom Hanks as a Southern redneck,

We'd seen Che earlier that night and Amala had already committed his routine pretty much to memory. She loved the bit where he asks Hanks about loving all God's creatures.

Ella cut in and looked right at me. 'Well, that's it, isn't it? That's the question we all want to ask. Mark. Do you love him?'

Suddenly sober, Amala, stopped arsing about and said, 'So, Mark? What are you thinking? A fling? Bit more? What's the deal?'

We were all the worse for wear but I could tell from the look that went between them that they had been leading up to this point.

Amala trailed off, realising that they were now at the part they wanted to talk about. They stopped laughing in unison and looked at me. I felt myself blush.

Tears came to my eyes. They were forcing me to look harder than I wanted to. Mark was hot and he was thoughtful and I knew he kind of made me a better person. But also, I knew what they meant. Why they questioned me and him as a couple. He was making me smaller. I looked at my two favourite people in the world and realised for all the messing about they were worried. Ella looked deeply uncomfortable. She had obviously geared up for a difficult conversation. She spoke first.

'Millie, he's a nice guy. He is gorgeous and all those Memphis manners are charming and all that but, you know, he's a bit, you know, a bit of a dick.'

'Why? What do you mean? Why do you think that?'

She had obviously rehearsed the conversation with Amala, who chimed in. 'He's very smooth but, you know, a bit sort of, controlled. Well, uber-controlled, really, and a bit controll*ing*. You know, everything is so much in moderation. He eats really well, he goes to the gym almost every day, he never gets pissed up. That apartment is like a showroom.'

I jumped to his defence whilst feeling a gnawing anxiety build. 'So you think he is too perfect or too rich or too nice?'

Ella picked up. 'Listen, Millie, it's not that. You know he is all those things but he's kind of not you.'

I bristled. 'What, so I am not nice and not perfect, and I'm a bit lairy?'

Ella smiled. 'Well, you are nice and you are lairy but, no, you're not perfect. No one is. Not even Mark Carter but he seems to want to make everything perfect, including you. You know the whole thing about the apartment. No shoes. You can't use the cloth for the sink on the kitchen bench. The dishwasher has to be stacked in a particular way and God forbid you might put a drink down without a coaster.'

I didn't want to see it. I didn't want to listen.

'Well, it's an $80 million apartment and I guess none of us would want it covered in coffee cup rings.' Even in my head that sounded lame.

Ella took my hand and stroked it. 'Millie, you know you are really great. We know when you exaggerate and make your stories bigger. It's funny. It's you. I hate the way he does that voice and says, "Oh Millie, that's a bit much. Or, "Let's tell it again without the drama". Don't let him take away the drama. Don't let him fade you.'

Amala looked at me. Her huge brown eyes were full of concern.

'Mille, lovely, I love you like a sister. So does Ella. We are the Nofas, we look out for each other. He's a nice guy. Have a fling. Enjoy New York with him, but just be careful.'

'As long as it is fun, Mills. Plenty more fish in the sea, you know, and maybe it will feel different when you are at home. Maybe you will start to breathe a bit more easily…' Ella trailed off.

We didn't say anymore.

TODAY

Tuesday 25th May 13.32

MILLIE

I think about more recently. Alone Mark was relaxed and funny but in our gang he was always a little on the outside. Ella tried hardest. He was always the quickest to find the poetry in her stuff. They swapped books and talked literature.

He is my rock, though. Was. He anchored me and made it safe. Easier to be a mum. Easier to be me. Always picking me up when I went too far. Always forgiving me. Until now.

I kick myself for being distracted. I need to get my head back. I think back over what Nusayabah said. Day of Reckoning. That must be the link to Touchstone. Judgement? Armageddon? Har majiddoon?

Rehan Ali is making calls. I ponder out loud to him. 'Is there something specific I am missing about a day of reckoning? Something in the Quran?'

Rehan turns to me as he finishes the call. 'You think it's today? Do you think she is preparing us for some sort of judgement day? Yes, it's in the Quran. Let me show you.'

He pulls up the text. We read it together.

But when there comes the Deafening Blast – that Day a man will flee from his brother, and his mother and his father, and his wife and his children. For each one of them that Day will have enough preoccupations of his own. Some faces, that Day, will be bright – laughing, rejoicing at good news. And other faces, that Day, will have upon them dust. Blackness will cover them. Those are the disbelievers, the wicked ones. (Quran 80: 33-42)

Rehan explains. 'The Deafening Blast is the nearest translation of the term, *As-Sakhkhah*, one of the names of the Day of Judgment in Arabic, the end of all delight and enjoyment. If you hear the Arabic word, you would know that it carries a very sharp tone; it almost pierces the ears.'

'Bloody hell.'

I read it again. 'Do you think it's something about the whole Hackeem family? Judging them all? You don't think Aafa's handed over his father too?'

'I have just spoken to Abdul Hackeem. Now that it is on all the channels, he was bound to see it and, I wanted to reassure him that everyone was working hard to get Amala back. That poor man. That poor family. This is a nightmare for them. Jean Norton had already spoken to him this morning. There is police protection at their home and he is there with the rest of the family.'

'God, he must be frantic.'

I can't imagine how they must be feeling about Aafa.

Rehan Ali says, 'I think perhaps we should look at the papers again and see if there is anything we have missed. Anything else about a day of judgement. You are doing so well Millie. You and Neil. It must be so hard.'

I nod. 'It is. I just wish I believed we had all the facts. What do you think is going on with Mitford? He brought something in for Thompson and Norton that clearly spooked them but nothing's been said?'

'Yes, I saw that but I have not been taken into their confidence either. Millie, I am an old man and I have been in this country since I was a small boy, but still they don't fully trust me. I have always tried to do the right thing but that's not always enough. You know Dalgleish was part of the woman's group in Tower Hamlets. She'd been there for months. Her cover was blown and I warned them to get her out. Even then, they can't quite trust me. I am not the same as Siddiqui or Nusayabah. I want to find Amala, but it's hard when underneath all the nice spin they tar us all with the same brush and don't really ever trust us.'

'I don't think they trust Neil and me either. And I sure as hell don't trust them.'

Tuesday 25th May 13.40

MILLIE

We are both deep in the dossier. Looking for any clues. Desperation making it hard to focus properly. Looking at the most recent entries, they seem to show Nusayabah has turned Emily.

24th April

The previous day a cell of six suspected terrorists from Ealing were arrested. One died of an asthma attack whilst detained.

Glancing at the next set of exchanges it is clear Emily is now referring more and more to less well-known passages from the Quran; showing a deeper knowledge.

Emily

I am really confused now. My boyfriend says he loves me but he tries to push me too far. He can be so cruel. Then he switches back and says he loves me. If he loves me there should be no despair but he ignores me when I cry, even though my tears flow down like a river. He says all girls have sex before they are married. I don't want to have sex with him. I haven't winced or cried out loud. Even though I want to. I didn't have the nerve to say no at first but then I thought of you and I did. I don't fit here. I tell him I want to get away. I want to get beyond this place of wrath and tears. I want to be the master of my soul. Or mistress. I don't want to feel the pressure of his rage.

Sometimes when I am alone and I think about him, I feel life is not having and getting but being and becoming. I saw the pictures at the weekend of those six boys that were taken to the PPC in Shepherd's Bush. They say that one died because he had a really bad asthma attack but I don't think that can be true. The others say they were tortured. What do you think?

Nusayabah

Sister, you and me we both know that our brother Majid did not die of an asthma attack. He is in paradise now and has given his life for jihad.

I think you know what you have to do. Join us. We do not judge fat or thin here. We are loving and care for our own. We keep you safe and honour you as a sister and a mother of the mujahedeen.

Sister, we can make the hijrah (the journey) *together, May Allah grant us shahada* (faith) *together and unite us in Jannah* (paradise).

26th April

Ackwaat (sister)

Nusayabah, I am no longer Emily. I am Ackwaat. I am a sister. I am ready to give my life to the struggle and to make my duty to Allah and only Allah. I live for the struggle. I will see the Kaffir dead in our streets just like our brother Majid. And our other brothers trying to fight oppression.

I am ready. Tell me how.

Quran (8:65) 'O Prophet, exhort the believers to fight'

Emily, now Ackwaat, is ready to die. Is she the one with Nusayabah today? The one with the knife? I call Toni Roberts.

'Hey, Toni. I am looking at the shift from Emily to Ackwaat.'

'Yeah, it's classic stuff. Just like most of the kids we've seen come through our deradicalisation programme. Looks like Nusayabah knows just how to find the lost, lonely and anxious and is smart enough, Svengali style, to make Emily feel valued and worthy. It's not rocket science but you can see where she has tapped into Emily's deepest fears; the most raw emotion and vulnerabilities.

She adds, 'I am pretty sure Emily has made that tiny step that moves belief to violence in the same way I think Aafa has. Nusayabah may be a link in Aafa's radicalisation too. It would add up. My reckoning is Aafa saw Amala as part of the price he has to pay. I'm guessing Emily has come to the same conclusion if she's heading to the women's group meeting today.'

Sadly, I can't help but agree. 'I think you're right about Aafa. We are trying to work out now if there is anything else going on today. Nusayabah talked about today as a day of judgement. Are you guys picking up anything else that says more people might be involved in this?'

'Nothing specific, Millie, but we are all over it. I will let you know as soon as anything else comes up. Promise.'

'Thanks Toni.'

I am not sure she will. Her loyalty will be to Alex Dalgleish who along with Mitford, Norton and Thompson know something. I just need to work out what it is.

Tuesday 25th May 13.46

MILLIE

I drop another quick note to Daisy Woo.

'Hey, Daisy, any thoughts on the Emily/Ackwaat exchange yet?'

Instantly a message back says, 'Is this about Amala? It's all over the news.'

'Yes.'

'I'm already on it. I'm with you my friend. I am sending over what I have done so far.'

'Thanks. I owe you x'

Daisy's reply is instant. 'No. You don't.'

I swallow, making myself concentrate. Thompson has reluctantly agreed to let Neil go to the Rockeem offices on the strict understanding that he will keep everyone informed. The world press is still trying to piece the story together. They are trying to work out who Nusayabah is and if she is affiliated to a known group, but it won't take long. Scuttling to locate voice experts, terrorist experts, bomb experts. Anyone to help grab an angle. Relishing the story. Caught up in the drama and excitement. Fiercely speculating on who is in the burqa. Convincing themselves it is Amala. Like vultures clawing at a carcass.

Thompson's Head of Communications, Elliot Mitchell, looks like he is earning his crust for a change and is now in the room next door with Thompson. The door is closed, but even through the frosted glass it is clear they are having a disagreement. Mitchell is gesticulating and his voice is raised but not enough to make out the words being said. Chances are Thompson is looking for someone to blame for the story getting on the networks and Mitchell is a handy punch bag. Mitchell slams the door hard as he leaves.

My phone beeps. There is a picture of Mark on the screen. My heart does a little somersault.

'Millie, switch to the Diginews channel. Nusayabah is on again'

I flick the computer screen, keeping Mark on the line.

There she is again. Swathed in black. The pixilated pattern and the black standard behind her.

'Today we showed you the infidel Amala Hackeem. Blaspheming, taking God's name in vain. A spy. A dog of war. She is not alone in spying. Her partner is Neil Rochester. Rochester is in the pay of this government. A government that kills in the name of so-called democracy.'

The screen switches to a picture of a drone blowing up a village near Mogadishu. It was the suspected hiding place of a Har majiddoon cell. The intelligence was flawed and, in fact, the drone had blown up a school. Thirteen children had been killed.

There are pictures of Neil and Ella dressed up at the Royal Opera House in Covent Garden, they had been to see *Carmen*, Neil's favourite. They both look glowing. It then switches back to the terrible pictures of the thirteen children lined up in the dirt, dead.

'Mr Rochester. You did this. Their blood is on your hands.'

My heart jumps when the picture shifts to the inside of Neil and

Ella's house. The camera pans around the living room. It takes in the floor to ceiling windows, the polished walnut wood floor, the Degas on the wall. The camera moves to the kitchen. Bright, light and with every conceivable gadget. The kitchen table I have sat at a thousand times.

'Oh my God,' I hear Mark say. 'Millie, are you seeing this? They're in Neil and Ella's house. How the hell did they by-pass the security? Their place is like trying to get into the Pentagon.'

I realise it isn't live. The kitchen wall is painted a pale yellow and a few weeks ago they had repainted it lime green. So when was it taken?

The camera pulls back. There is Aafa.

'Hey, man, don't film in here. Ella and Neil will go mad.'

I watch, enthralled. Aafa is feeding KK, Ella's dog. He is their dogsitter whenever they are away.

The camera shakes. Whoever is operating it is laughing. It moves back and we follow the camera through the hall, up the stairs and into Ella and Neil's bedroom. It hones into a desk in the corner.

My heart is in my mouth. I say to Mark, 'Oh my God, Aafa must have let these people in. I can't believe he would do that. Ella trusted him. He has the key and all the alarm codes.' I trail off as the camera operator sets up the camera so we can see him open a drawer and pull Ella's diaries from it.

I feel sick. Ella has written diaries since she was eight. She writes pretty much every day. No holds barred. It has everything in there.

The camera man has a mini copier. A sophisticated gadget that copies the whole book in a few seconds. Her every thought. Her every feeling. Things she didn't tell anyone, probably not even Neil.

I groan, 'Oh my God. Poor Ella. Poor Neil.'

Mark says, 'Who is that with Aafa? Who's got the camera?'

'I have no idea.'

The camera switches again. Back to Nusayabah.

'So Mr Rochester, how does it feel to be spied on? It all made for such interesting reading. Those barriers you put up were pretty useless once we were in your house and at your wife's computer.'

She pauses. 'I have a question for you. What did your wife know about Touchstone? It's all over her computer. We know because we have been reading it. Every day. Why don't you ask your friend, Simon Thompson? Why don't you try a little spying on him?'

The screen goes black.

Mark says, 'What's Touchstone?'

'I have no idea,' I say. 'We think it has something to do with Judgement Day. The final reckoning. It must have something to do with Thompson, but he's not giving it up whatever it is. It's all over the blogs, mail and chatter from Nusayabah. Sounds like Ella knows something. Sounds like it is on her computer. It must be her big story. She's doing this thing on women and radicalisation. Telling it from individuals. The human side …' I stop, my mind clicking back to a few days before. 'Hang on, she's working on two stories. She spoke to me about it the other day. Something to do with arms to ATF50. I need to ask Neil. I need to check.'

'Listen, I am almost at Rockeem's offices. I'll find out what Neil reckons.' I stare at Mark's face. I know every line. I can see he is in a cab. It seems odd to see the sun and the bright blue sky behind. I can see Green Park as he heads up Piccadilly, looking stunning with the hawthorn blossom bursting out.

'Ok.'

Mark sighs. 'Poor guy, Neil will be ripped apart. At least Ella can tell us about this Touchstone thing. There's something else though, Mills. Aafa's stuff. He's got some pretty big cash flows going on. Doesn't stack up for a student. I'm going to dig into it.'

'Yeah, Toni Roberts mentioned that too but she hasn't offered up anything else. Not to me anyway. You know, I just can't believe Aafa has betrayed us all. Do you know the whole family is under guard? Amala's dad is getting hate mail. I guess we never really know someone. Not completely.'

I don't say anymore. It's a bit too close to home.

I try, 'Bye love.'

Mark is suddenly brisk. 'Bye Millie.'

I turn back to the dossier. I click 'Find' and type in 'Touchstone'. I look through. Always capitalised. Always beside Thompson.

The phone rings again. It's Neil. Before I answer, I take a deep breath. Could this day get any worse?

Neil's voice is ragged. 'I can't believe it. He loves Ella. She is forever slipping him twenty quid to top up his student money. She will never believe he would let people in our house. She'll die if she knows someone has been reading her diaries. Sure, I've never even read them and now some nutter has them. I don't even know if she's seen it. How could he? Seriously, I'll kill him when this is over. First Amala and now this. Ella's still got her Ezylocate off. Bloody Amala showed her how. They thought it was hilarious that she could out techy me. Oh Christ, how am I going to tell her? And what has Touchstone got to do with her?'

Tuesday 25th May 13.52

MILLIE

My smart block buzzes. It's Mark. All business.

'Millie, I am here with Neil. Listen, we are looking at Aafa's accounts. So, the first bit you know. Tracking back from January there is a series of payments to this dawah account and the Education and Light Programme. I think Neil told you about them and it's in the BSU data. Both are registered as charities but the money seems to be leaving the accounts pretty quickly. There's something else though, something much bigger. It looks like Aafa has a set of accounts that are linked to a bank in Bermuda. There are some real serious transactions going through there. I mean hundreds of thousands of pounds. I am trying to piece it together. Does the company Kardax mean anything? It looks like Aafa has been buying shares. Where would he get the money for something like that?'

I click on the Kardax website.

I read, 'It's a £28bn company with interests in mining, manufacturing and arms. Looks like it also has a series of government contracts for training and maintenance in military bases.'

'Yeah. That's what I saw. I'm wondering what it's got to do with Aafa, and has it got anything to do with today?'

'What I can see is that there have been some real issues. Environmental damage, sweat shops, child labour. The lot. They look pretty shitty.'

Neil adds, 'Hey, don't you remember there was something about Kardax contravening trade embargos. Weren't they selling arms to Iran through some sort of sham company?'

I jump at a sudden noise from the office next door. A mixture of raised voices. I am alone in the meeting room. I can see Thompson and Norton huddled in the office next door with Dalgleish and Mitford. There seems to be a lot of activity but everything is muffled. Something must have happened. I can sense a shift.

'Mark, Neil, I've got to go something's happening here.'

At the same moment I hear Sean Menzies calling to Neil.

Tuesday 25th May 13.54

MILLIE

Norton charges through the door. Like a force of nature and barely able to get her words out fast enough she blurts, 'We've got her. We've got Amala. We've found her and Aafa. They are in the Mulberry Estate. Our guys are moving in now but it's a positive ID on Aafa and there is a woman in a burqa with him. We should get to her in the next six or seven minutes.'

My block pings. It's Daisy. I ignore it.

Relief sweeps through me in waves. I feel as if I have been holding my breath for hours. I hug myself, rocking back and forth. I can barely believe it's over. Almost over. They just have to get her out. Her and Aafa. God, Aafa. I feel a visceral surge of hatred for what he has put us through.

Norton tells me to wait. She needs to direct the extraction. I realise I am not going to be allowed to see how they will get her out. After everything I've done I can't believe she's going to leave me sitting out here. Screw her.

I presume ATF50 are going in. I need to see it.

It strikes me like a lightning bolt. No one will just hand her over. They will kill them both first. A dead Amala would be a much better story in their web of hate than a rescue.

I have got to see this. I wonder if Norton has told Neil. I message him and his face appears on my screen. Mark is beside him.

'Hey, I was just starting to call you. We tracked her down. My guys were able to find Aafa. He must have put his Ezylocate back on. The ATF50 guys were able to get drones overhead. I'm looking at the screens now. Listen, Millie, Amala and Aafa are in a flat in The Bush. There are four heavily armed guys shielding them. They look like they're holding Kalashnikovs.'

My heart starts up the drum beat again. It isn't over. Not yet.

'Millie, flick your screen to auto and I'll patch you into all our screens here. You can see it live.'

I do what he says. Within a few seconds a different picture appears on my screen. It is from the drone. It's a live feed. I can see the Mulberry Estate in a quarter of the screen; there are riots everywhere. Half the screen shows a flat and the last quarter is from a high definition infra-red drone, it shows a slightly blurred picture of a woman in a burqa, Aafa and three guards. It catches me out again, they are all women. It just seems so much more shocking. They are wearing hijabs and Kalashnikovs. The flat is on the third floor of a six-storey block. Each level with a long corridor and chest high balcony.

Aafa and the woman are sitting on the floor at a small table. They are huddled close together but it is impossible to make out their features. The room is dark so the blinds must be closed.

In the half screen of the flat I see two guards standing by the door, standing head up and legs apart. A show of their duty, training and vigilance. My throat is dry and every muscle is tensed. A supercopter has been hovering above the Bush Estate all morning, monitoring the riots. I watch as it drops eight officers on to the roof of the apartment block.

They begin to move with stealth and purpose. My nails push into my palms. Two remain on the roof, whilst two pairs move to the stairwells at either end of Amala's corridor. Two more are already in the corridor one level above where she is being held. For a moment they pause until everyone is where they should be. With a silent signal they move as one.

In the left stairwell one of the senior firearms officers bangs a dustbin lid against the wall. The guards look startled but are too smart to both move away from the door. One starts to head along the corridor, tense and alert to trouble. As she reaches the door to the stairwell the SFOs have her by the throat and quickly shove her to her knees, cuffed and gagged before she realises what has happened. The two above the flat drop like bats from nowhere and grab the other guard. They have her immobilised and moved from the door in under four seconds. They drag her to the stairwell.

The officer knocks on the door. A voice from inside shouts, 'What?'

The officer knocks again. My eyes are locked on the screen. I know we are all watching. Neil and Mark and the ministers next door along with Mitford and Dalgleish.

One of the women inside the flat pulls open the door, 'Parsa, what the...'

Before she can get any further. The two SFOs grab her and pull her out onto the balcony. She tries to pull herself from their grasp and reach for her gun. Before she can get near the trigger, a shot hits her neatly in the forehead, quickly followed by another. A sniper on the roof opposite, I hadn't even known was there. The SFO holds her so she falls to the floor gently, without making a sound.

I am horrified. I have never seen someone shot. Killed in cold blood. There are five SFO officers in the narrow corridor now. No one hesitates as each steps over her dead body. Half my screen switches to the head camera of the officer at the front. The image jerks as he moves forward. The whole team moves in a tight formation through the door. I can hear that they are being told, through their earpieces, the positions of everyone left in the room. The first two sweep into the cramped room, weapons at the ready and without hesitation point their rifles at the last guard. I hear them shout, 'Drop your weapons, armed police.'

The last of the hostage-takers looks up. Her face frozen and framed by a hijab. She reaches for the Kalashnikov and, as if in slow motion, I watch as the officer in front shoots her in the arm. The hostage-taker is thrown back onto the small table, falling into Amala and knocking her to the floor. She drops her weapon and falls to her knees.

The second officer grabs her by her injured arm. He drags her screaming to her feet and cuffs her.

The SFO speaks to the woman in the burqa, 'Are you Amala Hackeem?'

I hear Amala's voice, croaky and terrified but clear enough. 'Yes, yes I am and this is my brother Aafa. He is not with these women. They tricked us into coming here.'

I am so relieved to hear her voice. The officer is so close I can hear her breathing. As she pulls off the veil and I see her face I think I will burst. She looks terrified, she steadies herself on the table, and as she stands I see the blood stains on the burqa. I speak to Neil through the smart block.

'Are you seeing this?'

'Yes, I am. I can't believe it. I can't believe it's over. She's safe.'

I hear Mark giving up a prayer of thanks.

The SFO speaks into his radio. 'Both assets confirmed as Amala and Aafa Hackeem.'

Just then I hear Thompson's voice. 'Well done, Captain Murphy. A job well done. We have an ambulance thirty seconds out to take Ms Hackeem to the hospital. Please take Mr Hackeem to the supercopter. We need him back here as soon as possible.'

'Will do, sir. Thank you.' He turns off the camera.

Tuesday 25th May 14.01

MILLIE

I let out a long breath. My screen switches to Neil. I see him clasping Mark in a bear hug.

'Hey, thank God, Millie. Thank God, we've got her. I'm going to head to the hospital. Shall I meet you there?'

I can hardly get the words out. I feel so lightheaded. The relief is overwhelming. I try to stand but my legs won't hold me. The blood rushes from my head and I have to hold on to the chair.

'Yeah, I am going to tell Norton and I'll get there as quick as I can.'

Just then Norton appears. Not looking quite as sharp as she had at the start of the day. 'We have Amala, Millie. She is on her way to the Royal London.'

'Thank God, I can't believe it's over. I can't believe she's ok. I am going to meet Neil there.'

I pause. The hair on the back of my neck stiffens. Something in her stance is off. It's not just that she looks less sharp. It's more than that, I don't see relief. Her face is grim. There's no sense of having won, having outwitted Nusayabah. Why is that? Is she worried how it will play out in the media?

'Millie, I am really sorry but it's not quite over yet. We need to find Nusayabah. We need your help to talk to Aafa about the group that held Amala. We need him to help us crack open Umm Umarah. We are also asking Mr Rochester to continue to support us. We know that the filming was not done in that flat and we need to pin down her location. Nusayabah is due to make contact in less than an hour and we are working on the basis that she might still do that. We need to talk to Aafa before then. Can you help us for a bit longer?'

I'm a bit bewildered by that. Why would Nusayabah make contact now? She's got nothing to bargain with.

She sees my look and says, 'She is still out there and still dangerous. We haven't managed to find the person that torched the Faith to Faithless offices and we are still analysing the films she put out, including the one breaking into the Rochesters' home.'

Before I answer, I turn to the large screen on the wall. Amala still wearing the sky blue burqa but with her hair and face visible, is being escorted to an ambulance. Blood spattered across the front of the heavy material.

Aafa is handcuffed and they are taking him to a waiting supercopter. His head is bent and I can't see his face.

Someone in The Bush must have been filming the rescue. It is now playing on every channel. A piece of high drama showing on never ending repeat. It is flicking between Amala and the riots.

I turn back to Norton. She says, 'The prime minister is just going to make a short statement and then we will focus on finding Nusayabah.'

I breathe in and out. Trying to stay calm. My legs still feel jelly like and I have to sit down. I nod and tell her I will wait for Aafa.

I feel a physical yearning to hold Amala tight. Just to prove she is really alive and she's going to be ok. For the three of us just to be together. The Nofas. Normal. With a cup of tea or a bottle of wine or some vile concoction Ella has made. Like always.

What a day. God, Ella will never believe this. She will be desperate to comfort Amala. She will be desperate to comfort me. I check my phone. Still nothing from her. I leave a quick message saying to call me as soon as she can.

I still want to know about Touchstone. It's still the missing piece of the puzzle.

Tuesday 25th May 14.15

NUSAYABAH

Meticulous planning and patience.
Everything according to plan.
Inshallah.

Tuesday 25th May 14.16

MILLIE

Aafa is landing at Horse Guards Parade. There is a police escort waiting to bring him here. I watch on the screen. As usual, tourists are milling around hoping to see the horses. Thompson is obviously looking for the TV shot because the line of cars head down Whitehall rather than just taking the short cut to the back door. I see the cavalcade pass the memorial for the women of World War Two, before turning into Downing Street. I need to get ready. I don't know how I should handle it. Part of me is full of rage and part of me feels desperately sorry for him.

I start making a list.

Who is Nusayabah?

Who turned him – Abdul Izz al-Din?

What is Touchstone?

The cash – where did he get it?

The Light and Education Centre – is it a front for something?

The Kardax shares.

Before I can get any further my phone rings. It's Neil. I hear the relief in his voice. He sounds about ten years younger.

'Hey, I'm on my way back. Thompson and Norton still want help tracking down Nusayabah. They seem to think she will still make contact at three. I dunno if she will. Your boy, Mark, has done the business though. He worked out how to get the money into the account with an invisible tracker but thank God we don't need it now. He's going to stay at Rockeem in case he's needed. I can't wait to see Amala. I don't know whether to kiss her or slap her first. What was she thinking turning off her Ezylocate?'

Suddenly he pauses. 'Do they want you to talk to Aafa?'

'Yeah, I don't really know how to handle it. I don't feel as if I know anything anymore. I would have laid money that Aafa would never do anything like this.'

'I know, Mills, but you've said often enough, it's sometimes the good guys who get persuaded to do bad things for what they think are good reasons. If anyone can get through to him it's you. He trusts you. Hey, have you heard from Ella yet? I really wish she wasn't so paranoid about protecting her sources. It must be a good story. I've told her to call urgently but I didn't want to freak her out. The PM's officially confirmed that it's Amala but that she is ok. She's bound to see it.'

I am nodding but distracted. 'Listen, I can hear a commotion. That must be Aafa arriving. I'll see you in a bit.'

It is Aafa. I stand. I am so furious and so deeply hurt that I can barely look at him. But he looks so young and scared, surrounded by armed officers. He is shuffling forward, his wrists and ankles in cuffs. I can't help it, my heart leaps out in sympathy. Whatever's happened he's just a kid. Not bad, just young. A naive kid who has been manipulated by people smarter than him.

I try a half smile and raise my palms in a how did we get here kind of way. Aafa is staring at me. He is dazed. He is breathing heavily and there is sweat on his lip and brow. The police officers push him into a chair as Norton crashes through the door.

'Mr Hackeem, you have no idea how much trouble you are in. I'll get right to the point, there is no option other than to cooperate with us. We need to know who Nusayabah is, we need to know where she is and we need to know right now, so you had better start talking.'

Aafa blinks hard several times, trying to focus on what she has just said. He looks over to me.

'What is she talking about? Who is Nusayabah? Millie, what's this about?'

I say, 'Aafa it would be much better for you, and for Amala and your family, if you just tell us what you know. Anything you do to help us now will help you later on. We know you persuaded Amala to go to Tower Hamlets today, and we know you haven't been going to university these last five months, and we know you have been paying your fees to some Islamic group.'

He stares at me. Norton has obviously decided she's bad cop. I am irritated as she wades in without any thought of how to properly handle someone who has been radicalised and is probably now in shock.

'Listen, Hackeem, your friends kidnapped your sister and threatened this government. I don't have time for your games. This is the serious league, son, and you better start talking.'

Aafa looks genuinely bewildered.

I say, 'Aafa, this is really bad. For Christ's sake, they butchered Amala.'

He stares at me, his mouth opening and closing, trying to form the words. He looks aghast. 'Who butchered her?'

Norton, livid now, jumps in. 'Nusayabah. Or one of her stooges. We need to know where she is. Where is Nusayabah?'

I am watching Aafa very carefully. Every move. Every reaction.

Every micro reaction in his hands and eyes. The two places people give themselves away. He needs a bit of help and time to calm himself down.

'Look, Aafa, we know everything. We saw you two weeks ago, waving the black standard, at the rally where Abdul Izz al-Din was preaching. Talking about Glastonbury. Refusing to condemn it. Praising it even. We know you persuaded Amala to go into The Bush today and we know that someone convinced you to do that. We need to know who and we need to know where they are now.'

Aafa blurts out in a rush, 'I asked Amala to meet me at the Education Centre. There was a special women's group today so I said she should come and talk to them. Listen to them. I told her they are nice people and I thought she should give them a chance.'

Norton sneers, 'How many nice people do you know who feel the need to carry Kalashnikovs.'

'And was it this women's group that took her? Is that where she met Nusayabah?' I ask.

'Why do you keep asking me about Nusayabah? I don't know a Nusayabah.' He sounds genuinely confused

'Aafa, you must know her. You let her, or someone in her group, into Neil and Ella's house. They've put the film out all over the internet. Aafa, you even let them take Ella's diary.'

Aafa's eyes bulge, his Adam's apple bobs up and down. He bites his lip and his eyes fill with tears.

Despite the shake in his voice he tries to be firm and push back. 'I don't know who this Nusayabah is. Why do you keep talking about her? I only brought one person into their house. Hassan, he's a friend. We met on the Education and Light Programme. He's a film student. He films everything. Stupid stuff. Like just walking along the street. He sometimes comes with me when I walk KK. I told him not to film in the house but I didn't think it would really matter. He films hours and hours of stuff and normally he just films over it.'

I try to be gentle as I say, 'Well, he didn't this time. This time he gave it to Nusayabah and she is using it against Neil.'

Aafa is crying hard now. Tears falling unbidden. He looks terrified and heartachingly young.

'Aafa, something isn't adding up. Where did you get the money to buy the shares in Kardax?'

Norton glances at me. She obviously hadn't expected me to know that. She must have known about it though because she's not that surprised. I have no option but to tell her what I know. Even though I know she's not telling me everything.

'Mark Carter, my husband, is a banker. He is investigating Aafa's accounts over at Rockeem's offices. As well as using his university fee money to support various programmes and dawah stalls, it looks as if Aafa has been buying up thousands of shares in a company called Kardax. It is traded through Bermuda. Mark is still looking into it.'

Aafa's stopped crying. His eyes bulge even more. His mouth is opening and closing like a fish.

'Millie, what the hell are you talking about? Shares? Bermuda? How the hell am I going to get enough money to buy shares? Yes, I gave my fees to the Education and Light Programme but I've never even heard of Kardax. I don't know this Nusayabah. I don't know who or what Kardax is and I don't have shares in anything. Millie, you know I don't have that sort of money.'

Norton pipes up, 'Exactly. So where did you get it? Did you get it from your sister?'

'No, I didn't. I wouldn't ever ask her for money. I haven't got any shares. I haven't got an account in Bermuda. I have no idea what you are talking about.'

I change tack. 'Aafa, why did you tell Amala to come to The Bush today? When you knew she would be hurt, maybe even killed? How could you do that? How could you let them burn and mutilate her?'

He looks horrified.

'They didn't hurt her. Amala's not hurt. She came to The Bush this morning, that's true. I asked her. She was going to meet me and then she was going to go to the women's group. She fainted. She passed out because she was really hot and got up too fast. One of the women told me I could go and see her. When I found her, she was already in the flat with the guards. We were kept there all day. There were guards with us all the time. No one would tell us what was going on and then ATF50 stormed in. Amala wasn't hurt. They didn't hurt either of us. I swear it. I swear it on the Quran.'

I look at Aafa. I know he is telling the truth.

I say it quietly, trying to make some sense of the confusion, 'But the blood? The blood on the burqa?'

'The guard's, when the ATF50 guy shot her, she fell on Amala.'

I stare at him. Then I turn to look at Norton. She won't meet my eyes. She knew. She knew Amala had not been hurt. Why? Why are we going through this charade? She moves off the subject, pushing him to tell us about Nusayabah.

I look directly at her. My tone hard.

'What's going on?'

She doesn't reply.

And then I know. I feel the cogs shift and change. The pieces fall into place.

The burqa. Sky blue. I stand up, ignoring Norton's call to come back. I walk out. It's not over. Not even close. It's just beginning.

Tuesday 25th May 14.25

MILLIE

I am watching the press conference, allowing the pieces to fall into place. Visualising what I had been trying to grasp all morning. Thompson is on all the networks. I watch him. I watch him very carefully.

'I am delighted that we have managed to rescue Amala Hackeem today and I would like to offer my deep and personal gratitude to the ATF50 team. They entered a dangerous situation and have captured three of the terrorists, all of whom are on their way to Paddington Green. We have a medical team there on standby.'

A journalist shouts, 'What about Nusayabah, sir? Has she been caught?'

'The whereabouts of the terrorist calling herself Nusayabah is subject to a live operation and I will not comment at this stage.'

'What about her demands? What about the PPCs?'

'As I said, we remain in the midst of a live situation and I will answer no more questions at this stage. Again, my sincere thanks to ATF50.'

They keep shouting. 'Sir, sir, did you promise closures?' 'Is that why she's been allowed out alive?' 'Mr Thompson, what about the riots in The Bush? They're getting worse and the smart money says they are being coordinated?' 'What's happening? How many police are in there now?' 'Did Aafa Hackeem set up his sister?' 'Have you got anyone for the Faith to Faithless bombing yet?'

Thompson, now looking mightily pissed, turns away from the cameras and, head down, walks off. Back here. Good. I have some questions for him.

Tuesday 25th May 14.28

NUSAYABAH

I pull back the curtain. Light floods in and I step back a little, making sure I am completely hidden from view. The riots are only a few streets away and are masterful in their choreography. I feel a sense of satisfaction. Like a ringmaster, or a conductor of an orchestra. Making sure everyone is playing their part.

Unbidden, my favourite Brahms piece flits across my mind. I can hear the Clarinet Sonata Number Two and I begin to hum. For a moment, I am transported back to a lifetime ago, to that girl in the orchestra. I see her licking her lips ready to play her part, clarinet in hand. Dad in the audience, nodding to the music.

I turn back to the screen and see Thompson and the spell is broken. His deceit. His lies. His broken promises.

It's my turn now.

I place the call. He picks up on the first ring.

'Ready?

'Yes, ready.'

He asks, 'The whole amount?'

'Yes. Clear the accounts. The rest will arrive in under two hours.'

Meticulous planning and patience is about to pay off.

I stare at the cracked mirror. I allow myself a moment of contentment as I think of them all scurrying around. They will be feeling so smug to have rescued her, never thinking they might still be looking in the wrong direction.

Tuesday 25th May 14.30

MILLIE

I am sure now. Daisy has seen it too but she doesn't know the significance. Apart from me, right now the only other person who knows the significance is the person who wrote it. I know who and I think I know why. It isn't Ackwaat that is the significant name. It is Emily.

Suddenly Neil barges through the door. He grabs me and whirls me in the air before I can stop him. His exuberance and excitement spilling out and saying over and over. 'Oh my God, Mills, I can't believe it. I can't believe it's actually over and she's ok. We won. We won.'

He laughs again. Just then the door opens and Amala bursts through like a bullet. Heading straight to both of us, arms outstretched, looking more like herself in jeans and t-shirt, crying and laughing at once. She sweeps us both up and pulls us tight.

'I told them there was no fucking way I was going to the hospital. I'm fine. I made them bring me here in the next supercopter. They're cool those copters. I need to talk to them about Aafa. He's innocent in all of this. I know he is. Stupid but innocent.' Amala can't stop talking. She's like an express train.

I can't find the words. I can't. I don't want to.

'God, what a day. I had that fucking burqa on all day. I was sweltering. God, it was a nightmare. They kept us in that dingy room for hours. No one would tell us anything. So much for welcome and hospitality, eh? Oh God, I can't believe I'm back here with you guys. How's Ella?'

She can't stop. She's gabbling. 'It was pretty freakin' scary. Seems Aafa has been skipping uni and using the money for some education group. Fucking hell. He's a mug. He's in some deep shit, though. I tried to get the story from the guys that brought me here. But they kept schtum. They think he was part of the gang keeping us locked up. They were talking about Umm Umarah.'

She looks at me. 'Hey, Mills, don't you know them? Aren't they the ones in your research? I have to tell you when ATF50 arrived I couldn't believe it.'

I try to make them hear me but there is such a cacophony of noise I can't make my voice loud enough. I look out from the Amala and Neil hug to see Aafa, staring through the window from the next room, looking exhausted and deathly.

Behind Aafa is Thompson, Norton, Mitford and Dalgleish. They come into the room looking grim and determined.

Thompson speaks first. 'Ms Hackeem, we are delighted to see you here unharmed. Please can we all take a seat? We need you to tell us exactly what took place today. It's important we understand everything.'

Neil suddenly steps back. Holding Amala at arm's length. 'How come they let you come here and not the hospital. What about your hand? Your ear?'

He grabs Amala's hand, turning it around. He turns to Thompson and Norton, trying to work out what's going on.

Before he can say anything, I say in a voice louder and stronger than I feel, 'What's Touchstone?' I look straight at Thompson. He would have made an excellent poker player.

'Look, I hardly think we need to worry about that now. Some lunatic radical spouting off about something none of us have ever heard of. I would have thought, Dr Stephenson, the most important thing is to have your friends back safe and sound and very much in one piece.'

Somewhere I find the strength and focus. I stand up and with two hands on the table. I stare straight at Thompson. 'Don't patronise me, you arrogant fucker. Touchstone is important. I watch people for a living. I know when they're lying, and I know when they're scared, and I know when something is important to them, and I know that Touchstone matters to you and I think it's going to matter very much to all of us.'

I see him swallow and lick his lips. He is angry but he is also scared. I don't care. Norton is taking it all in.

I say, 'It's all over Ella's computer. And so is your name.'

The clues were everywhere. Why didn't I see it earlier? Ella's questions about my work. Talking to Aafa, getting him to talk about getting picked up by the PPCs. God, her Ezylocate. Getting Amala to show her how to switch it off so even Neil can't find her. Cancelling today. Saying she had a story but not telling us what it's about and where it is. Deeper than that. Her frustration with constantly being referred to as Neil's wife. Not being taken seriously as a journalist by us as much as anyone else. Desperate to make her name with some real journalism.

Shit. Shit. Shit.

The clip from their house. Touchstone on her computer. The blaring silence from her today. Then I had seen it. The burqa. The burqa in the videos was black. Not Amala's. Amala's is sky blue. The traditional colour of Afghanistan.

I move around the table to Neil. I crouch down beside him and take his hands in mine.

'Millie, what is it? What are you doing? You're freaking me out? What is it?'

'Neil, it's Ella. They have Ella. It was never Amala. Nusayabah has Ella. I am certain of it. Neil, I am so sorry.'

He looks at me in utter disbelief. I pull his head to me, cradling it and trying to soothe him, the way I would Grace.

Amala kneels beside me. 'Millie, how can you know? How do you know?'

I pull her to me too and for a moment just breathe them in, summoning the energy for what's to come. Neil moves out of my grasp. Asking questions, part to me and part to himself.

'What are you talking about? Ella's on a story. You know she is. I told you. I told you that. That's why we haven't heard from her. She's on a story.'

He keeps saying it. 'She's on a story.'

But I can see something shifting. He presses the quick call on his phone and immediately a picture of Ella appears. In rude health, on a beach with a broad smile. It rings out to her voicemail. 'This is Gabriella Russell, please leave a message.'

He presses again. Voicemail. And again. He checks her Ezylocate. Dead.

Amala lifts the phone away and takes his hand.

Neil looks at me. Almost too soft to hear he asks, 'How? How do you know?'

Before I can say anything, he starts to answer his own question. Pieces falling into place like a deathly nightmare. 'It's a diversion. Of course, Amala was a diversion. There's no furniture in the clip. Just that table. In the clip the wallpaper is peeling off and there's no carpet on the floor.'

He is seeing it all with monstrous clarity. His throat catching, he says, as if to himself, 'Someone has her. Someone has Ella. Someone is hacking her to pieces. Someone with no mercy. Oh my God, someone who will kill her.'

The look in his eyes is unbearable. Stripped naked. His mouth is in a grimace of unadulterated fear.

Neil tightens his grip on my hand. His eyes brim over. He tries to speak. Just a whisper. 'No.'

Again and again. 'No, no. No. Not Ella. Not my beautiful Ella. Please God anything but that. Not Ella.'

He slumps forward in the chair like a rag doll, no control over his limbs. Amala is rocking back on her heels, her hands over her mouth battling panic. She moves to hold Neil. She puts her arms around him. He keens like a childless mother.

Tuesday 25th May 14.40

NUSAYABAH

Ella Russell. God, she is pathetic. We've been watching her for months. We didn't even have to break in. Aafa let us in. A very helpful boy. So sincere and so willing to believe everything he is told. We started by talking to him about the Education and Light Programme, playing to his need to spread the positive word of Islam, convince people we are all peace-loving. Never guessing Hassan was no more a film student than me, but a hardened foot soldier who had fought in Mogadishu when he was only sixteen. Hassan had even given that ugly dog a mild tranquiliser to be sure it stayed docile. What a fool.

Once Hackeem had started paying his tuition fees to the Education and Light Programme, it was a matter of minutes to hack his bank account and use his name to start buying the Kardax shares through phantom charities. We now have nearly enough shares to create a panic on them. And we would have more than enough before the day was out. But all in good time.

I open Ella's diary. The date is from thirteen years ago from when she first met Rochester. I skim through it. I've read it all before.

July 2010

It didn't start well. I hate this day. The anniversary of Mum's death. But it was Amala's party and she loves a party.

Then it got worse as this guy arrived at the same time and made me jump out of my skin by leaning over me to press the doorbell. I jumped so much I dropped the bottle of wine on his shoes.

He was really good about it and then I looked at him! Looked properly. He smiled. He was gorgeous. The colour of mocha coffee, the beginning of some stubble and the warmest brown eyes I have ever seen. He stuck out his hand. 'Neil Rochester, workmate of Amala's. I think we must be heading to the same place? Sorry I startled you, you looked like your hands were full.'

Just then Amala opened the door. How come she is always so stunning? She was wearing a scruffy t-shirt and jeans and her hair was pulled back in what looked like an old rubber band and yet she could have just walked off a Christopher Kane catwalk.

Thank God Amala's Mum, not her, had cooked. But enough of that. Neil. Neil Rochester. And now I know THE Neil Rochester – Amala's 'freakin genius' mate that she keeps talking about.

I chatted to Millie for a bit. I told her how much I hate working for 'Write on Us'. Every time I say it I hear their stupid strapline: 'Specialising in giving your corporate communications a human voice.' It makes me want to gouge out my own eyes. I told her I was especially pleased to insert in the recruitment brochure of a shampoo company, the Walt Whitman line, 'Whatever satisfies the soul is truth.' Now if that doesn't attract what they keep calling top talent I don't know what will.

But… back to my Mr Rochester (how cool that he is Mr Rochester!!!!)

Neil came over to talk to us. I was like a total dork because I gulped my drink too fast and he had to pat me on the back as I choked. Millie thought it was hilarious and left us, after telling him I really couldn't hold my drink – that was after he had shown her his red wine stained suede shoes.

I felt the heat of his hand through my shirt when he patted my back. For the first time in my life, I felt a surge of desire like a torpedo.

We started to talk then about how we knew Amala and what we did for work. I realised he was the guy Amala has told us loads about. She sees him like a brother.

I found myself distracted, constantly looking at his hands as they held the wine glass and imagining them on my body. I felt my body pulsing. In my mind, I pictured him naked. Pictured him on me and inside me. It was so intense and so real. His skin looked so soft, so smooth it was all I could do not to touch it, feeling every tiny cell in my body pulse.

I am sure he could see right into the carnal pictures in my mind.

I could smell Amala's mum's cooking wafting out of the kitchen. She had made chicken karahi. I knew it would be awesome (it was). He grabbed a couple of plates but I couldn't eat it. I was actually shaking. I am crap at chatting up men. He kept smiling and so did I.

Then he said, 'You are so beautiful.'

And I could think of nothing else to say but, 'So are you.'

He put his glass down and reached for mine, placing it on the table. He took my hand in his. He turned it over and stroked my palm with his thumb very gently. It could have been my whole body for the impact it had on me. My breath was stuck in my lungs and I could feel my insides turn to fire.

I put my lips to his and didn't move. I could feel his lips, soft and full, and the graze of his stubble. I could smell the wine and the food and just a hint of something citrus. I could feel his hand tighten its grip on mine and I knew he was aroused. Not just erect but every part of him was electric. I pulled on his bottom lip very gently.

I thought, if I don't get out of here I am going to fuck him right here on Amala's table.

We broke off. I didn't do what I normally do and over-think it. Neil said, 'Shall we get a cab. We can be at mine in ten minutes?' I didn't hesitate. 'I live around the block we can be there in three.'

'Let's go.'

The walk was a blur. I was like liquid. Molten and on fire. I could feel every inch of him. Once inside the flat, it was frenzied. I touched every part of him. I breathed him in. Never ever wanting to let him go.

The first time was fierce and urgent. I wanted to possess him. For him to possess me. Afterwards we lay side by side. Neil raised himself on one elbow. I looked at him and it was like a mirror of what I felt. His eyes were glistening. What he saw must have been right because he visibly sighed. He took me in his arms. I tightened my arms around him and relaxed into him. Something I had never done before with any man. I leaned my head on his chest as he said, 'You are the most beautiful person I have ever seen.'

The next morning, I woke with a jolt to the sound of my phone buzzing. Of course it was Amala. She sounded a bit like Tigger on speed. 'Hey, Ells, you can pick them. I have never seen Neil go out with anyone. He's like obsessed with his work. He's the guy I told you about. The one I'm working on the translation software with. He's a freakin' genius.'

I looked at Neil in my bed. Replete and grinning in his sleep. I wouldn't have cared what he did or even if he was a freakin' genius.

I read on a few pages, she's still going on about Neil Rochester.

I sit back and watch her. Let's see how much you love her, Rochester. Let's see how much power you really have. Let's see if you can save her. The diversion has worked like a dream. That was the prelude and now for the main act. I tuck the diary into my pocket. I'm going to need it later.

Planning and patience.

Tuesday 25th May 14.45

MILLIE

Thompson and Norton have stepped outside. Neil and Amala are frozen together. She's holding him, stroking his hair, trying to stay calm herself, her jaw clenched and silent tears pouring down her cheeks.

In front of me are Daisy's notes. As usual they are clear and concise.

1. *Emily is more interesting. The reference to sex with her boyfriend uses quite strong language. A bit old-fashioned.*
2. *The change of name has feminist overtones. She sees herself as a sister first before she sees herself as a fighter.*
3. *She is older than she is pretending to be.*
4. *There are some incongruous phrases like master of my soul. That sounds like a quote or something she has used before somewhere. I'm checking it out.*

I must have known somewhere deep, deep in my psyche that it was Ella. Something in my brain was triggered by Norton's reaction and then I saw it all in forensic detail. It hit me like an inevitable surprise, in my consciousness, fully formed. I should have been paying more attention.

Lifting my smart block I highlight the exchanges between Nusayabah and Emily/Ackwaat and hit 'check plagiarism'.

I watch as the blogs and e-mails run through the plagiarising software, knowing it would pick up lines from poems. Ella's signature. I stare at the screen.

I say to Neil and Amala as gently as I can, 'There it is. The poetry. The lines hidden. Hard to find. Only her mates could find them. All from the 19th Century poets she loved.'

I look at my two beautiful friends. I feel Amala's tears as she leans over to hold me in her arms with Neil.

I carry on, 'The name, Emily. Two of Ella's favourite poets. Bronte and Dickinson. There they are, the lines. They are all from major poets. The lines from her messages lined up beside the titles.'

I hold up my screen. Neil reads the first few. His lips moving as he takes in the words. So irresistibly Ella. So well hidden.

Sometimes when I am alone and I think about him *I feel life is not having and getting but being and becoming. (Matthew Arnold 1822 -1888)*

If he loves me *there should be no despair* but he ignores me when I cry even *though my tears flow down like a river. (Emily Bronte 1818-1848)*

I *haven't winced or cried out loud. ...* I want to get beyond *this place of wrath and tears. I want to be the master of my soul. (William Ernest Henley 1849-1903)*

I don't say anymore. They are the poems and essays Ella had read when she was a teenager, at her most anxious, scared and vulnerable. Just like the thousands and thousands of teenagers reaching out, seeking help and answers. She had channelled that to become Emily and then Ackwaat.

Amala speaks first, her voice gruff. 'Ok, let's think. What are we going to do? How do we get her back?'

Neil looks up. He has his phone again and keeps pressing redial.

He says very quietly, 'Simon needs to agree to Nusayabah's demands. There's no option. Christ, when I think what we've done for him. He can't refuse. No way. No way can he refuse.'

I'm not so sure. I'm infuriated with myself. I feel so stupid. It had taken me so long. Thompson is still giving nothing away. I say it aloud. 'Touchstone. What is Touchstone?' I picture Thompson's face when he heard it. I saw the tell-tale twitch of his upper lip, the slight tightening of his jaw, the tiny backward movement of the head and his eyes look to the right as he composed the lie. He had worked hard not to show any emotion. Worked very hard. Not a flicker unless you were really looking. I picture him in micro detail. So where does it fit into today? What does Ella know?

I say, 'Neil, unless we can work out what Nusayabah has on Thompson we are blindsided.'

Neil moves and swivels his chair to face the screens that have been there since morning. In just a few key strokes he is into Ella's computer. He searches 'Touchstone'. Pages and pages of notes appear.

Without looking up, Neil says, 'There's a document here called Touchstone Themes.' He reads aloud. 'Thompson and Robson – what's the connection? Robson now on backbenches. Wife is a barrister and also non-executive director. Is she involved? Kardax. Arms? Government deal. Procurement process – check it out. Transparency.'

He scrolls down. 'There is a link here to some clips.' He connects. On his screen is a recorded news story from Mediawatchers, a left wing organisation scrutinising media bias. Amala and I lean in to watch. It's from about ten years ago. It shows the MP, Matthew Robson, selling his sportswear company to a big conglomerate called Kardax. Beside him is his wife and daughter.'

None of it makes sense.

Neil says, 'I'm going to get Mark to come here. If it's about the shares he can help us.'

I look back at the notes I had made about Touchstone. I re-read the dictionary definition. 'There are various companies called Touchstone but I've already looked and found nothing linking them to Thompson. I don't know if Touchstone is Kardax. Kardax fits in somewhere?'

'Will Aafa know anything?' Amala asks.

I tell her I've already asked him about Kardax but he'd looked blank and I believe him when he said he had never heard of it.

She rubs her hand through her hair and looks to the room where they are still questioning Aafa. 'Maybe he knows more than he thinks. We need to check.'

I say, 'I think there is a Touchstone in Shakespeare. It kind of rings a bell. It might be a code name. People often use Shakespearean figures as code for something. I've seen it loads of times. It would be typical of Thompson to do that. He would think he was being super clever.'

I click on 'Touchstone in Shakespeare.'

I read aloud. 'Touchstone is the court jester of Duke Frederick, the usurper's court in *As You Like It*. There are no demonstrations or expressions of affection by Touchstone, as by the fool in *King Lear*, yet he is not lacking in loyalty.'

Amala says, 'Do you think Touchstone is a person? A loyal person? Why has she got Matthew Robson in her notes? What's his connection to Thompson?'

'I'm not sure what it is. I thought today was about judgement and judgement day. Nusayabah talked about a day of reckoning. I spoke to Rehan about it. I just don't know.'

'You're right, though. If we can work out the connection then maybe we can get Thompson to negotiate,' says Neil, desperate for something to hang on to.

Thompson and Norton are coming back in.

I glance down at the rest of the highlighted pieces from the plagiarism software. I don't need the affirmation but it's all there. I see Neil read it and wince like he's been punched in the gut.

What mad pursuit. What struggle to Escape. (John Keats 1795 -1821)

I believe what lies behind us and what lies before us are tiny matters compared to what lies within us. (Ralph Waldo Emerson 1803 -1882)

The dreamers of the day are dangerous people for they dream their dreams with their eyes open and make them come true. I will make it so. (T.E. Lawrence 1888-1935)

We need answers. Fast. The next contact is in ten minutes. I know she will keep the appointment.

Tuesday 25th May 14.48

NUSAYABAH

I stare in the mirror. My eyes look back. Focused and determined. No room for doubts. It's almost like a dream. I've prepared so long for this day and it's hard to believe it's finally here.

I think back. It was Faiza who told me to look harder at Kardax. I remember digging. Following the money. I was good at that. I understood money and how to make it and how to hide it. I knew what money could do to people. I knew because I had learned from the best.

I watched all those smug celebrations when Kardax bought Clemco. Back then I didn't know just how dirty it was. I had suspicions but it was only later I saw just how bad it really was. Kids in workhouses, sweat shops for a pittance. Like Dickens.

Worse than Dickens. All over the world.

Faiza pointed me in the right direction then I did the digging. I read everything I could get my hands on. Every story pointed to the devastation Kardax left across the world from greedy people doing dirty deals.

I look again now. I click 'Kardax' and 'Who are we', up comes a picture of Jack McClelland, the CEO.

I know him.

I click on 'Non-executive directors'. I see her picture, Jennifer Robson. I read her profile. I definitely know her. I gaze at her photo. Memories tugging. Meeting Simon Thompson. Smug bastard.

7 YEARS EARLIER

NUSAYABAH

'Simon, welcome, welcome, come in, come in. You too, Kate. How lovely to see you both.' Jennifer Robson, already two vodka tonics down, kisses them both enthusiastically and ushers Mrs Harris, the hired help for the night, to take their coats almost curtseying in her effusiveness. The woman from the village gawps at Simon Thompson, fully aware that in less than a fortnight he's likely to be the next British prime minister, riding the post Brexit wave of nationalism. Thompson, as ever, never one to miss the chance to press the flesh and win a vote, turns his famous 100-watt smile on her and says, 'Thank you so much. I do hope you will be out to vote next week, Mrs…?'

'Harris,' she supplies.

'Well, Mrs Harris, I do hope we can count on your support. I'm sure Matthew here will do this constituency proud for another five years. He has been a marvellous local MP, always fighting for what is best for the community.'

'Indeed, sir, yes sir,' she gushes, as the old Etonian with his in-bred confidence walks off, having already forgotten her.

Leading them both into the large reception room, beautifully furnished from top to bottom by an interior designer and with not a single trace of personal style or taste, Jennifer Robson busies herself with the drinks, surreptitiously pouring a double measure of vodka into her own glass and knocking it back in a swift gulp. I see it all from the side lines, before they draw me in desperate to gloat about the upcoming election. I was such a fool. Taken in by all their crap.

TODAY

Tuesday 25th May 14.50

MILLIE

Alex Dalgleish, looking as composed as she had at ten o'clock this morning, speaks first. Her voice calm and clear, 'Mr Rochester, Neil. I am very sorry but Dr Stephenson is right. In the last hour or so we have had proof that the hostage being held is indeed your wife. We tested the DNA and knew it was not from Amala but it took us some time to cross reference on the national database and confirm that it is your wife. Since it was confirmed we've been doing everything in our power to locate her.'

Mitford adds 'The courier who picked up the, eh, eh…' He struggles for the right word. 'Package this morning didn't know a lot but he had collected it from the Welcome and Hospitality Centre at The Bush. It led us to believe at first that it was Ms Hackeem's here, given that was her last sighting.'

Neil turns to Thompson. 'Simon, I know how things need to look in public but you have to do something. You just can't let Ella die.'

Thompson looks uncomfortable. I see him steal a glance at Jean Norton, who gives the slightest of nods.

'Neil, look, I know how this must feel, how utterly desperate you must be, but we cannot be seen to negotiate.'

Amala is scathing and immediate in her response. 'I think we all know that's not true. Neil's wife, and our friend, is being hacked to bits and I think we are feeling that maybe a bit more than you. And as for negotiating…'

Neil cuts across her. 'Listen, Simon. You and I go back a long way. Amala and I have done more than most to help your government deliver its agenda and not just ID cards through Ezylocate. Much more.'

He stops, his voice catches. 'Not once have I refused you. Never. Despite not always being comfortable. Are you telling me now that it was all for nothing?'

His voice rises at the end as he watches Thompson's impassive face.

Jean Norton cuts in. 'Neil, we are really optimistic that we will get Ella back. All our resources are working on it. We believe that she is still in London and has been all day. We've been watching all traffic in and out of The Bush…' She trails off.

Before anyone can move, Neil suddenly leaps across the table and has Simon Thompson by the collar. Their faces only centimetres apart.

'So what, Thompson? Tell me. You fucker. You stupid, arrogant little fucker. You were going to keep it to yourself? You knew. You knew they had my wife but you were going to distract us all. How long have you known? How long have you sat there while they have been slicing off body parts? You complete fucking shit.'

He pulls Thompson even closer. 'If anything happens to her so help me I will ruin you. I will completely obliterate you. I know enough to do it so you better start moving your people to really help and you better start thinking about convincing this mad woman that you will close the PPCs. And whatever the fuck this Touchstone is, we'll find it. It's all over Ella's computer with your name on it.'

I see the blood rush to Thompson's face and spittle shoot from Neil's mouth as he slightly loosens his grip but keeps his face right up to Thompson's. 'Do not doubt I will pay the ransom and I will find Ella and if you do anything, anything, to jeopardise that, then I will stop at nothing to make you regret it for the rest of your life.'

Neil pushes him back in disgust, turning his face away. Thompson leans back and straightens his collar.

He is trying to compose himself but Thompson is rattled. He's never been the down and dirty street-fighting kind of politician, preferring the smooth back room deals in the juice bars of North London.

Alex Dalgleish continues smoothly as if nothing has happened. 'Mr Rochester. Please sit down and I will tell you what we know.'

Reluctantly, Neil sits. Amala and I move in beside him. Holding on to each other, dazed and terrified but totally focused. We look at Dalgleish, each of us trying to garner some hope from her quiet authority.

'This is what we know. The woman known as Nusayabah has Ella. We know it is Ella from the DNA. We have just confirmed that in the last forty-five minutes or so. The terrorists had spiked the finger with various chemicals, which made the DNA tracing extremely difficult. We don't know where she is, but we do believe she's in London given the timings of the movements established so far, and we have a strong suspicion she's in the Mulberry Estate. As you know, we believe the riots are coordinated. They're making access to some parts of the estate extremely difficult. However that, too, may be a diversion. A ploy to keep us looking there. The attack on the Faith to Faithless building has also required significant resource, we believe that is also only part of the story for today. At this point we are not ruling out anything, including the possibility of other attacks or other hostages.'

There is a pause as each of us hears the clock move to three o'clock. Bang on schedule, Nusayabah appears, a dark crow of death. Again, only the black standard and the geometric picture behind her.

'Mr Rochester, I take it you now see that I do not lie. We do have your partner and we will carry out our threats. You have missed the deadline for payment. I can only assume that with the arrival of Ms Hackeem, you saw no need to pay up. How wrong you were. I will now give you an additional one hour to pay the money. The money must be transferred by four pm and I will be back in touch at four thirty pm. The stakes are higher. The price has risen. The payment for your wife is now £200 million. Let's see if you think she's worth it. Our second demand stands. Both must be paid in full.' She pauses. 'As I said before, Mr Rochester, you know a lot about this government and so does your wife. In particular, her investigations into Touchstone have let her see just the kind of man your prime minister is. Perhaps you should look at the other names in her files.'

That's it. The screen goes black.

Tuesday 25th May 15.03

MILLIE

For a moment, we all continue to stare. This time I was more prepared. I had paid close attention. She sounds as if Touchstone is personal. Who are the other names? I cycle back in my mind. Matthew Robson? Is that it? His wife? The barrister?

Norton breaks the silence. 'We have ninety minutes before she is back in touch. The priority is to determine Ella's location. Let's regroup. There's no point in arguing amongst ourselves. Time is not on our side.'

Dalgleish turns to me. 'Dr Stephenson, we've read your analysis of the blogs and correspondence and combined it with other intelligence from Toni Roberts and her team, plus we have what Dr Ali was able to ascertain for us today.'

'We believe Nusayabah was the wife of Abu Bakr, the terrorist and strategic commander of Har majiddoon. You may remember he was wanted for atrocities both here and in the US, and was killed in a raid around last Christmas.'

I shiver, realising that as his wife, presumably she's just as devoted and ruthless.

As she talks, I'm looking at what was in the dossier about Abu Bakr,

I glance down to read the news report at the time of his death and my blood turns to ice.

Bakr is the person who masterminded a series of explosions at Glastonbury last summer, killing 47, maiming close to 280 others and striking fear throughout the country. Bakr was in the top 10 of most wanted global terrorists. Wanted by both US and British Authorities... He is believed to have entered Britain in the spring of last year with false papers and had been supported both in hiding and financially by the Tower Hamlets Mosque.

I read fast.

Bakr was killed as Special Forces raided a flat in the Mulberry Estate. James Mitford, from the Met's Anti-Terrorist Squad said: 'At 07.45 this morning officers from ATF50 were despatched to a residential flat in the Mulberry Estate following intelligence received... Six heavily-armed men were in the flat... Abu Bakr was killed instantly as were three other, as yet unidentified, associates... The two remaining terrorists are being held at Paddington Green.'

Rehan Ali, who had been sitting in silence, looking increasingly anguished, nods, 'I'm pretty certain his wife is British and part of

Umm Umarah. It fits. I heard she was recruited by Faiza Siddiqui and spent time in Syria.'

Dalgleish continues, 'Your analysis of the blogs shows a shift from the general to the personal just before Christmas last year when Abu Bakr was killed. They also increased in their targeted viciousness.'

She glances over at Thompson and Norton when she says this.

She looks back at Neil, 'Two of his men survived and have been working with us. They told us that Abu Bakr married an English woman who had turned up in Syria a few years ago. They have a son. We also know that Nusayabah has access to significant funds. We have played her voice to Bakr's men and they have confirmed it's his wife and their view is that she will have been devastated by the loss of her husband. They genuinely loved each other and were devoted to working together to create an Islamic state here in Britain. She's likely to be well-equipped, strategic, well-planned and lethal. I'm sorry to be so blunt, Neil, but we have very little time.'

'Thank you and thank you for being straight with me.' Neil's struggling to hold it together. 'My whole team are on it. I'm calling in favours where I can. I'm getting updates every few minutes but we still haven't pinned down the location.'

He looks at his screen. 'There was something that came in earlier from Sean, just before Amala was found, so I didn't pay too much attention.'

He reads. 'There is a faint trace of something like Yorkshire or Lancashire. We're still working on pinning it down to a town or village. We'll keep listening and get back to you.'

He says, 'Have Bakr's men told you anything else about her?'

'They say she is very well acquainted with the British establishment. She knows a lot about how things work,' Dalglish replies.

Neil glares at Thompson, 'You and I are not done. Not by a long way.'

I speak up. 'That all makes sense. It was after Abu Bakr was killed that Nusayabah became more specific, naming Mr Thompson, Mrs Norton and Mr Mitford. I quote from my file, reading fast.

'20th December

Fight and kill the unbelievers, take them captive, harass them, lie in wait and ambush them using every stratagem of war.

Quran 9.5

Thompson, Norton, and Mitford we are coming for you. We will get you.

Thompson for you I will take my blade and I will cut out every organ until you bleed like a dog on the street. I will cut you to ribbons. You are the TOUCHSTONE for all Kaffirs. I will take everything you have. I know where you are. I know where you go and I know what you have done.

Norton. I will come for your devil's spawn. So proud to bare everything to feed your brat. I will take that boy and put a spear through his heart. And I will laugh in your face when you have nothing.

And Mitford. For you we have something very special. Not just for you but for the abomination that lives with you.'

I stop there. There's a clip next to Mitford's name. I had looked this morning at the special prize in store for him. It shows a young man in a cage with three wild dogs ripping him apart limb from limb. It had been yet another low in the last few years of lows as a Sharia council had used that particular inhumane torture against two young homosexual men. I had clicked off. I couldn't bear to watch it. Mitford's well known as gay and in a long-term relationship with his partner.

There are a few more blogs like this. All personal, all mentioning loved ones – Thompson's wife, Norton's son and Mitford's partner. All have something about Touchstone next to Thompson's name, always capitalised. I pause. I look straight at Thompson, pushing forward, trying to catch him out and gain a foothold. 'I'm asking again, Mr Thompson, who or what is Touchstone?'

Thompson doesn't speak. He's obviously calculating his next words and actions very carefully. He looks caught. I feel disgust as he weighs up his own political future and whether to trade it for the truth. And a life.

Norton speaks, 'Simon, we have very little time. This has disaster written all over it. Is this Touchstone something that can help us?'

Dalgleish keeps looking at the clock, watching its relentless countdown. The tension in the room is suffocating. Neil starts pacing and looks ready to strangle Thompson given the opportunity.

Dalgleish moves in for the kill. She has clearly had enough and is not prepared to tolerate any more delay, coyness or political calculations. 'Mr Thompson, you should know that we have spent much of today tracing Touchstone and have been able to draw some conclusions. We are aware of the connection to Matthew Robson and we have arranged for Mr Robson to be collected from the House. He will be here any minute.'

So, is Matthew Robson Touchstone? He features highly in Ella's notes.

I never take my eyes from Thompson. He's shrewd but he's caught. He's about to trade what he knows.

Norton, looking puzzled, says, 'Simon, what has Matt got to do with this? He's a backbencher. He no longer has access to anything likely to matter here today. Nothing to help locate Nusayabah and Ella. What's going on?'

Dalgleish is not going to help him. Her look is steely and although her tone is neutral, it's clear she will brook no argument. Her eyes hold nothing but contempt. A woman prepared to risk her life for queen and country, who has spent years undercover, likely eschewing her friends and family. She watches and sees, as I do, a political animal still working out how he might save his own skin. Knowing he's caught. Knowing his options are narrowing by the second.

'Mr Thompson, we have all the brains and insights around this table to help us locate Ella. Let's not hold back with something that might impede our progress and be regretted later.'

The implicit threat is loud and clear and Thompson knows it.

Norton says, 'Simon, I think you had better tell us what's going on here.' This is a mission in full media view and it's not going to fail on her watch. Ruthlessly ambitious, she will not protect him from Touchstone, whatever it is. She, too, is calculating the future.

Neil whispers, 'Mark's on his way back.'

What I can't quite piece together is the link between Thompson, Touchstone, Nusayabah and now Matthew Robson the Tory MP. Robson is known to be a long-term mate of Thompson's. An astute businessman who had made a fortune before being elected. He'd sold his company before taking office. Mark can look at that. But there's something else. Not just the money. He'd rather surprisingly made a move to the backbenches a couple of years back. I couldn't quite remember why. He had been destined for one of the big jobs.

Tuesday 25th May 15.06

ELLA

Someone's coming back. My heart's pounding, making my chest hurt as I try and draw a breath. I hear myself whimper and will myself to stay calm. I pull into the corner, curling into a tight foetal ball; bracing myself for what's coming next.

The door opens. It's her, Nusayabah. She's holding a knife. Twirling it, casually. Nonchalant. I can't help it, I push further back into the wall.

She speaks, venom dripping from every word. 'So, we've just had a little chat with your husband.'

I feel my breath stop, trapped in my lungs. Is he here? Is Neil here? Has she got him too?

She keeps spinning the knife. 'So, let's see how much he thinks you're worth. What do you reckon? £10 million? £100 million? More? Much more? Easy for him to get money, eh? Awash with the cash he gets for all the poor bastards he runs down for Thompson. Ezylocate has made him a very rich boy. But let's see if it's enough?'

She throws the knife high in the air and catches it without even glancing at it. 'You see, sadly for you, the money's only part of it. We need more than that. He needs to get his great mate, our egomaniac prime minister to do what he needs to do to get you out of here? Now, that might be a little tricky. We really need to make it worth his while.'

I stare at her. 'What do you mean? Persuade him to do what? Is Neil here?'

The toxic hate that floods my body when she laughs gives me the strength to spit out, 'What has Neil got to do with this? What has Simon Thompson got to do with it?'

She's still playing with the knife. 'Do you know this knife can take the head off a chicken with one slice? Takes a second. It's true, you know, they do run about headless? Bit like your infidel husband right now. Running about like a headless chicken. No idea how to find you.'

She gives another bitter laugh.

I can see she's thinking. Calculating. But what. I wince as I feel her hard stare.

Tuesday 25th May 15.15

MILLIE

We all turn at the sound of a knock on the door. Matthew Robson is there, escorted by a couple of casually dressed men who nod at Dalgleish and make their exit. Robson looks furious. He's visibly out of breath. He has the air of a man more used to expensive lunches than being hauled to account. He has no idea just how bad his day is going to get. I train my eyes on him, watching his every move, poring over his every word.

'Simon, what's going on? A couple of apes from MI5 just about manhandled me out of the tea room and without a word of explanation brought me here.' He surveys the room, clearly knowing some but not everyone there. 'What the hell's this all about? Is everything ok?'

Thompson sighs and points to a chair. Robson sits, looking to Thompson for assurance. Trying hard to assess the situation and failing.

Dalgleish speaks, her voice crisp and clear, 'Those apes are highly-trained agents who keep the likes of you safe in your bed at night. But that aside, we are here to talk about Touchstone.'

If she's hoping for a reaction she gets one: first the blood drains from Robson's face then he turns a startlingly bright ruby red. He's known as a man fond of a scotch or four and has the colouring of a heavy drinker. I miss nothing. I feel a flutter in my belly. A breakthrough. We're getting closer. I can feel it.

Without realising he has already given himself away, he turns to Thompson and blusters, 'What's she talking about? What's this about?'

Dalgleish speaks again. 'Mr Robson, we have intercepted a series of messages between you and the prime minister that mention Touchstone. There are no further written details but we now need you to talk to us. We have an escort bringing your wife here too so that we might question her. We understand she continues to look after some of your business interests, so we thought she may be able to shed some light. It's pertinent to a live security situation. I'm sure even you are aware that a woman calling herself Nusayabah has taken a hostage and threatened the government today, so I advise you to hurry up.'

Her tone is menacing. She's an impressive operator. Robson looks stunned. Ten minutes earlier he had no doubt been enjoying a cup of Darjeeling and a strawberry tart with nothing more on his mind than when he might have the first scotch and soda of the day. He gulps hard trying to catch Thompson's eye. Thompson is studiously ignoring him.

Neil starts calmly. 'Mr Robson, I am Neil Rochester and I am half of Rockeem Technologies along with Amala here. I'm heavily involved in much of the current technology and surveillance issues—'

Robson cuts him off. 'I know who you are. What I don't know is why you are here. Have you been bugging my computer?'

Neil can't help it. The full force of his fury and panic comes unconstrained, and he flies at Robson. 'No, you stupid little fucker, I'm here because some nut job terrorist has my wife. She has her in a location we can't find and bit by bit she's hacking off body parts. So I'm here to find her and if you know something about that, you had better start spitting it out, or so help me I'll fucking kill someone. And I don't give a fuck if that person is you, you fat cunt. Her computer has pages and pages of notes about Touchstone and Kardax and it has your name and Simon's all over it. So don't waste my fucking time.'

Robson's mouth opens and closes in astonishment. He looks at Amala. 'I thought you were the hostage?'

Dalgleish answers. 'Amala was a decoy. The woman calling herself Nusayabah has Mr Rochester's wife.'

I am missing nothing. Something is falling into place.

Robson turns back to face Thompson. Thompson sighs and with a voice weary with resignation says, 'Touchstone is the code name for a contract to sell training, logistics and maintenance services to Jordan, Lebanon and Syria. It was a contract to help rebuild after the civil wars there and the devastation caused by ISIS and then Har majiddoon. It is a contract delivered by Kardax. Kardax is the company where Matt was a director before quitting all his commercial roles for one of public service. It was just after the Brexit vote and everyone was obsessed with that at the time. Everyone was worried about how Britain's place in the world would be impacted. It was critical we had a reliable British company in the area, and at speed, or we would have lost all the profitable contracts to the Americans and Russians. We just wanted to help the procurement process run smoothly.'

Norton speaks very slowly. 'Simon, both elections were won on a ticket of absolute transparency. Everyone was shouting about compromises and trading with companies and nations with appalling human rights records. Your voice was the loudest of them all. After Brexit, you guaranteed we would still be a trading nation without losing our integrity. Are you seriously telling me that this contract did not go through the proper channels?'

Thompson's nod is almost imperceptible. 'Jean, you know as well as I do how hard it was to sign that contract. We visited the Levant dozens of times. I went twice myself. Signing the deal was massive. We didn't have time for a beauty parade through the proper channels. Kardax were ready to go.'

Norton speaks very deliberately. 'You also knew that Kardax did not meet the criteria we set for companies working on government contracts. And you would have known that at the time their human rights record was abysmal. They were caught using child labour for God's sake. They dropped poisonous waste in the Amazon. Never mind the whole Iran debacle. Kardax was, and is, toxic.'

'It was that or delay for months and we didn't have months. They were already working in the Levant. They had all the infrastructure in place.'

As Thompson talks I scan the Kardax web page again. More pieces start to fall into place.

I say, 'Kardax is a £28 billion pound global company run by your old Etonian mate Jack McClelland. The same Jack McClelland that had to do a volte face after one of Kardax's divisions was found to be selling arms to Iran, in clear contravention of government policy. And yet the contract in the Levant was never investigated. In fact, two years ago Kardax won another government contract to sell weapons to ATF50 and other armed forces according to this. A contract that you personally oversaw, Mr Thompson. Even more interestingly, Kardax is the same company that Mr Robson here sold Clemco, his sports clothing company to, for £19.8 million, and the same company where his wife now sits on the board. Well that's all very cosy but I wonder what has it got to do with Nusayabah and Abu Bakr?'

Tuesday 25th May 15.18

NUSAYABAH

I stare at Ella Russell. What a waste. I think about everything she knows. I handed the story to her. Handed it to her on a plate. No matter how this day ends. One thing is certain. She will die.

Time to talk. I need to know what she did with the story.

I had told the whole story one time before.

If I close my eyes I can still feel the heat. Taste the warm pita, just made and steaming hot.

Abu was listening. He lit a cigarette and settled down to hear about Simon Thompson. He wanted every tiny detail. Nothing left out just in case it became important.

I began, 'I can't believe who I was back then. I was living in a bubble.'

He pulled me close and said, 'And now this is the girl who can slice the head of a chicken with one swipe of a knife?'

I told him everything.

Tuesday 25th May 15.25

MILLIE

I ask again, 'What has it got to do with Nusayabah and Abu Bakr?'

'I don't know,' Robson says, looking anxiously at Thompson.

A look passes between the two men. Long-time allies. Mates with a secret. Robson wipes the sweat from his top lip and I see his hand tremble.

Norton says, 'Matthew, you need to keep talking. You need to tell us everything about Kardax and the contract in the Levant.'

Neil is apoplectic. He's looking between Thompson, Dalgleish and Robson. 'We need to find Ella. We can't sit around here talking about contracts. We need to search for her. There are notes about Touchstone on her computer. Sean has them and is pulling them apart. That can come later; right now we need all our resources looking for her.'

He speaks without realising tears are pouring down his cheeks. I have never seen another human being look so desperate and so fragile.

Dalgleish interrupts. There's real sympathy in her voice. 'We have all our best people on it, Neil, I promise. We're narrowing down her location. We know Ella was picked up at 08.30 this morning. Her Ezylocate stopped working at 08.44. We know she was last seen at St Pancras station. We have CCTV footage of her and we know that she went to the ladies' toilets opposite the Eurostar and changed into a burqa. We know she met a woman and the exchange looked friendly. They exited by the back door at the side of the British Library. They all got into a blue van, which we traced to a man known to us. He's a cleric in a North London mosque. We've spoken to him today and he claims the van had been parked at the mosque, but the keys are kept in his office, and he has no idea who took it. We are still interviewing him. The van entered the Mulberry Estate at 09.13 and we lost them after that. The van was later seen leaving at 10.30, driven by some kid who says he was asked to drop it back at the mosque. So, to the best of our knowledge Ella is still somewhere in The Bush.'

Neil is slowly nodding, 'Ok. Now what?'

I'm desperately trying to make the next connection. Robson and Nusayabah. I'm watching Dalgleish too. Is that everything now? Are we finally being told everything? Dalgleish starts talking again and I turn my attention to Robson.

She says, 'Neil, I suggest you and I take a look at the footage, cameras and data. We have our teams working with yours. Our tech guys and the BSU are pulling the threads together but you may see something different. Mitford's team are still questioning Aafa. He is going through every detail with them and is cooperating fully.'

Neil says, 'I want Mark Carter to talk to him too. About the money and the shares. Mark will be here in a few minutes.'

My eyes never leave Matthew Robson. He is sweating and deeply uncomfortable. He constantly plays with his wedding ring, twisting it first one way and then the other. He's loosened his tie but is still red in the face. He looks as if he might expire.

Neil stands. Amala, who has been silent throughout, looks up from the geometric shapes she has been repeatedly drawing then discarding and speaks for the first time. 'I'm coming with you. We can work the data and I can help.'

Looking at Amala, James Mitford says, 'I think we need to understand a bit more about what happened to you and your brother. As yet we don't know if we're looking at coincidence or connection.'

'Can't that wait? I can be most help to Neil trying to crack where Ella might be.'

'You have a unique insight into what happened in The Bush today and as far as we know this could be a coordinated attack,' he counters. 'Give us ten minutes. It may be invaluable and only you can help. Then you can work with Mr Rochester.'

Amala sees his point and reluctantly agrees to be debriefed by Mitford. She grabs the papers with the doodles and walks out. Norton and Thompson stand to go and I look at Matthew Robson.

'Mr Robson, I wonder if we might talk further and see if there is any way you and I can piece together the more confusing parts of the picture?'

He looks at me as if I am dirt on his shoe, 'I don't think so, Miss…?'

Dalgleish steps in. 'I was about to say the same, Dr Stephenson. Mr Robson, Dr Stephenson will explain her credentials and I strongly advise you to fully cooperate with her. You heard Mrs

Norton, we need more explanation so we can see what the connections are. How it fits into the day.' Again her implicit threat roars like a foghorn.

I fire myself up. I need to nail this. What good am I if I can't work out who has Ella and how to get at her? There's no way he's slipping through my net.

I say with all the authority I can muster, 'My name is Dr Millie Stephenson and I am an expert in radicalisation. I came here this morning to brief the prime minister on the increasing number of young British girls tempted and drawn to radicalisation.'

Bingo.

Robson's eyes bulge. He swallows hard and moves his hand to his mouth as if to hold in any involuntary sounds. His Adam's apple bobs up and down like a cocaine-fuelled pole dancer as he wipes the sweat from his top lip.

Alex Dalgleish intervenes again. 'As I said, I think you could be very helpful Mr Robson. Alternatively, I could get a couple of my apes back to talk to you.'

With that she walks out with Neil, giving the slightest of nods to me.

She knows something. I have a hunch we are onto something and I am becoming clearer and clearer as to what it might be. I look at the time. I can hardly believe it is only half past three. It feels like hours have passed.

Thompson pauses by the door, he's grey, his eyes hollow. He knows he's holding a busted flush. Weary, he says, 'Matt, I think you may want to help Dr Stephenson here. I think you need to tell her everything. And I mean everything.'

Hearing the emphasis on the word everything, Matthew Robson looks as if he's been stabbed in the back. Except I think he's just been stabbed in the front.

Suddenly, I'm certain. I can't feel sorry for him. I need answers. 'How long has your daughter been part of Umm Umarah?'

Tuesday 25th May 15.27

NUSAYABAH

I am still picturing it. Ella Russell is waiting for me to speak. I savour the memory a minute longer.

Abu was so proud of me, of how much I could remember. I had to tell the whole story again. To Har majiddoon

I saw them all waiting. Not used to listening to a woman but knowing I had the last pieces of the jigsaw.

The meeting had started. The atmosphere was charged, we could all see Abu's strategy coming together. The plans were audacious. London street maps were blown up to cover the walls, key personnel in the British Har majiddoon cell were patched in. I could see them on the screen, all alert to what was to come. Proud to be part of Abu Bakr's men. Faiza was beside me. In front of her were details of the major bank accounts across the globe financing the mission. They wanted to know about Touchstone.

Tuesday 25th May 15.28

MILLIE

I ask him again. 'How long has your daughter been part of Umm Umarah?

I let him talk.

'I don't know if she is. She left home seven years ago. She had everything, a place at university. The world at her feet and she threw it all away. God, I loved that girl more than life itself. She started to turn to Islam when she was seventeen. At first, we kept it all to ourselves. She didn't visibly change at the start. She was always sensitive. Bit highly strung, I suppose, and we think she got drawn in by the idea of being part of something she thought was important. She met some girls online and they persuaded her to start going to a mosque. She started going to all these classes. We never saw her. We didn't know what she was doing to begin with. We thought she was just out with friends, same as before. But then over that summer, she stopped going to parties, or even to the cinema, she wouldn't watch films with us. She stopped having a glass of wine with us. It still didn't click, though. We didn't really know what to look for. She still looked normal, if that's the word. Now it's all anybody talks about, but not back then. It's yet another thing we have to look for, think about. But back then it was unheard of. A nice, white, middle-class girl. For God's sake, she went to church.'

He rubs his eyes. He looks very old all of a sudden. 'It sounds daft now but then we didn't know to be worried. We began to notice no one ever came to see her any more. We didn't see any of her school friends. Around the time of her A levels, the school rang to ask us if everything was ok at home. We thought she was maybe moping after some boy. She'd been dumped by someone. We put it down to a broken heart from a first love but something she would get over.'

He gives a sad laugh and then sighs, almost talking to himself.

'One morning, she came downstairs wearing a hijab. We were appalled. I thought it was a joke. Her mother started to say it was offensive. Until we realised she was serious. We tried to talk her round. We tried everything. We pleaded with her, tried to ground her and stop her going out. Then one day she just left. About a week before she was due to go to university. She called her mother once to say she was happy. She never called again. Not one word. She broke her mother's heart. And mine.'

He looks down. His hands are shaking. A single solitary tear rolls down his cheek. I can smell sweat and alcohol in his pores. All the bluster is gone.

'Do you know where she is now?'

'No.'

It's the truth. He is empty.

Tuesday 25th May 15.30

NUSAYABAH

'I thought you were a big shot journalist, desperate for the big story?'

I watch as she lifts her chin. A tiny act of defiance. I have to admire her courage. She's got guts. I thought she would be begging for her life by now.

'What story? What are you talking about?'

'Touchstone. I fed you everything.'

I want to see her face. I pull off her veil. She falls back with a jerk. Her eyes are bright but focused. I push her head up so she is looking right at me.

I have my finger under her chin; she is rigid but hiding her fear as best she can. 'Were you worried about exposing your dirty-dealing husband? The story wasn't even about him. You had everything. No questions asked about how fast that sweet deal went through the procurement process. Not just that but to a company that had blood all over it. Sweat shops, toxic waste and arms to any dodgy dictator. Arms to those racist bastards in ATF50. No mention of Matthew Robson, MP and great chum of Simon Thompson, and all the shares in his blind trust.. His wife, a non-executive on the board, and still you didn't tell the story.'

Ella pulls herself up as far as she can. She looks down at her ravaged hand. 'Is this what this is all about? A contract? Me not writing a story?'

My frustration pours out. How can she be so stupid? So naive?

'It was a complete sham. Thompson was elected on transparency. His pitch was about being a global player without compromising British values, and then one of his first acts is to turn a blind eye to Kardax, an organisation selling arms to any buyer.'

I take off my veil. I want her to see me. I want her to know what she's done.

She's trying to work it out. 'I was planning to write it. I was building the story. It's a complex piece. There's a lot to check out. You can't just libel people these days. Not now everyone is so paranoid about fake news.'

Ella Russell twists herself up a bit further, wincing in pain. She looks deathly pale. Blood clogging her hair. She's tougher than she looks, I'll give her that.

'I was going to run the story. I needed to find the right place for it. I wanted it in the mainstream. No one will publish now without checks and double checks.'

'And what about Simon Thompson, were you scared of upsetting him?' I spit at her. 'And your husband. He colludes with Thompson and this government. Colludes and helps to kill innocents. Thompson, Robson and Rochester all have innocent brothers' blood on their hands. Their arms and surveillance are working hand in hand to massacre Muslims.'

I look at her in disgust. She is shaking her head, denying

Rochester's part in this. She's either blind or stupid. I see her close her eyes and wish she was anywhere but here.

I walk out. It's time.

Tuesday 25th May 15.32

ELLA

There's a lot of noise. Something is happening. I can hear movement and voices, furniture moving around.

I have given up trying to wriggle out of my bindings. It's not like the movies where there is always some sort of sharp edge and the hero manages to cut free.

And I'm no hero. I am sore. So sore. There's nothing. Just my thoughts. I make myself think the good thoughts.

I think about Neil. The best thought. Our wedding.

The little church was so beautiful. The sun was shining and everyone was there. Holding Dad's arm, I felt him shake but he held it together. Walking down the aisle was like a dream. I could see Neil waiting, doing that thing where he worries at his lip with his teeth when he's nervous. I could see his eyes mist over as he saw me. The music was stunning. The day was perfect.

Everyone giggled when we got to the bit 'for richer or for poorer'. As a wedding present, Neil bought me the world's ugliest dog, Kubla Khan, KK, a Pug Schnauzer cross with an alarming overbite from Battersea Dogs Home.

It was the best day of my life. Millie and Amala did a really funny speech. They had all these photos from Edinburgh. We looked so young. They even had the photo of me trying to rescue Millie's bra from the moose antlers in the student union.

Tuesday 25th May 15.35

MILLIE

Robson is weeping.

'I loved her. I still do. I love her with all my heart. She's still my little girl. I pray every day she'll come back.'

I know it is like salt in a wound but I need to understand. And fast. I try to keep my voice calm, controlled, 'What was it that turned her?'

'I don't know. Maybe we put too much pressure on her. You know, perfect grades, best at sports, best at music. Maybe it was all too much. I've asked that question a thousand times and I still don't know.'

He's nodding as he speaks but he's playing a part now. There's something he isn't saying. It is too off pat. I can smell it. He's staring straight at me. He's trying too hard to hold eye contact. Too keen to look convincing. I need the rest.

'Normally,' I say, treading carefully, 'there's a trigger. It's usually a couple of life-changing, or life-challenging, events that create a vulnerability and then that vulnerability is exploited. Do you know what it might be for your daughter?'

'No.' A bit more emphatic.

My guess is she had been Daddy's girl and somewhere along the way Daddy hadn't quite passed muster.

I try a different approach. I find his eye line. 'Could she be Nusayabah?'

He looks genuinely astonished.

His voice is made stronger by agitation, 'Of course not. To our knowledge, she's not even in the UK. She might have fallen in with this group, she might be feeding them information to harm me, to harm Simon, but she's not a murderer. That woman was married to a mass murderer. She's hacking another woman to bits. My daughter may have taken a wrong path but she's not a murderer. Clemmie wouldn't do that.' He runs out of steam. 'No matter what.'

But I can see he is starting to wonder. His eyes are darting all around. He's trying to find some solid ground. Something he can hold on to. What if his daughter really is that lost?

I'm pretty certain she is.

Tuesday 25th May 15.36

NUSAYABAH

I see her in the next room. She's got a stupid smile on her face. What has she got to smile about?

I have read all the stuff in her diaries, not just the stuff about Rochester but about her fairy tale childhood before it got ripped from her. I have read all about how she felt then. All alone. I know how that feels.

She said she had found a new family when she met the other two, Hackeem and Stephenson. Well, the whole family is about to be blown apart. All of them. I hate them. All of them.

That rage I had calcified into a searing, clinical desire for revenge the day they killed Abu.

Killed by weapons sold by Kardax.

Killed by murderers trained by Kardax.

Found by surveillance created by Rockeem.

She's not that different to me. I had never been a joiner. Neither was she. I never really joined in. Until now.

Tuesday 25th May 15.38

AMALA

'For God's sake. Can I get out of here now? I'm fine. Apart from the fact my best friend is going to die unless we find her.' I know I'm screaming like a banshee but I don't care. The debrief has gone on and on. I know there will be more later and I know they're still talking to Aafa.

I could hardly answer any of the questions about Aafa: was he turned? Who had turned him? And where did he get the money? I was as much in the dark as them. Jeez, my baby brother and I hadn't a Scooby what he'd been up to.

I had seen the shock and hurt on Aafa's face when he arrived at the flat courtesy of the Kalashnikov-wielding jihadists. He was devastated. Gutted. Horrified at what he had got us into. I keep hearing the desperate howl of pain when the guard was shot and the feeling of sheer and utter terror that it would be me or Aafa next.

A woman died today. No matter how the day ends none of us will ever be the same again. I know Aafa will never forgive himself for his part in this nightmare.

Aafa, my baby brother, is such a good and kind boy. Gullible but not cruel. Naive for sure, but not a violent extremist. The police aren't going to see it that way, though. I know the media will have a field day. They've got rich pickings. I saw the stuff running about me: bi-sexual, mega rich tech entrepreneur. They think that's all I am. A set of labels. It's not even original. The fact so much has been on live TV and across thousands of websites means this is going to run and run.

I ask, 'Can I see Aafa for a minute? I just need to check he's ok then I really need to help Neil.'

Surprisingly, I'm allowed.

I grab the pages I was working on and run to Aafa.

I put my hand to his hair and stroke it. 'Hang on in there, bro.'

He looks totally bereft. He moves to speak, to say sorry but no words come. Only tears. 'It's ok,' I say. 'I know you couldn't have known. Don't blame yourself.' I rub his head gently and move to the door.

In a tiny voice he says, 'Amala. I am so sorry. I had no idea…'

'I know. I know you didn't.'

He asks the question none of us can answer. 'Will they get Ella? Will they save her?'

'I hope so. Pray for her, baby brother. Pray hard.'

His only protection right now from the demons that will haunt him for the rest of his life is his deep state of shock.

I leave the room and walk over to Neil. He looks deranged

'Where are we up to?'

'Millie is still in with Robson. Mark's here. Working on the money. He's sent it with a tracer. They're trying to follow it now. Aafa's still with Mitford's guys. They say Mark can talk to him in ten.'

'Yeah, I just saw him. Neil, you know he didn't know. He would never have let anyone hurt me and you know he loves Ella like a sister, right?'

Neil doesn't answer. I see him swallow hard.

'Neil, he's stupid but he's not bad. He would never let anyone into your house if he knew they would film it or do anything to harm you and Ella.'

Neil looks up briefly. 'Yeah, but he did. How do you know he didn't help them put the stuff out about you? Who knows what else Aafa's done. There's a lot of stuff still not adding up.' He puts his head back down, looking at the screen. 'And do you know your dad's getting hate mail?

Hate mail? My dad? I feel like I've been sucker punched. The stuff about me is crap but it's all been out there before. But my dad, he wouldn't hurt a fly. My mum will be beside herself. Hate mail. I can't believe this. My whole family dragged into this.

I can't process that now. It will have to wait. I have to get down to business. Do what I'm good at. I feel my head clear. Zoning in to what we need to do. I look at Neil's screen.

'It might be worth me looking at the anti-tracer stuff. Mark's good but he won't know the tech stuff to look for.'

Neil nods not looking up, pointing with his head to the room next door. I can see Mark hard at work. Even today he makes me feel awkward. Even today there's not a hair out of place.

I walk in. 'Hey, Mark. Can I help?'

He looks up and gives a weak smile. He stands and, to my surprise, hugs me tight.

'I'm glad you're ok. We all thought it was you.'

He holds me at arm's length. 'Come on, let's do this. Let's find the money and let's hope it gets us to Ella. There's no other option. Millie won't be able to bear it if anything happens to her.'

Tears prick my eyes and I say very quietly, 'Me neither, Mark. Me neither.'

I move to the desk. I know what to look for. They said she's good, but I'm better. I give Mark's arm a quick squeeze and move him to the side. I'm going to get this bitch. 'Let's go. Let's see where this money's going. Let's nail this fucking Nusayabah.'

Tuesday 25th May 15.40

NUSAYABAH

The money should be here. I check.

Yes.

Mark Carter will no doubt have put a trace on it before he sent it. Men and money. It makes them blind.

I feel my hair. I haven't put the veil back on yet. I'm going to talk to her again and I want her to see my face. To show her what she has done.

Her and the rest of them. Rochester, Hackeem and Stephenson. They're to blame.

They've made this happen.

Tuesday 25th May 15.42

MILLIE

The door opens and an elegant but dishevelled woman in her early fifties appears.

'Jennifer,' says Robson standing up.

I recognise Jennifer Robson as soon as she walks in. I realise she's a top-flight barrister known for taking tricky cases. She had once been stunning. She still has the poise of the trained ballerina she was. She's as thin as a whippet and no amount of money or excellent tailoring can hide the bones peeping through from her open-necked shirt nor the rosacea that goes with too much drinking. My God, these two must really put it away.

She looks at her husband then at me. Her impeccable manners

not quite quick enough to hide the slight sneer as she takes in my hair, piercings and Doc Marten boots.

I pull myself to my full height and go for the jugular. I need the reaction before her husband has a chance to warn her.

'Mrs Robson, I am Dr Millie Stephenson. I am a Professor at the LSE, specialising in radicalisation. You may well have seen the footage earlier today of a hostage taken by an Islamic extremist and the demands made by a woman dressed in a niqab.'

She nods, suddenly on full alert.

'We have very little time so you will need to forgive my bluntness. We have reason to believe that the woman in the niqab is your daughter.'

I'm watching Jennifer Robson intently. She's clearly intelligent and absorbing everything I say. She stands stock still clutching her bag to her chest as if it might protect her. I can see her breathing change. Inhaling deeply but unable to catch enough breath as the blood leaves her already pale face. She looks as if I've just driven a stake through her heart.

I carry on. I can't leave any space for Robson to warn her. I need to control this. 'The woman she has taken is not Amala Hackeem. I'm sure you will have seen the news today including Amala's rescue. However, she does have a hostage and her name is Ella Russell. Journalist and wife of Neil Rochester. If we're going to rescue Ella…' my voice falters. I clear my throat and blink hard. I try again, my voice thick and hoarse. 'If we're going to rescue Ella then we need your help. This is what we know. The woman in the niqab is likely white British, well-educated, with a Yorkshire or Lancashire accent and we are fairly sure she's in her twenties.'

I know this is brutal. 'She calls herself Nusayabah and so far she's hacked off Ella's finger and an ear.'

I swallow, trying to shift the dryness in my throat.

Jennifer Robson sits down with a thump, still clutching her bag. 'What makes you think it's Clementine?'

'The profile and voice fit. MI5 and GSOC have traced a connection. Nusayabah continually mentions something called Touchstone which she has made public. Touchstone is linked to you, your husband and Simon Thompson. Your husband has explained that it was the code name he and Thompson gave to a dodgy procurement deal.'

At this, Matthew Robson bursts out, 'No one said it was dodgy. We've told you it was the best option and the best provider we just needed to speed up the process.'

He looks over at his wife, pointedly. 'Jennifer knows that too.'

I've had enough. His reputation doesn't even feature on my top 100 list of worries. 'That's why it needed the secret code name,' I roar. 'Nothing to do with your shares, your wife on the board and let's not even talk about what Kardax sold to Iran. And just so we're crystal clear here. The guns used by ATF50, the ones made by Kardax and the ones that killed your son-in-law, I suppose they're all squeaky clean too!'

Jennifer Robson speaks very softly, 'Son-in-law? What do you mean son-in-law? Is Clementine married?'

I look at her. She's dazed and desperately trying to piece things together. She looks so small and vulnerable. I have to remember this woman is a mother and this was, is, her daughter.

I rein in my fury and kneel in front of her. I hold her gaze. 'Jennifer, I cannot imagine how hard this must be but we really need your help. Ella Russell is my best friend. She is a good and true person and she has less than two hours to live if we can't get to her. Please, please help me.'

She nods and whispers, 'What can I do?'

Tuesday 25th May 15.43

AMALA

I look up, one of Mitford's guys is at the door.

'Commander Mitford says you and Mr Carter can have ten minutes with your brother, Ms Hackeem. He says you want to ask about the money.'

Mark and I stand and follow him.

Aafa, still chained, has his head on the desk, he's weeping uncontrollably. The police officer beside him looks at him with complete disgust.

Aafa looks up. Tears all over his face.

'Mals, I didn't do these things. I didn't sell out you or Ella. I'm not an extremist. I don't support anything this Nusayabah is doing. I've never met her. I would never have let Hassan into Ella's house. You've got to believe me. I am not what they say. I swear I am not a radical. I'm not a jihadist. I hate violence. You know that. They're talking about me in a photo with Abdul Izz al-Din. I swear I wasn't there. Hassan photoshopped me in. They've just showed the film to me. I was not there. I swear. I know where they took it from; it was Hassan. He filmed me waving at him. He took that picture. He told me to look angry and shout. He said it was for something he was making at college. They fitted me up. Mals, Mark I promise, I swear I didn't do this.'

I stare at him. He's choking and sobbing, snot and tears falling into his lap.

I move to hold him. The police officer steps in front of me.

'Please, Ms Hackeem, sit on the other side of the table and do not make contact with the prisoner.'

'Prisoner? For fuck's sake, what happened to innocent until

proven guilty?'

Mark touches my elbow and guides me to the seat.

He says, 'Aafa, for now we need you tell us what you know about the money going in and out of your account. It's being used to buy up Kardax shares. Also, there's money going to this Education and Light Programme. Tell us what you know.'

Aafa sighs. 'Honest, Mark, everyone keeps asking me questions that I can't answer. I swear, I don't know anything about the money. I've told them I was fed up at uni. I couldn't tell my dad. He'd go mad. I wanted to do something else. I wanted to move to a teaching course. Dad would have thought that was a waste. He wants me to be an engineer, but I hated it. I thought I would love it but I didn't.'

I sense Mark's impatience. 'Aafa, what about your fees. They went to this Education and Light Programme?'

'I know, I know how it looks but honestly it's exactly what it says. It's about teaching Islam, not hate, not jihad but peace. It's a charity. It's to train teachers that go out to schools and youth groups. That's what I want to do, not be an engineer. I've been training as a teacher.'

I hear the police officer mutter something and see his look of disbelief. I glare at him until he lowers his gaze.

Mark says, 'Why didn't you tell us, Aafa? Why didn't you say anything?'

'Because my dad would be so disappointed. He would think I was throwing away an opportunity.'

I look into his bloodshot eyes and say gently, 'Aafa, Dad loves you, we all do. If teaching was what you wanted to do, we would have been cool with that.'

Mark speaks before Aafa can answer, 'Listen, mate, we need to talk about some of this later. For now, we really need to understand how the big sums of money went in and out of your account.'

'Mark, Mals, I wish I could tell you but I swear on my life I have no idea.'

I turn to Mark. 'I believe him. Let's go.' I look back at my brother. 'Aafa, I believe you. You've been played.'

He nods, and sighs from the depths of is soul.

'I just hope everyone else believes me.'

Tuesday 25th May 15.45

NUSAYABAH

I'm still watching her. I have my own memories tugging and pulling me back. Even though they feel like a lifetime ago I can still see him. My dad: the big man, the indestructible force; or so he thought. Hubris writ large. Flawed and corrupt. He was a "Thompsonite" through and through. Known as Matt to his mates, my dad was a big man in every sense. Six foot and with the build of someone well-acquainted with the rugby front row and with the crooked nose and bashed up ear lobe to prove it.

I close my eyes and think back to just before Thompson's landslide election win.

'Simon, Simon, great to see you. Welcome, welcome' he boomed, grabbing Thompson enthusiastically and pulling him into a bear hug, patting him hard across the shoulder.

Waving one arm in the general direction of the drinks cabinet, and with the other still around Thompson, he roars, 'Come on, Jennifer, let's get this party started. Simon, so fantastic you could spare the time to come here. You must be exhausted. You've covered the entire country at least twice in that battle bus of yours. It's been worth it though. The polls are fantastic. There's no way we can't win this time, Simon. It's all rosy in the garden. Come on, Jennifer get a clip on, get some champagne going here. We're parched.'

Mum's back stiffened and she looked down, her hands shaking as she tried to compose herself. Steeling herself to turn back to them, she made a slightly faltering circle and forced her mouth into a smile, sharing her brilliant white cosmetic dentist teeth with the room. Her face was set with false vivacity that on closer inspection revealed nothing behind the eyes.

'Just coming, darling,'

Grabbing Kate Thompson in one swoop and extravagantly kissing each cheek, Dad then moved like a dervish to open the champagne, wrestling it from Mum just as she was about to pop the cork.

Seeing me at the door, Dad abandoned the bottle. Distracted by a new shiny possession to show off, he swept me in to be paraded in front of Simon and Kate Thompson.

'You remember my beautiful and talented daughter, Clementine? Apple of my eye. Top marks all the way, in all the top sports teams and plays the clarinet like a professional. Not that I am biased. Well, maybe just a little.'

He chuckled, knowing his pride was evident and so any boasting would be forgiven.

'Of course.' Thompson smiled. 'Although the last time we saw you, Clementine, I think you were at the pony show. That must be what four or five years ago? Would that be right? Now what year are you in at school?

I smiled and, just as I had been taught over the years, engaged in a nice conversation with the grown-ups.

'Hello, Mr Thompson, Mrs Thompson. It's lovely to see you

both again. Yes, I'm almost eighteen and just waiting to go on to university in Durham.'

'She got all A stars too,' interrupted Dad, beaming.

'Well, I worked really hard but I'm really pleased I got in to Durham to read Economics.' I smiled.

'Very wise choice, and I'm sure you'll do brilliantly. Clever just like your mum.' He slapped Dad on the back so he could appreciate the wit.

Dinner included a few of the most senior local party members all basking in the anticipated glory to come and spirits were high.

I tuned in and out of the conversations. Most of the time I was ignored. I had Kate Thompson to my left and some totally boring local farmer to the right. Simon Thompson was next to Dad, upsetting Mum's boy – girl pattern at the table, but he had insisted that 'there are just a few things to sort out', and it was vital he sat beside the 'next PM'.

I blink, coming back to the present. I remember telling Abu the whole story and how by then I had already decided I was leaving. I had my own money from the Kardax shares, supposedly to 'secure my future'.

Abu had leaned back on his heels and laughed at that. 'Maybe not quite how Daddy saw the future though!'

Tuesday 25th May 15.48

MILLIE

I take Jennifer Robson's hand in mine, it's tiny and cold and she's shaking but she's holding it together.

'We believe she married Abu Bakr, the Har majiddoon strategic commander. He was killed in the ATF50 raid just before Christmas last year. We think she's not just a committed jihadist but has a personal grudge linked to Kardax. We think there are also connections to Rockeem Technology for their surveillance. We think she's taken Ella because her husband owns Rockeem Technology. But also, Ella has loads of information about Touchstone on her computer. Nusayabah has made two demands. She wants £200 million and for Thompson to close the PPCs starting today.'

I wait as the pieces start to fall into place for her. To her credit, Jennifer Robson holds my gaze.

'Somehow your daughter must know enough about the Kardax deal to make life very difficult for Thompson and your husband and she's prepared to make whatever she knows public. Neil has gone through Ella's computer and much of the information came from one person, someone calling herself Citrussister.

'We have people poring over it as we speak. She's trading on two things. That Neil Rochester will find a way to pay the ransom and Thompson will make a deal to start closing PPCs in order to keep Touchstone out of the press. Her timing is brilliant, she knows Thompson has the party conference coming up and he won't want any challenges that might shake their confidence that he should stay leader for a third term.'

I realise some of this is only properly falling into place for me as I explain it to her.

Her voice, when she speaks, is suddenly clear, 'What can I do? How can I help you?'

'I need to piece together a picture of Nusayabah. Clementine. I need to understand what makes her tick. What her vulnerabilities might be. Tell me why you think she would have turned to Islam and what would have convinced her to be radicalised and risk her life.'

Jennifer sighs deeply and closes her eyes, no doubt thinking back to her little girl.

I prompt her. 'Normally there are a couple of events that shake someone. Something that makes them question the life they lead and the beliefs they hold. Can you think of anything that may have done that to Clementine?'

She nods, 'Yes.'

Tuesday 25th May 15.55

AMALA

I flick through the code. My thoughts are moving fast. I can hear the musical notes in the digits, an orchestra only I can hear. It's clever and it's very sophisticated anti-tracing technology. But I can see the path. I always can. Thank God.

I say to Mark, 'It's going through these banks in Bermuda, there are a few reroutes but it looks like it ends up with this same broker here in London.'

He looks at the screen, already tapping the information into his own device.

'I don't know the broker and they will likely have pretty heavy client privilege contracts, but I have a few contacts that might be able to help. I'm going to call them.'

I pat his shoulder and say, 'Thanks, Mark.'

He's already dialling. I hear someone pick up and he says, 'Hi, Mark Carter here.'

I mouth, 'I am going to help Neil.' My head is buzzing but I stop in my tracks. I can see my little brother in the corridor. They are taking him away. Jean Norton is there with Mitford.

She says, 'Your brother will be questioned further by trained officers. He's on his way to Paddington Green.'

I watch him walk away. His head bowed and his feet shuffling in the leg chains. I look away. I can't bear to watch Aafa. Rehan Ali comes towards me. He takes my arm and leads me away.

'Come on. We all need to stay focused and work together. I have some intelligence about the riots. I think they're being coordinated by someone known to the authorities. I have asked Alex Dalgleish to check and we are pretty certain it is Hassan Yacoub. The same person that convinced Aafa to let him into Ella and Neil's house. He is a fierce fighter and is now commanding over 200 people in The Bush. The police are struggling to cope. They're trying to pin down where he is.'

'Thanks, I'll take a look. I am going back in to help Neil. If we can see the pattern in the riots, it might help to locate Yacoub and it might also help lead us to Ella.'

Rehan turns to go back to the table. I grab his elbow and show him the screen shot on my smart block.

'Rehan, look at this. What does it look like to you?'

He stares at the block, taking it from me and turning it to see the pattern from different angles.

I say, 'It's the screen behind Nusayabah. It's like she's obscuring something. Pixelating a picture. If you look, it looks like an Islamic Pattern'

'Yes, you're right.' He traces his finger along the interlocking lines.

'It's basic Greek geometry. A circle in a square divided into twelve equal sections. It could be a clue to where she is.'

'Or it could be from any mosque in the world or anywhere else with Islamic art on display, Amala,' Ali says slowly, his hand gently on mine.

I nod. I can't help but agree but it's bugging me.

I quickly squeeze his hand. Turning from him I pick up pace and shove hard on the door. Neil's crouched over three huge screens. I can see them from here. In an instant I can see the constellation, another pattern. I say to Neil, 'What have we got?'

Tuesday 25th May 16.00

MILLIE

Jennifer Robson sits up straight. Without a pause she says, 'When she was twelve, she came home early and found her father, whom she adored, in bed with the au pair. She never looked at him the same way again. Until then her daddy was the most important person in her life. I never got a look in. Everything she did was to please him. The sport, the music, the grades. All she wanted was to be the perfect daughter to the perfect father. She later found out that the au pair wasn't the first and she definitely wasn't the last. There were many nails in that particular coffin.' Her voice is harsh and bitter. Every word telling of a life lived in pain, lies and humiliation. And I suspect, latterly, at the bottom of a bottle.

Matthew Robson looks down at the table and puts his head in his hands.

She isn't finished. 'Clemmie really was very bright. Even though she never idolised her father the same way again she was always interested in his business life. Matt gave her shares and taught her how to follow the market, work out what and when to buy and sell. She had a nose for it. He gave her shares in Clemco. It made her a rich young woman. Later, when she was older, she started asking questions about why he had sold Clemco to a company that had been exposed as having terrible human rights. They had a massive row about that.'

'Kardax?'

She nods. 'The only thing I ever did that won Clemmie's approval was my job. She was proud of my record on fighting difficult cases. I lost that respect the day I joined the board of Kardax. She took to sending us both every press release that showed Kardax exploiting vulnerable people all over the world. I'm not proud of my part in it either.'

My heart is racing, I need her to keep going and I need the whole story. There will be more. 'Thank you. I know that can't have been easy for you. I'm sorry to be so probing but there's no time to be gentle. Why didn't you leave him? You were financially independent with a strong career of your own?'

I need to know if she is hiding anything else in the family dynamic.

For the first time, she breaks eye contact. Sitting back in the chair she says quietly, 'I was ashamed. I didn't want to be known as the barrister fighting for women's rights who had put up with a serial adulterer.' She pauses and carries on in a small resigned voice. 'And I believed what a million women before me have believed. I was stupid enough to think he would stop.'

My guess is she probably also liked the five-star lifestyle a little too much too.

I wait for her to blink away the tears. This is something Jennifer Robson will have to deal with herself later. I can't help her right now. It feels brutal but I need her to focus.

'Did something else happen to Clementine when she was maybe around seventeen or eighteen? Something that would have created an opening for her to be exploited?'

She looks down, a single tear falls in to her lap.

She swallows hard and looks straight in my eye.

'Yes.'

Tuesday 25th May 16.02

NUSAYABAH

I can't stop thinking about back then. I picture the me from before, tucked away on the window seat. I could feel the damp from the condensation on the sash window and the lights from the garden reflected in the glass. Back then I didn't realise the significance of what I was about to hear, nor how useful it would be a few years and one lifetime later.

Mum was in the kitchen, swaying as she had one more for the road. Kate Thompson was with her listening to her drone on.

Dad and Thompson were back in the reception room with two large whiskies. I was tucked in the corner reading. I wasn't deliberately hiding but they didn't see me, and I kept quiet.'

Thompson was upbeat, 'I really don't want to tempt fate, Mattie boy, but it's looking good for us. This next four years is for us to really make our mark. Our place to shape the economy and Britain's place in the world for decades to come. Not since Thatcher in the eighties has our party been so well-placed to make the seismic shifts we need to hold our own with the super powers. With the tax breaks we've lined up we can start to get the big boys back into the City and get the scroungers working again, just lowering that net a bit more. Enough bite to get the lazy back to work, not sitting on their arses waiting for a handout. Yep, putting the Great back in

Great Britain eh? No, this is it, I can feel it. This is our time.'

Thompson picked up his whisky, a rich tawny swirling in the heavy bottomed crystal glass. He lifted it to his nose, inhaled deeply, appreciating the rich peaty smell before taking a long swig. He sat back, looking smug. Looking every inch a man with the world at his feet. Dad leaned over and patted Thompson's knee, a little jagged in his movements as he tried to control his words, which were just slightly slurred.

'Simon, we're twelve points ahead. No one's catching us here. Labour are in total disarray. Christ, they can hardly hold their own MPs together; no one's going to trust them to run a corner shop never mind the bloody country. Nah, the whole "Global outlook, local focus" is genius. We've got the message out that Britain can be a big trading nation again but keep the immigrants out at the same time. Bloody genius.' He burped slightly as he sat back in the chair.'

Lowering his voice, he leans forward again, 'Listen, Simon. I need to talk to you about this deal with Kardax. I've tied everything up with Jack McClelland. He is a good guy and a CEO who knows what side his bread is buttered. My shares are, of course, all tied up in the blind trust but we have agreed that Jennifer will sit as a non-executive director on the board. You know, she'll keep an eye on the training, logistics and maintenance division. After that debacle when we left Afghanistan and the National Audit Office was all over the MoD like a rash and the bloody accounts were qualified, you can't be too careful.'

I wasn't even pretending to read, I listened intently as Dad was obviously building up to something. He had said qualified with his fingers making quotes in the air and his mouth set in a grimace.

It struck a chord from A Level Economics. I knew what he was referring to. There had been a huge inquiry that had lasted years into the money spent in Afghanistan and one of the recommendations issued a few years before had been about clearer budgeting and auditing within the MoD. Mainly because the answer to how much did the war cost was, 'we don't really know.' Thompson had promised that there would be greater transparency so 'The great British public could never again be misled on the true cost of war.'

I hold my breath and lean further towards them, catching every word. Dad was still talking and looking red-faced and pompous.

'We need to be much smarter. Remember the headlines at the time – How much does it cost to fly a soldier to Kabul? The press get hold of that stuff and it just gets mis-messaged. Then Joe Public gets all het up working out what they could have done with the money, without actually understanding any of the context.'

Dad was warming to his theme, his voice rose to a slightly higher pitch when he was emotional. He was speaking more quietly now. 'Jack's a smart guy. You don't get to run an £28 billion conglomerate by being slow. He knows how to milk an opportunity but he knows just as well how to keep quiet too. He knows we need to get our guys into the Levant pronto to clear up the mess. They can do that for us. They can do it with no big drama. In and out. Bish bosh. Job done."

Thompson looked at Dad. 'Listen, Matt, there can be no fuck ups here. Is there anything in any of the other Kardax businesses that can come back to embarrass us? You know they've been involved in some deals that are pretty close to the wind and we can't afford any scandal.'

'I'm really confident. Don't worry. Also, remember Jennifer will be on the inside and she can pick up on anything we need to know.'

'Yes, but she's sitting at the top of a sprawling conglomerate. She might not hear about specific divisions. Kardax is all over North Africa. They're mining for coal, copper and diamonds. I'm not going to find hundreds of black miners in townships working for a pittance or a bunch of kids in slave labour factories making high end fashion for pennies, am I?'

'Simon, Simon relax. It's all good. The main thing for us is that Kardax wins the Levant contract. No fuss. It just needs to run through procurement like a ferret up a drainpipe.'

'Ok, ok. I trust you.'

He was sounding completely sober now. 'Listen, Simon. It's better if you're not seen as too close to this. As long as I know you agree, let me handle it so you are distanced from it. When we need to talk let's not put anything in writing and if we need to discuss it lets give it a code name.'

'Oh, very Le Carré.' Thompson grinned.

'No, I'm serious. This is our time. I really believe that. If we're confident about reshaping Britain and getting back to being a real global powerhouse we need to show we can stand shoulder to shoulder with the big boys. We need to start punching above our weight again and part of that is our presence in rebuilding the Middle East. We need to be in at the beginning, be strong, reduce the noise and create some stability.'

Thompson gave an odd laugh and said, 'And if Kardax, and by proxy Matthew Robson, can make a few bucks along the way then all the better.'

Dad at least had the decency to redden a little. 'Well, that's business, Simon. But it's also the right thing to do.'

Thompson smiled. 'So, a code name? What are you thinking?'

Dad paused and Thompson looked up still smiling, 'I know, what about Touchstone? The court jester in As You Like It. The witty fool, the one who says the unsayable to the king. That's what I need. Someone wise who will tell me as it is. Sooner we get you into the Home Office, Matt, the better I'll feel. Jean Norton's naked ambition for my job means she'll bide her time and then find a way to cut me off at the knees as soon as she can and clear a path for her to the top. I need an ally in there.' He smiled more broadly, winking at Dad. 'If he'd thought of it, Shakespeare would have made Touchstone a canny Yorkshireman.'

Dad laughed. 'Touchstone. A wise fool. But it's also a stone used to test for gold. What could be better?'

'I need to get going,' said Thompson and the two clasped hands whilst I closed my book and tip-toed out. Thinking about Touchstone. A wise fool and a way to test for gold.

Tuesday 25th May 16.05

MILLIE

Jennifer Robson looks totally distraught.

'She fell in love. A boy at the neighbouring school. She was besotted with him.'

She gives a weak smile and says, 'I'm not the psychologist here but I think everything she had poured into her father was transferred to this boy. They were together for about eight months. He was the first boy she gave her heart to. It seemed to go really well and then suddenly it all stopped. She wouldn't talk about him, she wouldn't tell me what had happened. It was as if she just went into a shell. It was months later when I found out from one of the mother's at school that Joe, that was the boy, had posted naked pictures of Clemmie.'

She pauses, looks down at her shaking hands and then says in a rush filled with heartache for her daughter, 'The pictures were of her performing oral sex. He posted them after an argument. They were traded like football cards across the school.' Her voice falters.

‘My poor baby. I tried to talk to her but I think it was too late. I think by then she had turned to another path. She was betrayed twice. First by her father and then by him.’

And just in time to be picked up by Faiza Siddiqui, I think

I can hear Matthew Robson weeping but Jennifer Robson is completely composed. She has become robotic, staring into space, trying to reconcile the little girl with the pony, with the teenager giving a blow job for all the world to see, with the radical terrorist hacking off body parts. I have no idea how she will fare when this is over.

I have what I need. I just need to work out what to do with it.

Tuesday 25th May 16.10

NUSAYABAH

I smile. I stare at the numbers. £200m. That easy. Along with the other shares more than enough. Enough to bring them down. All the dodgy deals, the pain and exploitation. Coming home to roost. Payback time.

I place the call that will start a panic in Kardax. I allow myself a moment of pleasure. Revenge. It’s a cliché but true. Best served cold.

I look at the newspaper picture from December. The headline reads, ‘*ATF50 kill world’s most wanted*.’ Inside is the analysis. All the self-congratulatory guff about another terrorist off the street. Don’t they know it’s an idea? A philosophy. You can’t kill an idea with guns and bullets. You only fuel it.

The banner headline is ‘*Inside the mind of a murderer*’ by Dr *Millie Stephenson.*

I skip to the end. I have read it a hundred times but that has not dulled the piercing pain in my heart.

'So, what is terrible and abhorrent to us, is following the path of Allah to him. And anyway, if he dies he will have eternity in paradise. We see him as a violent extremist, a deeply vile person who cares nothing for our way of life. He likely sees himself as on the side of the righteous.'

I delete it from my smart block. I don't need to read it again. Now it's time. Time for a little taste of her own medicine. Let's have a look inside the mind of a liar, Dr Stephenson, the head of a hypocrite.

Tuesday 25th May 16.13

MILLIE

I leave the Robsons together. I realise Neil is back. Amala is with him and then I see Mark too. My stomach flips. I don't know how to react. Before I can say anything, he comes towards me and holds me. I hear him whisper in my ear, 'It's ok. Let's just get Ella back. Nothing else matters.'

I let my body sink into him just for a second. He smells of lemon verbena. It's like home.

Neil says, 'I agreed it with Dalgleish. She reckoned it would be best if Mark worked from here. There are a couple of guys from Rockeem with him. He's following the money. Mark put a trace on it. It bounced all over the globe but it ended up in a brokers in London via Bermuda.'

Mark gives my hand a quick squeeze. 'Amala was amazing. I've never seen anyone work that fast. They had serious anti-tracing on it but she saw it almost immediately. She just honed in on where it ended up.'

Amala says, 'We make a good team.'

I gawp at her just for a second. She gives a tiny shrug and an even tinier smile.

Mark continues, 'I was able to talk to a few people. The money is buying Kardax shares. My guess is she's going to sell them short.'

He's gazing at me and smiles a little. He knows he's explained that to me before, more than once, but I can never remember what it actually means.

'She's selling a lot of shares at once, she's doing it through multiple channels, covering tracks just enough so it looks clever but not so clever that it means other traders won't notice and start digging into Kardax to see if there's some sort of problem. I suspect that's what she wants them to do. She might start planting stories about the dodgy deals. Touchstone maybe?'

'She's stiffing Kardax,' I say. 'Like seriously stiffing them.'

Mark nods, a trace of a smile. He touches my belly, butterfly soft, before moving to the room next door where the rest of the Rockeem team are working.

I put my hands where his fingers have just been.

Amala says, 'Listen I'm going to work in there. Rehan Ali has come up with the guy coordinating the riots.' She turns to me. 'We've created a picture. The riots are being tightly managed and look to be protecting a couple of areas in The Bush. Neil and I have pulled a map together so Dalgleish and Mitford can start directing their resources.' She then turns to Neil. 'Neil, if you keep on the links and media breaches, I'll take a quick look and see if there is an obvious central control point.'

She looks right at me and Neil. 'Mills, we spoke to Aafa. Mark and me. He's been set up. Right from the start. Nusayabah played him like a violin. She got to him through Hassan, the supposed film student. She controlled everything. He's not an extremist. He's just stupid.'

I stop staring at Mark in the other room and give a little shake.

I nod. I'm not sure what to think about Aafa. I wonder what else he might be able to tell us. Who else he met that might lead us to Nusayabah. Most people in times of high drama, high stress will contact the people closest to them.

I say, 'Where is he now?'

'They've taken him to Paddington Green.'

'I think we should get him back here. He might be able to help us work out how to get to Nusayabah. He's probably got a better idea than any of us of who's where in The Bush and he might also know other people who might be useful to us.'

Amala nods, talking as she walks, she says, 'You're right. I'll tell Norton.'

I start to fill Neil in on the conversation with Matthew Robson and his wife. He is looking behind me, distracted.

'Millie, I think you had better see this.' He's looking at something online.

He says slowly, 'It's Nusayabah again. What now?'

I turn to see. She is holding something in her hands. She holds it up to the screen. I know instantly what it is, a pale blue, old-fashioned moleskin book. Ella's diary.

My heart jumps into my mouth as she starts to speak.

'An important person in everything that happens today is Millie Stephenson. Here we are just four weeks ago, getting right up-to-date in the life of Dr Millie Stephenson, holier than thou psychological profiler, courtesy of her good friend Ella Russell. Ella has been so helpful in sharing her every tiny thought about her friend, Millie.'

Millie is pregnant. I can't believe it.

Neil and I have been trying for a baby for so long and Millie seems to get pregnant easier than falling off a bike.

It is Nusayabah talking, but I know instantly they are Ella's words.

I know what's coming. I feel shame wash over me. I hold my breath and brace myself. I look at Neil, his face is contorted in fresh pain. Nusayabah keeps going. I think about the millions of people across the world about to hear a story no one knows. Only Ella and Amala. And soon the world. And Mark. Mark oblivious in the room next door.

Nusayabah is a mix of sarcasm and saccharine. Pouring scorn on to my own personal heartache.

Mark doesn't even know about the abortion.

My heart is racing.

In that hideous voice she says, 'And now we come to the good bit just a few weeks ago, four weeks ago… poor Millie is not well and has to be rushed to hospital but thankfully her good friend Ella is by her side. Again.

Millie started bleeding this morning. Thank God I was with her. She was weeping. Making deals with God to keep her baby safe.

Poor Mark, he didn't even know she was pregnant. He was so excited when he got to the hospital. Excited and anxious for her. He looked so besotted at that moment.

That was then. It all changed later, when he overhead a junior doctor talking to the consultant, saying she'd had a termination seven years ago.'

I feel sweat form all over my body. My hand shifts to my belly. The tiniest bulge not quite showing.

Nusayabah says, 'And there's more. So much more.'

Reading again.

Of course, Mark asked her about it. He's completely against abortion except in the most extreme situations. He made her tell him everything. He now knows the abortion had been just after she left NY. I can still remember that time. She was so hard. So callous and so sure it was all her decision. I hated the day I took Millie to the clinic. I hated her too. Just for a bit then. She got drunk that night and started crying. She was a total mess. All that Catholic guilt. Kept saying she was going to hell.

It's not fair. All I want is for Neil and me to be a family.

This baby's safe. She's lucky. But Mark needed to know about the time before. He is many things but not a fool. It didn't take long before he asked her the most incisive question. 'How many weeks pregnant were you?'

When she had told him twelve, he could do the sums as well as she could.

It wasn't his baby. They hadn't really been sleeping together then. Now he knows about the fling before she left NY. She had never told him, not even when they got back together. She figured ignorance was bliss.

He didn't even ask her if this baby was his. He just looked disgusted with her.

Nusayabah stops reading. Looking up she says, 'Well, Ms Stephenson, are you listening? Not nice, is it? To be judged. An affair and an abortion and all kept secret. Shame on you. You're nothing but a whore.'

Neil turns to me. 'Oh, Millie, I'm so sorry. She just wants to hurt us. All of us.' He stands and holds me. I have my head on his shoulder and I can see Nusayabah still on the screen. Behind the veil she must be smiling.

How could she do that, knowing her own life had been ruined by her own secrets plastered all over the internet?

My phone starts buzzing. No caller ID. I ignore it. Call after call. I ignore them all. I look up. I see Mark, head down, working on the money.

Tuesday 25th May 16.17

MILLIE

I need to talk to Mark. I watch him work for a few seconds. He's engrossed, working alongside the guys from Neil's team.

He looks up, his eyes crinkle and he smiles his sexy smile. He knows I love it and now I'm going to blow it all apart again. 'Hey, Millie. We're definitely getting somewhere now. The broker looks like a front for a bigger operation.'

He stops. He looks at me and says, 'Hey, what's up? Is it Ella?' He moves towards me and I step out from the doorway and into the corridor.

He takes my hand. 'Is it Ella? Has something else happened?'

I look at my feet. 'No, it's me. Nusayabah has read out Ella's diary. It's trending everywhere.'

Quiet, composed and hesitant. 'What does it say?'

I look up. I can't bear this. I had such a hope. 'It's about the abortion. My abortion.'

Mark drops my hand. He doesn't speak. I can see his hurt. I feel the power shift back to him.

'Mark. I'm so sorry. I'm sorry for everything. For embarrassing you in front of your friends. For lying. For the affair, the abortion. Everything. I know I ruined everything. I am so sorry. Please forgive me. Please. Grace really misses you.'

I want to tell him how desperately I miss him but I don't trust his response.

Mark, suddenly all business-like says, 'Look, let's both just do our jobs. The most important thing right now is Ella.'

He walks away. 'Sam, anything new?'

Tuesday 25th May 16.20

AMALA

Norton agreed and Aafa's on his way back

I head over to Neil. My heart lurches. He is tapping at all the devices open on his desk and barking orders into a headset. He looks frantic. I know that look but this time it's not good. It's like he's on speed.

I speak fast, 'I've given some options to Sean to work through. They're looking at the pattern across the riots. Trying to see if it triangulates to a specific area, an area that's being protected. Rehan got the name of the guy coordinating it. Rehan's also connected with the Tower Hamlets Mosque but so far, they're not giving anything up. What have you got? Anything new?'

He looks up at me his eyes scorched and dry. I pretend not to notice. Both of us need to hold it together. He fills me in with ruthless efficiency.

'Millie reckons there's a good chance Nusayabah is Clementine Robson. Matthew Robson's daughter. She's twenty-four, widow of Abu Bakr. She formed a special services style splinter group out of Umm Umarah. Millie is working out more details with the BSU.'

'Where is she? Where's Millie? We need her here.'

'She's gone out. Nusayabah put some really personal stuff out about her. About the abortion when she left New York. She read it all out from Ella's diary.'

'Out? What do you mean? On line? Shit. No one knows about that. Oh my God, does Mark know it's out there?'

'He does now. Along with the whole world.'

'Oh my God.' I shudder. 'Poor Millie.'

Neil swallows and says quietly, 'And the bit about the baby not being Mark's. And about how much Ella wants a baby. It's trending on every website and blog. They're repeating it on all the networks.'

'So, where is she?'

'In the bathroom. She's pretty upset'

'I'm not surprised. But we've got so little time. We need her on this too. She needs to get her act together. She can cry later.'

Shit. I can't deal with that right now. Sympathy will have to wait. 'Ok, what's new with the search?'

Neil shows me the screens. I try to clear my head. He speaks at a gallop, 'We're pretty certain Ella still hasn't left The Bush. ATF50 are all over it but you've seen the riots and blockades everywhere. It looks like a war zone. Every single thing about this day has been planned in meticulous detail. Spike's got his guys at Fort Meade doing what they can. I am calling in every favour I know. GSOC are working with us. They have their best guys in the cage working on it.'

The cage. The room that holds the cryptographic 'keys' that generate and break encryption codes. The next contact will be in less than ten minutes and that will be the final golden hour before time runs out. I look at the images on the screens in front of Neil. One shows ATF50 working their way through the Mulberry Estate. There are people flooding the streets, causing road blocks, throwing bottles and stones. Organised chaos.

My head starts shifting gears. I can feel adrenaline pumping and I get myself back in the zone. 'OK, let's crack this.' I push Neil a bit to the side so I can work on the main data screen. It is rolling through masses and masses of code. We are not so much looking for a needle in haystack more like a piece of hay. I push that to the back of my mind and start trying to interpret what's on the screen. Where is she? Where is she recording the live stuff?

I say, 'Who's doing phones?'

'Sean's got a team on it.'

'Who's looking for Faiza Siddiqi? If she's the one who turned her she must be key?'

'Alex Dalgleish has people on her.'

Just then Millie walks in and with no preamble and in full professional stride says, 'We are pretty certain Nusayabah is Clementine Robson. Her parents are listening to the tapes to confirm it's her voice. This is a woman who loves. She loved her daddy until he started fucking the nanny; she loved her boyfriend until he posted pictures of her giving him a blow job; and she will have loved Abu Bakr. She's a romantic. She has passion and commitment. She believes in justice, equality and fighting for the underdog. She has moral issues around how Daddy made his money and Mummy spent it. She's also educated, rich, well-informed and knows everything about the Kardax deal. Feeding the story to Ella was meant to draw her in. When that didn't work, Ella gave her a perfect new opportunity when she decided to do the Ackwaat undercover story. Everything about her screams planner. From the way she did her school work to getting to Syria to this. She's been watching us all for months.'

Millie sits on the edge of the table. She is talking very fast. She's on fire. I've never seen her so pumped and just so brilliant at what she does. She's awesome.

She tells us the rest. 'She was radicalised online at seventeen by Faiza Siddiqui, who is well known to the authorities. She will have helped Clementine get out of the country and also back in. Inside her marriage to Bakr they will have been partners. She will have shared everything she knows from inside the establishment. Killing him shifted her from recruiter to murderer. She will have covered all the bases. Ella will have been her target all along. Amala was a decoy. There is one weak spot, we know from Bakr's men, that she has a son. My guess is she will talk to him before the day is out. Find Omar and we'll find her.'

We both stare at her. Part in awe and part in empathy. She blushes a deep red. My heart goes out to her and I move to take her in my arms. She puts a hand up and says, 'I know. I know it's fucking crap. I know what everyone will be saying and thinking but I'm not going to let that bitch win. If she thinks that's going to knock me down then she picked the wrong fucking enemy. I am going to kick her ass because we are going to find her son and I'm going to make her give us Ella back.'

We get back to work.

I whisper to Neil, 'Glad she's on our side.'

I keep looking for needles in haystacks. Hay in haystacks.

It is 16.23.

Tuesday 25th May 16.23

ELLA

She pulls up a chair and sits beside me. Her voice has a hint of a Yorkshire accent. You have to listen hard to hear it but I can. I've been a mimic since I could talk. She hasn't put her veil back on. I can see the hate and determination in her eyes, in the set of her jaw. I feel how much she hates me.

'So, Ella Russell, what did you think you would gain by pretending to be a girl struggling with her identity? Pretending to convert to Islam and desperate to come to a Muslim women's group, when you could have been writing the story of your life?'

I feel her disgust as she judges me. I pull myself up. Forcing myself not to wince. A rush of adrenalin sweeps through me. Fuck it, I'm not going down without a fight. I summon up the last drops of energy and say, 'I wanted to write a story. A woman's story. To understand what it would be like to be part of a cult that oppresses women at every turn, but can still attract young girls with everything to live for, and brainwash them.'

'How dare you.' Her body looks rigid as she points at me and spits out, 'Islam is not a cult. You talk about oppression. That's because you apply your own Western standards. You think just because I'm covered I'm oppressed. It's all bullshit.'

I blast back, 'No, Islam isn't a cult. In its true sense it is like any religion. It's based on love, morality and fairness. What you have concocted is not Islam. It's an interpretation straight from the dark ages. Brainwashing and filling vulnerable people with notions of hate. It's based on power and oppression. That makes it a cult. A cult full of hate and rage that suppresses women at every turn. Swathes them in cotton, stops them having an education, thinking their own thoughts and treats them like a chattel. Fair game to rape and abuse when they don't fit the misogynist crap being pumped out. That's a cult'

Suddenly, she has her knife again, she spins it in her hand then throws it in the air, catching it deftly by the handle before lurching towards me. Instinctively, I jerk my head back. Panic catches my breath as she grabs my hair by the pony tail and cuts it with one ferocious swipe.

With real venom she spits, 'You're an illiterate fool. You have no understanding of Allah or Islam. You judge me and women like me by what I wear not who I am.'

I try to control my breathing, feeling the sting in my scalp and the air moving around my neck, as I see my hair fall in my lap.

I bite back. 'At least I'm free. Free to work, to think, to have an education to wear what I want. '

I shift my position so I can see her eyes. 'So what do you want? Why am I here? Are you after money? Is that what it is?'

She snorts a laugh then hisses, 'You think you can buy your way out of this? Just because you have a rich husband. You think that's enough. He'll make it alright?'

'No, I am asking what you do want. With me. If it's not money what is it? I'm not particularly important, so what do you plan to do?'

'I plan to bring down Kardax and then I plan to bring down the Thompson government.'

I'm stunned. I sink back against the wall. The storyteller in me is intrigued. Even through the pain and terror I want to know. I need to know.

'Don't look so surprised. So innocent. I gave you everything you needed to make the case against Thompson but you sat on it. The big story. You could have made a name for yourself but you didn't want to rock the very expensive boat you and your husband are in. You're a coward. You're nothing.'

'I told you. It was a complex story. I was still checking it out. I was working on it at the same time as the radicalising women story.'

'Really? Or was it because Thompson and your husband are so cosy. So locked into creating a future of them and us. A future where Muslims are spied on and victimised every day.'

'That's not who my husband is. He created Ezylocate to help find children that had gone missing and to help in a major crisis. He gives millions of pounds to help refugees, many of them Muslim. He and Amala set up Teachers in Tents. Thousands of people have had food, water, shelter and an education because of him.' I'm shouting and so is she.

'It might have started that way but Ezylocate is the Trojan horse to state sponsored spying. Why do you think so many people are turning against the PPCs? Coming over to see things our way? Take your good friend Aafa Hackeem. Is he a terrorist? Is he a bad person? If not, how come he's in and out the PPCs every week? Same guys picking him up. Just like thousands of others. Thousands you can't see from that pedestal in your ivory tower. Paid for in blood money.'

'Well maybe if people like you were prepared to listen and talk and allow non-Muslims to live their own lives in their own way rather than blowing them up we wouldn't need the PPCs.'

'And maybe if people like you were prepared to listen and talk when we say we are harassed and abused in the street you wouldn't be sitting here tied up.' Her visible rage is so powerful I feel the fight ebbing from me.

Her voice catches but she carries on. 'Rockeem technology is like a wild dog sniffing out easy prey. Serving them up to the authorities and selling them for baubles. Claiming Ezylocate is colour blind, race blind and religious blind and all that rubbish about "making life easy for you". It's a facade. A facade for snooping, profiling and selling data to the government. Well data is people. Real people with real lives and real families.

'Not just your husband but that infidel Amala Hackeem. We gave her a little scare today too, see how she likes it. To be tracked and watched. She has the death of a loyal soldier on her hands today. A soldier who died because of her. Martyred and in paradise. Inshallah.'

She stands. She looks at me for a long moment. 'We've been following you too. We know everything about you. We're not so different you and me. We both need a cause. Something to believe in. We both want to be part of something bigger. We both had to find another family when we had no one else.'

With that she walks out.

I can't make any sense of it. What does she know about me? What does she mean no one else? What is she talking about?

I start to think about everything she said. I wish my head wasn't pounding so hard. Something drifts across my brain. It was a few months ago. I had come in from work. Come home and felt something not right. As if the peace had been disturbed. KK had been asleep. He never slept when anyone came in. He always rushed to greet everyone. Yapping loudly and skittering about like Bambi on ice.

Something else had bugged me that day. In my desk I kept a paper diary. All my diaries since I was eight. The drawer hadn't been quite closed. I never locked it but I always closed it. I asked Neil if someone had been in. He laughed it off, something about an overactive imagination and that maybe the cleaner had changed her day. But she hadn't. I checked. Then I'd forgotten all about it.

Someone has been in my house. Someone committed and smart enough to bypass the security. Someone committed and smart enough to read my diaries.

The door opens. There are two of them. Two of her soldiers. They're holding something. They're coming towards me.

The woman from before is back. She has the knife. I can't help it. I start to panic. I'm pleading, scuttling backwards.

She takes the knife and puts it under my chin. Forcing my head up. I can feel it. I can feel the cruel, cold metal sting and break the skin. I feel blood trickle down onto my chest. She moves it a tiny bit, cutting deeper. The pain is intense. My jaw's gripped tight. My breath's coming fast. Through my nose. I can feel her move the knife, back and forth, back and forth. Twisting.

She slices the ties keeping my hands together, they sting painfully as the blood supply returns. She moves back, grabs the burqa and slices it down the front, ripping it in half, turning it into a lecturer's gown. I can see my blood still on her knife from before.

She pulls off the torn burqa and I feel my heart thudding in my chest. They are pulling on a heavy vest. A suicide vest. I scream and fight. Lashing out wildly at both of them. It's useless. I feel it pulling and dragging on my neck and shoulders. They throw the burqa back over me and tie my hands. I realise I've wet myself. I can feel the damp on my legs. The smell mixing with the sweat and the ever-present stench of blood and burnt flesh.

My mind jumps like a monkey through a forest torturing me with what's to come. The bondage of wires and the explosives locking me in. My own modern-day noose. The pain in my hand and ear is beyond excruciating. I can feel blood sticky and lumpy in my hair. My mouth tastes like iron filings sickening me to the stomach. I'm so scared. So afraid. My heart's pounding. Beating a tattoo ready to burst through my screaming skin.

I slump to the ground. This is it. This is where I am going to die.

My brain is still trying to work it out. My diaries, but I can't get anything to fit into its rightful slot. The pain in my hand and ear is so brutal it almost feels as if it has happened to someone else. Thoughts are drifting in and out. I can't grasp them.

I want to keep the good memories but she has forced the bad ones in. That's not going to be my last thought. I won't allow it. I will not allow it. I try to stop the thought but it comes in savage technicolour.

It's all shifting and jerking.

A kaleidoscope.

It hurts.

I don't want this.

Something's not right.

Mum and Dad are at the kitchen table.

'Hey, what's up? You two look grim.' There's ice in my veins. I feel it spike through me and I claw at my flesh.

I sit. Mum. I can see her. How she was. Before she was ravaged. Before. Before.

Before when I was loved. When I was precious to someone.

I don't want this.

'Ella, darling. Listen, this is hard to say but it's going to be ok. Ok? It's going to be ok.'

I am rigid. Fear coursing through me.

'I have cancer.'

There is a noise in my ears like the sea and it's blocking out everything.

It's too loud.

In my ears. My ear hurts.

Why can't I hear her?

'Gabriella, Ella are you ok? Say something.'

Mum is speaking.

I look down and I can see her hand in mine.

Her fingers are long like mine.

The nails are chewed. She isn't a nail biter. I stare at the nails wondering when she bit them. How come I hadn't noticed that?

How come they're bleeding?

Is it her hands I can see?

Or are they mine?

What's wrong with my hands? Why does my hand hurt so much?

I feel so tired.

'Ella, I promise it's going to be ok.'

She said it would be ok. But it wasn't. It really wasn't ok.

It was not ok.

I blink the memory away.

Another one pushes in.

I don't want to see this.

It's a long time ago. I don't want to see this.

The coffin is lowered. She's in there.

It wasn't ok.

Tumbling memories

I close the bathroom door.

'Ella, you in there?'

'Yeah, two secs.'

I don't have long.

My hands shake as I roll up my sleeve.

Am I shaking now?

I pull the straightened paper clip along the inside of my arm.

I go back over and over. Again and again until the blood bubbles up.

I feel relief.

I feel something.

I feel the pain.

I feel my heart.

'Ella, Ella, come out.'

His words are slurred.

Orphaned twice.

Cancer took my mum.

But Jack Daniels took my dad.

Then I had nobody.

Tuesday 25th May 16.29

AMALA

The heat is oppressive and fetid. It's hard to breathe. There's mess everywhere. Papers, cups, half eaten sandwiches curled at the edges alongside maps and smart blocks. But it's the atmosphere that's choking us. You can feel adrenalin and sweat hang heavy in the air.

The noise as the screen clicks on seems deafening. After a second or so Nusayabah appears on the screen. I tense. I feel such a surge of venom I know I could kill her with my bare hands. How dare she? How dare she do this to us? To Ella, to me, to Aafa and Millie and Neil. She's ruined everything. Nothing will ever be the same again. Ever.

I turn slightly as I hear Jennifer Robson give a tiny moan. Even hidden under the cotton something primitive must tell her it is her daughter.

Leila flashes through my mind. There is still a smell of kulcha shor on me from the burqa.

The eyes behind the niqab. Can I see them or am I just imagining the deathly focus and hatred that lies behind them?

She begins to speak, unhurried and calm. Jennifer Robson lets out a cry, like an animal in despair. All the affirmation she needs.

The screens scramble for a moment. Thompson has a host of experts working on stopping any more media breaches. For the moment, Nusayabah is only talking to us, not beaming to the world. The screen behind her is still obscuring a pattern. It's a rhombus, with four circles but there's a thick line running through it. Is it a mosaic? From a mosque?

Nusayabah speaks, 'First of all, Mr Rochester, I presume you now have your business partner working with you. I'm sure that is of little consolation. So much harder to watch the person you love more than your own life being ripped from you. Knowing you have no power. No power to do anything about it. But I thank you. I thank you for transferring the money we asked for in such a prompt manner.'

Thompson pushes his chair back and splutters, 'What? What's she talking about? We do NOT negotiate.'

Everyone in the room ignores him, totally focused on the screen.

'So, would you like to see your lovely wife, Mr Rochester?'

The screen switches suddenly and there is Ella. Slumped against a wall. I don't know what to think. I can't believe this is happening to us. Her hair is partially covered by a scarf that is slipping. Blood encrusted around the side of her head. Someone else must be in the room with her.

I try to do what I'm good at. I try to take everything in. The walls are dingy and there's a shaft of light coming in. There must be a window but it's covered. I try to work out the angle of the light. Half my brain is trying to calculate the direction. I don't know if it's any use. I can't help it. I need to try and solve this. I need to get her out. It's my fault. Maybe I should have kept my mouth shut. Maybe if I had listened to her and Neil maybe she wouldn't be there.

It's unbearable. I don't want to watch but I can't not. I look around. The whole room is gripped. A rigid and dreadful fascination. All eyes on the screen.

The soldier in combat gear comes into view. She hauls Ella up by her arm into a sitting position and takes out her knife. Ella is frantic. Shoving back against the wall, cornered like a wounded animal, hyperventilating behind the gaffa tape on her mouth. The knife is raised and Neil howls.

The knife pushes open the burqa at the front.

My stomach cramps and my bowels turn to liquid as I hear Ella's whimpers and Neil's scream merge into one. Underneath is a suicide vest. The countdown shows one hour and twenty-seven minutes.

The screen returns to Nusayabah. 'Mr Rochester has kept his side of the bargain but it means nothing without your part, Mr Thompson. Tim Ellis at Newsbreaker is expecting your call. If he does not receive your call confirming the closures of the PPCs then he will receive my full report on Touchstone and Ms Russell here will be blown to a thousand pieces. Inshallah.'

I turn to look at Neil. He is standing up, breathing heavily and staring at the now blank screen. Millie is transfixed. Unable to move from her seat. Gulping air. Pale as a ghost.

Thompson turns on Neil. 'For God's sake, Neil, what were you thinking? We do not negotiate. You know it doesn't make Ella any safer. You should have left this to the experts.'

He's such a prick.

Neil reacts in an instant. He looks Thompson straight in the eye. 'Experts? Experts? If it hadn't been for your greed, and Robson here sticking his cock into every twenty-three-year-old he saw, that woman might not be sitting there killing my wife. So don't lecture me about experts. I'm going to find her. So far your experts have done nothing. Fuck you and fuck your experts.'

He looks at the clock. It is now 16.36. One hour and twenty-four minutes.

Alex Dalgleish speaks. 'I think we should all calm down. We have less than ninety minutes to find her and we need to pull together. The money is only relevant right now if we can use the recipient account to help trace it.'

She looks at me, 'What has Mark come up with?'

Thompson says, 'Mark? Mark who?'

Norton is icy. 'Mark Carter is Millie's husband. He is working with the forensic auditors and Neil's team to trace the recipient account.'

Thompson looks apoplectic. 'And at what point was I to be informed of this?'

Norton says, 'You were tied up with Elliot managing the media. That seemed to be your priority. The money had already been transferred, so it seemed sensible to make the most of any advantage that would provide.'

I can't help but think no one very much cares what Simon Thompson thinks or wants anymore.

Thompson breathes deeply, trying to control his emotions. The set of his jaw and the nervous tic at his eye betrays his deep anger.

Norton turns to Neil and repeats Dalgleish's question. 'Let's just focus. What has he got?'

Thompson can barely conceal his seething rage.

Neil tells her, 'They have some pattern around the Kardax shares. The best guess at the moment is the money is part of a plot. They are selling short. It looks like they're selling enough shares to get traders interested and once they start poking around we think Nusayabah will leak something about Touchstone. It looks like they have enough control over Kardax shares to seriously hurt them. Mark says they have been quietly buying stock for months.'

Dalgleish turns to Millie. 'What do you think, Millie?'

Millie is quick and clear. 'I think she will contact her son in the next little while. If we can find out who has her son we may get some leverage. I'd like five minutes with Aafa just to check if there are any other significant relationships. He may know something without realising its importance.'

Dalgleish nods.

We both turn as Jennifer Robson lets out a noise that gets strangled in her throat. I see her grab her husband's hand. Now she's got to contend with being a grandmother.

Dalgleish turns to Ali and raises her brow questioningly. 'No one is saying where Faiza Siddiqui is?' Rehan Ali shakes his head.

Dalgleish sets off another set of instructions via her watch.

Neil says, 'We have people at Rockeem working on all of that. They're looking at phone records, accounts, traffic...' he breaks off.

I look at him. It is agony to watch. I can't help myself. I turn to Dalgleish. I ask the unaskable. I need to know. 'Do you think we will find her in time?'

Dalgleish gives nothing away. 'We're doing our best.'

Tuesday 25th May 16.38

NUSAYABAH

Time for the next step. I pick up the phone. I feel in complete control. I say with authority, 'Ready?'

'Yes. All units in place. The traffic is already starting to slow. We are waiting for your command.'

I savour the moment, just for a second. I close my eyes and I picture Abu.

I have made him proud today. I feel his presence in my heart. He has given me the strength to see this through on my own. I feel him warm me as I say, 'Project Deafening Blast is Green go. Green, go.'

'Allah Akbar'

'Allah Akbar.'

Tuesday 25th May 16.40

MILLIE

Rehan Ali and I are looking at known associates for Faiza Siddiqui. It's a vast network of cells. As well as profiles on my screen we have drawn a spider's web of contacts for Tower Hamlets, Umm Umarah and Har majiddoon. We are in constant contact with Toni Roberts. We are narrowing it down. I can feel we are getting closer.

Rehan says, 'You know, it's days like this that makes my job so difficult. I can see Norton and Thompson not quite believing I'm fully on side. They keep asking if I know where Siddiqui is. If I did, I would tell them. It was Faiza Siddiqui who worked out that Alex Dalgleish was an MI5 spy. I told them that. Without me they would have tortured and killed her, but still they freeze me out.'

I start to agree but before I can say anymore my screen changes. It's the background picture from Nusayabah's clips. My heart speeds up as we wait for her to appear, but she doesn't. It stays with the background, it's changing, clarifying. The geometric patterns are turning into something else. A picture starts to emerge. I look around the room. Every laptop, every smart block and every TV screen is showing the same image. It's getting sharper. It looks like a kite with four circles within it. The image sharpens again.

It looks like a road network. A complex network. It crystallises. In the corner it shows the time. It's a live image. The pictures are from a drone.

It's the M25. The orbital motorway that circles London.

The screens show the traffic at a standstill. An aerial view. I peer at the screen. It is where the M4 intersects the M25, right by Heathrow Airport. Nothing unusual about that. I hear it every day on the traffic reports. Half-term mayhem. So why is it on the screen? I look around the room. Norton and Thompson are also staring, trying to make sense of what they see.

Mitford and Dalgleish react first. Reaching for phones as they make the connection quicker than the rest of us. Something is wrong. Terribly wrong.

The camera zooms in. Five trucks are stopped across the northbound carriageway. In a line. The traffic is backed up. Penned in. Five other trucks are parked a mile back, traffic coming to a standstill behind them. Nothing moving.

An instant car park. Two hundred metres ahead, a lorry is jackknifed across the slip road.

The data in the corner of the screen shows it's the northbound M4 junction 4B / M25 junction 15. The camera moves. Two more lorries at the southbound exit. The link that takes traffic to Heathrow, to the west into the Home Counties or east into central London.

I hear Dalgleish, 'Are you watching this? What do we know?'

I see her nod. She grabs Mitford and presses her phone to speaker.

'Ma'am it looks as if we have a blockade. No warnings to any of the usual security services and no intelligence yet.'

Mitford is already dialling.

'What units do we have in the vicinity of the M25 and M4?'

He's listening but his eyes never move from the large screen on the wall.

The camera veers violently. The M4 eastbound carriageway at the same junction. Probably the most heavily used piece of road in the country. Another lorry stopped. Jackknifed.

This has to be coordinated. The trucks have created a complete standstill. Nothing can move in or out.

I hear a voice. 'Jesus Christ, they're like rats in a trap.' It's Thompson. He turns to Mitford and Dalgleish. It dawns on all of us at once.

They *are* rats in a trap.

Tuesday 25th May 16.42

Ella

I spit out the bile in my throat, coughing and spluttering like a hag. The dead weight of the vest is pressing hard on my chest and shoulders. I feel as if I'm already in my coffin.

She's coming back. What the fuck now?

I watch Nusayabah and the other one wheel in a huge screen. They have cameras, equipment. What's going on?

They're going to film me.

She pulls me up, the vest on full show. The screen is showing a road. A motorway. I can see it's the M25.

Suddenly there is an almighty blast. A deafening blast. The screen fills with fire and smoke. The camera pans back. The truck at the far end of the southbound exit has exploded. Black clad, machine wielding terrorists are dropping from the back of the other trucks.

I stare at Nusayabah. She's engrossed. She high fives the soldier.

'Project Deafening Blast. Allah Ackbar.'

Tuesday 25th May 16.43

MILLIE

Norton moves with the speed of a panther. She grabs the phone. She keeps her voice calm and controlled, 'Get COBRA back. We have a live and major incident on the M25 Junction 15. We are looking at a coordinated attack. Assume terrorist activity. Likelihood of multiple and serious casualties.'

Amala, Neil and I are stock still. Mesmerised.

Amala slams her fist on the table. 'I'm a fucking idiot. I should have seen that. Of course it's a road.'

We see eight terrorists jump from the back of one of the trucks. They hit the ground running, waving their semi-automatic machine guns in the air. Marching up and down shouting. Rows and rows of trapped vehicles. The drones are wired to pick up sound.

They're roaring, 'No one move.'

'Move and you will be shot.'

'Stay still. No one move.'

'Allah Ackbar.'

'Stay the fuck still.'

There are hundreds of people, mostly holidaymakers, families with small children dressed in bright t-shirts. I see them getting out of their cars. Terrified. Trying to hold their kids steady. I watch as some try to push their children back into their cars. Finding safety. Or trying to. Stunned to see armed terrorists racing up and down. There must be at least twenty of them, all heavily armed.

Thompson thunders, 'What is going on here? Is this footage real?'

Mitford is already in full command. 'Yes, sir, it's live and real. We have reports starting to come in. Road exits are blocked. We have choppers already in the air. ATF50 are two minutes out. Heathrow police units are on their way across the fields.'

I see two supercopters hovering above the road. A full-scale operation is now in motion. Something catches my eye. In the corner of the screen is a little boy. He's running, bolting for the fields. A woman sees him and starts to chase. I see a man, screaming, 'Helen, Helen stop. Don't move. STOP! Jack, stop, stop!'

The camera zooms in close. I see the boy, he's about three years old with bright blond hair. I see his striped t-shirt and blue shorts.

He's clutching a big pink rabbit. Grace's favourite. The camera zooms in closer. His face is filling the screen. Tears are pouring down his face. I see his mouth form the scream 'Mummy!'

She's almost there. Almost.

The camera pulls back to show a black-clad terrorist with the traditional kufiyah scarf around her face. She raises her AK47 and fires. The boy jerks into the air. Without a pause the terrorist is already turning back to the stunned crowd. The crowd gasps, already moving closer to each other.

I see the boy's mother fall to her knees and grab her son.

Her screams are beyond anguish.

Tuesday 25th May 16.45

ELLA

'Are you some sort of fucking barbarian? That's a child. They're killing children. What the fuck has that got to do with your sick revenge? That's not Thompson or Kardax or your fucking Touchstone. That's an innocent kid. Have you no mercy.' I run out of steam. 'Fuck's sake. It's a kid. A mother.'

She whips around, 'Collateral damage. Do you know how many innocent children have been killed in Syria? In Somalia? Iraq? No one's counting them. Or those mothers.'

I keep watching the screen, the soldiers are pacing up and down. Shouting and shoving the Kalashnikovs into the face of anyone that dares to catch their eye.

I can see rows and rows of cars. People everywhere. Stunned. Jabbing at phones, no doubt calling for help and sending messages to loved ones. I see the police and ATF50 start to arrive. They're landing in nearby fields. Riot gear and shields, moving into position. Moving together like a well-oiled machine.

I hear a voice.

'This is Commander James Mitford.'

Nusayabah turns to me.

'Now it's time for your TV debut.'

Tuesday 25th May 16.46

AMALA

Sickened, I pull myself away from the screen. There's nothing I can do there. Others are all over it. The time is ticking for Ella.

I need to focus on her. Neil has already reset his screen back to the Mulberry Estate. Fires are burning in almost every street. The gangs are pushing hard against the police. They're now throwing petrol-soaked rags in bottles. The Met has sent in back-up in full riot gear.

Mitford's passed command to a senior officer, David White, who has been with him throughout the day. White's now commanding his people on the ground in The Bush. Mitford is fully focused on the scenes at the M25.

Meanwhile, Matthew and Jennifer Robson sit in silence. Devastated. Heads moving between the motorway hostages and Neil's screens at The Bush. It's incomprehensible to me that such brutality could be so exquisitely masterminded. It must be beyond endurance for them, to know that the mastermind is their own flesh and blood.

Rehan Ali has his head in his hands and is openly weeping. Mark has come in at the sound of all the screams. He's holding Millie. I watch for a second. He's been amazing today. I hope they make it. Millie looks at him just for a second. I see her take a moment to inhale him.

The screens flicker and a picture of Ella, gagged and bound in the suicide vest appears on all the screens. Her face is bloody and uncovered. I register her hair has been hacked off making her look like a refugee.

The caption below reads 'Ella Russell, journalist and wife of government spy and murderer Neil Rochester. Close the PPCs or she dies.' Next to the caption is a clock counting down. It shows one hour, twelve minutes and fifteen seconds.

Counting down with a deathly regularity. 14, 13, 12…

Ella's poor beaten face is superimposed against the backdrop of the M25. The Kalashnikov- and AK47-wielding terrorists moving up and down behind her.

Nusayabah is beside her. 'Thompson, Rochester, only you can stop this. The soldiers at the M25 are awaiting my command. They are all prepared to die today. They are part of jihad. They will give their lives and be rewarded in paradise. Inshallah.

Neil is staring, his cheeks are soaked. Tears fall from his nose and chin. She disappears from the screen and is replaced by the ticking clock. Thompson looks deranged. 'Can someone cut this? It's all over every TV channel. Get it off the fucking screens,' he barks.

The screens are flicking between the M25 and Ella. Whoever has a hold of the media is as talented as they are ruthless. The screen splits in two. Half showing the terrified crowd on the motorway and half showing Ella. In a part of my brain it registers that it is in our interest to keep it public. More chance of someone calling in anything they might know. Thompson has other priorities, though. His own skin.

Mitford and Dalgleish are both talking into earpieces and jabbing devices at the same time. The split screens now have a countdown clock superimposed on the top.

One hour eleven minutes and eighteen seconds.

Nusayabah appears next to Ella, she is on every screen. Every device.

'People of Britain. We will kill one hostage every fifteen minutes. We have a very simple demand. This can be stopped. It can be stopped right now. Simon Thompson can stop this right away. All he has to do is close the PPCs. When the clock is at 17.00 hours one more hostage will die.'

At that moment, the camera shows a balaclava-clad terrorist grab a woman by the hair. She pushes her to her knees, the Kalashnikov at her head. The woman is screaming. The camera pans to a man being held back by another terrorist. He screams, 'Take me, take me. Please don't hurt her. Please. Please.' Two children are wrapped around his legs, screaming for their mother.

The clock is at 16.50.

I hold my breath.

Nusayabah says, 'Thompson, if she dies, her blood is on your hands and yours alone.'

Mitford's voice shatters the tension in the room. 'Sir, on your command we are ready to move.'

Thompson is gaping, hands to his mouth, blinking hard at the screen.

Norton says, 'Simon, we have to act. We cannot let this woman die.'

Thompson says nothing, just keeps staring.

Neil walks over to Thompson and Norton. His face is wretched. He grabs Thompson by the arm and pleads. 'Please, please, Simon, do something. Call this journalist. Tell him anything. You just have to say it. I beg you. I will do anything. Anything. Just do this one thing. Don't let Ella die. Please, please don't let her die.'

Nusayabah says, 'Less than ten minutes, prime minister.'

Thompson is shell shocked. He's staring straight ahead. The scenes on the screen from the M25 are showing that more supercopters have landed.

I am still connected to our team at Rockeem. My watch buzzes. It's Sean Menzies.

'Hey, Sean, what have you got? Please, please tell me you've got something?'

'Amala, we've traced a call to Faiza Siddiqui. Millie put us on to her. Aafa told her that Faiza Siddiqui was the person that introduced him to Hassan Yacoub. The call lasted three and a half minutes and we got the last ninety seconds. We were able to hear a woman talk to a very young child. We think it's Nusayabah's son. We have an address for Siddiqui.'

I stop him. 'Sean, hang on.' I grab Alex Dalgleish. I quickly tell her what Sean has found then say, 'Sean give us the address.'

'42 Rowan Gardens. Flat 6.'

Dalgleish is already relaying it to her team on the ground. They will be there in under four minutes. Dalgleish is brusque, 'Do not open fire, and do not harm the child. We need the boy. I'm going to give a line to Millie Stephenson. She will tell you what you need to do once you have the boy.'

Turning to me she says, 'Get Millie connected and get her to be really clear about how to handle the boy. He's all we have to trade.'

She turns back to Junction 15.

She says, 'Prime minister, it's almost five?'

Thompson looks between her and Norton.

Jean Norton says, 'Prime minister?'

Too late.

The sound of the rapid fire is deafening as the woman slumps to the ground.

Sean is speaking again. 'Mals, they will get to her son in less than four minutes.'

I turn to Millie. She is staring at the screen, the dead woman lying in a pool of blood. Mark is holding her. His face twisted in pain.

'Millie, we know where her son is. Get with this. There's no time.'

Millie is holding onto Mark like her life depends on it.

I shout at her, 'Come on, you need to brief Dalgleish's team. What do they say to the boy? Sean will have a trace on the source of the call any minute and we need to know how to deal with Nusayabah when we get to her?'

Mark nods at her. 'You can do it.'

Tuesday 25th May 17.01

MILLIE

'This is Millie Stephenson, who am I talking to?'

'Dr Stephenson, my name is Ahmed Hussain. I am in charge of Alpha Gamma team. We're less than two minutes out from Faiza Siddiqui. We're in Rowan Gardens.'

'Ok, Ahmed. First thing to know is if the boy is with Faiza Siddiqui then she's likely to be armed. She's a hardened jihadist, ruthless and brilliant. My guess is she will have agreed with Nusayabah what to do if her cover is blown. Omar is the only chink in Nusayabah's armour and Siddiqui will not risk the operation by handing him over. She will be prepared to die. She will likely kill the child rather than hand him over as a negotiating pawn. We're pretty certain Nusayabah has masterminded everything today so she will not have left anything to chance, including her son.'

‘Ok, got it. Get him out and get him out alive.’

‘Yes. Then we can talk about what we do with him.’

Neil’s beside me. I grab his hand then sit back and wait. Mark is perched on the table. I see him mouth ‘You’ll do it. We’re a team.’ Amala is by his side. We sit in silent prayer. Ella’s right, she always said there are no atheists in a foxhole.

Amala says, ‘Sean’s got a drone over her house. We can see Ahmed go in but we may not be able to see inside.’ She never breaks her intense staring at the screen.

We watch. Ahmed Hussain has four others with him. Armed and in position. They move through a small back garden.

Sean’s voice comes over the computer. ‘Amala, flat 3 is on the ground floor, third from the left. Red door. The guys are in the communal garden at the back. We can’t see any movement inside.’

‘Thanks, Sean.’

Amala stands and we hold each other tight. We see the five soldiers slowly move through the garden. Two are by the back door, one has moved to the front. We see Hussain kick the back door in. Then we are blind to what is happening inside. My jaw aches from my grinding teeth. Neil’s lip is bleeding again. Each of us praying to any God that will listen.

There’s a sound of gunfire. Semi-automatic weapons.

The clock is ticking. Fifty-five minutes and three seconds. Merciless. My stomach is in knots.

Behind us the screens show more supercopters arriving at the M25. Heavily-armed ATF50 teams are landing in the fields either side.

Neil can hardly contain his panic. ‘What’s happening? Why’s it taking so long?’

And then Ahmed Hussain walks out. ‘Dr Stephenson, we have the boy.’

He's holding a small boy in his arms. The boy has huge brown eyes and is wearing a bright blue t- shirt and matching shorts. He has a big pink rabbit and a little blanket.

Dalgleish is beside us. 'Well done, Ahmed, any casualties?'

'Faiza Siddiqui was alone. She went for a weapon. We opened fire. She sustained a shoulder injury. Toby's cuffed her and we are waiting for a medic.'

Interesting, she wasn't expecting us.

Nusayabah's first mistake.

Tuesday 25th May 17.06

AMALA

Norton is pleading with Thompson. COBRA is back. They're all arguing. I can hear them through the glass. They have less than ten minutes before another hostage will be shot. I'm watching the screen. A man is on his knees in front of a soldier, hands behind his back. There are screams from the crowd. Mitford's demanding a decision. Thompson has his head in his hands.

Neil is talking to Sean. 'Have we pinpointed where Nusayabah made the call from?'

'Not yet.'

A noise in the background.

'Hang on. We've got it. Neil, Amala, we've got it.' He sounds triumphant.

I grab Neil.

'Thanks, Sean. Give us the address?'

'She's in the Mulberry Estate. 19 Harman Road. I can see it on the screen. It's an old, end of terrace house. Looks like it's boarded up. There are cops and ATF50 guys in the next street.'

Dalgleish calls over to Mitford's number two, David White.

White grabs his radio and barks. 'Sara, Tom the address is 19 Harman Road. We are Amber. Repeat Amber. One street to the left of your current location. Perp believed to be there. Proceed with caution. We have back-up ninety seconds out. We know there is at least one heavily-armed guard. Likely to be more. Hostage is in a suicide vest. Likely to be traps. I repeat proceed with caution. We have two units trying to contain the estate. I cannot afford any other resources. All local units diverting to M25.'

I switch Neil's screens to full picture. It's fixed to the exact location. We can see the house in Harman Road. Millie is briefing Ahmed Hussain. I glance at the small screen in the corner showing the clock. Forty-six minutes and thirty-two seconds.

Over the speaker, Thompson is talking to Mitford. Mitford wants to move in before the next hostage is shot.

I hear him say, 'Sir, we are in position. We can attack on your command.'

Thompson asks, 'Can you guarantee the safety of the hostages.'

Mitford tries hard to hide his anger. 'Sir, this is a live situation. We count eighteen terrorists, all armed. We cannot guarantee no civilians will be killed.'

Thompson looks to Norton. 'Jean, this could be carnage.'

She nods, all colour has drained from her face. 'Simon, either way, it could be carnage.'

I hear Mitford, 'Too fucking late.'

Another hostage is dead.

Tuesday 25th May 17.16

MILLIE

'Ahmed, try and keep Omar calm. Tell him that he can talk to his mummy. Ask if he would like that?'

'He says he would.'

'Ok. Put him on and let me talk to him.'

The screen shifts. I see this beautiful boy, thumb in his mouth. The same pink rabbit that Grace has tucked under his chin.

I say in a voice as calm and gentle as I can manage. 'Hi, Omar. Is that the Big Pink Friendly Rabbit?'

He nods solemnly, never moving his thumb from his mouth. I garner as much control as I can so as not to scare him.

'I have a little girl. He's her favourite too. Do you like the song he sings? Rabbit Hop?'

I start to hum the theme tune. I watch him slowly remove his thumb and start to sing along.

I smile and say, 'Wow, you're a good singer. Does Mummy watch it with you?'

Another nod.

'Would you like to talk to Mummy? Ahmed can bring you. You can have a ride in the supercopter and then we can get Mummy on the screen for you. I'll be there and you can show me your rabbit. Would that be good? Maybe you could sing Rabbit Hop for her?'

A fierce nod.

'Good, ok.'

Ahmed appears again. I say, 'Quick as you can, get him here. Should only take ten minutes or so. Everything's cleared for you to get here. Land at Horse Guards and there's a car waiting.'

'Got it.'

Tuesday 25th May 17.17

ELLA

I stare at Nusayabah, she shows no flicker of emotion as the second hostage is killed in cold blood. Third including the little boy. She's acting as if it's nothing.

I feel sick to the stomach.

She turns to me. 'Simon Thompson's weighing it up. How to save his own skin. No one will ever remember anything else about him now, apart from today. He'll forever be the prime minister that caused death and destruction while he stood by and let it happen.'

She kneels beside me, I start to shake. She fingers the vest around me, gently tugging. The sweat runs down my back, cold and wet.

'So, let's see if he'll listen to you. How would you like the chance to save the day? Or say your last goodbyes?'

I stare as she hands me a piece of paper. I read: 'I am Ella Russell. I am married to a killer. His name is Neil Rochester and he is in the pocket of the infidel, Simon Thompson. My husband makes Ezylocate. It's used by the government to harass innocent people. Muslims who are held in PPCs and treated like filthy animals. Simon Thompson has the blood of the dead at the M25 on his hands. He could stop it now, but he won't; he's letting them die. If he agrees to close the PPCs no one else will die. If he doesn't then the soldiers will open fire and I will be taken to a location in London and more Kaffirs will be blown to hell. Inshallah.'

I look up, she says, 'You didn't think we were going to waste that vest just to blow you up, did you?'

Tuesday 25th May 17.19

MILLIE

Nusayabah's gone. At last, Simon Thompson seems to be moving. He's ordering Mitford to get ready to move in.

Mark, Amala, Neil and I move as one. The screens on Neil's desk are showing the same picture from three different angles. Harman Road. Nusayabah's HQ. Eight ATF50 officers. Terrifying in the masks and jack boots, heavily armed with Tasers and pistols as well as batons and the hugely controversial Heckler and Koch G36 Carbines. With speed and stealth, firearms poised and ready, they move with the sweet choreography of a Tchaikovsky ballet. My heart is thumping, my mouth is dry and my eyes are burning. It's like a movie but it isn't. It's real and it's Ella.

The ATF50 guys are lined up to move on White's signal. We are hooked in to the special firearms officer, Sara Martin's smart block. She's ready to get Omar on the screen.

I hear a commotion and a child crying. I turn to see Ahmed Hussain holding Omar, Nusayabah's son. Jennifer Robson, who had not moved from her chair since I spoke to her, suddenly sprints across the room.

She grabs her grandson and holds him tight, rocking back and forth and whispering over and over, 'Oh, my sweet boy, my sweet, sweet boy.'

Omar wriggles and pushes against her. I walk over to him and gently prise him from Jennifer Robson, who can't quite let him go. She kneels beside him and says, 'Hello, Omar, I'm your grandmother.'

He looks scared and confused. I say, 'Hey, Omar, I'm Millie. You sang your Rabbit Hop song to me.' I start to hum it again and he joins in smiling.

I take him by the hand and sit him on a chair, he immediately starts to swivel, smiling at me as he twists it faster and faster.

I laugh and say, 'Hey, how about we get Mummy to talk to you?'

Tuesday 25th May 17.22

NUSAYABAH

I make sure the screen is split between here and the M25. It's going exactly to plan. I radio Thumi. 'Get the next one lined up for 5.30.'

'Will do.'

Every media outlet all over the world is showing images of the M25 and Ella. Now they are about to hear her plead for her life and the lives of the trapped rats on the M25.

I turn to Ella Russell. 'Ok, let's get Thompson and your husband in this show. Let's see what you're worth.'

I reconfigure the screen. I can see into Number 10. They aren't expecting that. Maybe from here on in they'll check their IT contractors a bit more carefully. I smile. 'Stupid Bastards.'

The screen splits again. I can see Rochester and Millie Stephenson talking. I can see Thumi lining up the next hostage. A woman, dressed like a whore in tiny shorts. She's pleading, screaming. No courage. Pathetic.

I say, 'Mr Rochester. Get Simon Thompson. It's time we all had a chat.'

I see them look up in shock, register the screens. Register I can see everything. I see him look for his wife. Thompson walks into the room with that bitch that wormed her way into Umm Umarah beside him.

'Thompson, can you hear me?'

Neil grabs Thompson and physically yanks him to the screen. 'Talk to her. Do it. Please. I'm begging.'

I turn the camera so it's on Ella Russell, she's covered in blood around her ear, her hair is sticking up where it's been sliced and the suicide vest is in full view.

I spit at her, 'Read it.'

She picks up the paper. 'I am Ella Russell.'

She stops, takes the paper and chucks it at my feet.

'I am Ella Russell. I am married to Neil Rochester. I love him with all my heart.' She starts to speak faster and faster. 'Neil, my darling, my love. She'll never let me out of here. Never. She is a fucking mad woman. Millie, Mals, if you're there, I love you. I love you. She's mad. She's going to kill all the people on the M25.'

I grab her by the arm and push her to the floor, 'Shut the fuck up.'

I kick her hard in the head and leave her lying there.

I say, 'Take her out, get her ready to move.'

Tuesday 25th May 17.24

Ella

My mind keeps drifting. My memories are more real than this room. I think about a long time ago.

Freshers' week in Edinburgh. Even in the middle of September it's freezing. I have been here for three days now and I am already wondering what December will feel like. I pull my hat down, stick my chin into my scarf and turn the corner along the side of the David Hume Tower. I stumble in the wind tunnel that keeps catching me out and walk the last few steps to the Freshers' fair. I can smell the yeast in the air from the local brewery.

I think I'll ring Mum and tell her she was right, it does nearly blow you off your feet. Then I remember she's gone.

George Square is teeming with students, braving the cold and sitting in the gardens drinking coffee. Lots of excited people racing around with bunches of leaflets stuffed into their hands, looking to convince Freshers to join whatever club or society. I walk along the side of the gardens up to Teviot Row Student Union.

I see a girl from my hall that I haven't spoken to yet. She is dressed in purple Doc Martens, a vintage frock covered in pink tea roses and a chunky jumper, her nose and eyebrow are pierced and I don't think I've ever seen anyone who looks more comfortable in their own skin. I smile and she walks over. 'Hi, I'm Millie. I think I've seen you in Masson Hall?'

I can picture it so clearly, Edinburgh's student Halls of Residence – the gothic fronted dumping ground for most first years.

Millie. So funny and spiky. Her weird obsession with aquariums. So original and bright. She has a mind like a steel trap. She became my friend and my family. With Amala. Oh, Amala, what have they done to you today? The three of us. Our own tribe. Nofa's.

'Hi, I'm Ella, yeah I'm in 265 just along the corridor from you.'

Millie smiles again and sort of raises a hand in a semi-wave. Her wrist has about twelve bangles on it and I can see the beginning of a tattoo that looks like a thistle snaking up her arm. She says 'Ok, here goes, how many times have you been asked, where are you from, what course are you doing, what subjects did you do?'

She has a really lilting accent and a funny way of drawing out her vowels. It would sound mildly aggressive if she wasn't smiling all the time. She sounds a bit like Mum. I like her from the off.

I picture us as we climb the broad wooden staircase through the middle of Teviot Row House, laughing at the moose head stuck on the wall. We go for a coffee that turns into a beer that turns into tequila shots in the library bar, a beautiful room that looks like a library only in so far as it is lined with books. We have been through everything together. My memories are jerking around, like a film on fast forward. Meeting Amala. So brilliant. So funny. So drop dead gorgeous with a mouth that would shame a Docker.

The flats in Borough and St Johns Wood.

Cycling across at Waterloo. Looking along the Thames to Hungerford Bridge one way and Blackfriars the other. Millie used to make us sing 'Waterloo Sunset'. Every single time she would say it was Ray Davies' love letter to London. I hum it to myself now.

Millie, Amala and I had started talking twenty years ago and never stopped. I would give anything to talk to them one more time.

They have taken everything but not my last thought. I will not give them my last thought.

I close my eyes and will my mind to remember a day. An ordinary day. A June day. There is cherry blossom lining The Meadows in Edinburgh. The scent not quite enough to mask the smell of the brewery carried on the chilly wind. Chilly even in June. I picture it. Arthurs Seat and Salisbury Crag outlined against a watery sun. Standing bold and resolute for thousands of years. The university emptying of students, pouring out as finals are finally over.

The three of us are together. We have a picnic of stale pizza and cheap cider. It's perfect. We have a Frisbee. I throw it to Millie. She misses. She always misses. I smile at the thought.

Tuesday 25th May 17.25

MILLIE

Amala says, 'I've got it. She's still live. I've got control. We can link to her system, beam onto her screen.'

Simon Thompson leans in. He speaks rapidly but somehow still manages to garner some habitual authority.

'Clementine, stop this slaughter. You are not this person. Your parents are here. They want to talk to you. We can talk about this. We can talk about your concerns. Killing more people at the M25 will not work. Killing Ella will not help you. We cannot help you unless you put a stop to this.'

Nusayabah spins around, stares at the screen. She's tapping at something and we hear her say, 'Hold on the hostage until you hear my command.'

She turns her face to the screen. 'Thompson, you've got four minutes then on my word the next one dies. Ella Russell is on her way now. She's going to blow some of your voters to hell. You'll never find her. She's set to explode in half an hour.'

Jennifer Robson moves forward. She speaks, her voice querulous but audible. 'Clemmie, darling. Please don't do this. Your dad and I are here. No matter what we love you. We want you to come home. Please just do what they say and put the detonator down. Ella is not involved in this. These poor people on the M25 are not part of your fight. It has nothing to do with them. Please, Clemmie, we love you.'

Nusayabah stares ahead. 'Mum?'

I see her hesitate, stop in her tracks.

Alex Dalgleish nods to me. I move in front of the screen, take a deep breath and pull Omar beside me.

I'm ready for this. She's not going to win. I have the ace. No mother will risk her child.

'Clementine, this is Millie Stephenson. We have your son.' I hold him up, my arms around his middle as he stands on the table. 'We have Omar.'

In the quietest voice she says, 'Omar.'

He squeals in delight, 'Mama. Mama.'

Tuesday 25th May 17.31

AMALA

Things are moving at a pace. Simon Thompson has moved to the back of the room. The COBRA team are looking at him. Waiting for him to give the go ahead. The moment to move on the M25. He nods, Norton picks up the radio, 'Commander Mitford you are authorised to go. Green, go. God be with you.'

I turn back to see Millie holding Omar.

Also on my screen is the team at Harman Road. David White is in constant contact with them. Closing in on the end-of-terrace house. It looks derelict. Moving up the path to the house, two officers stand to either side of the front door, their sawn-off H & Ks moving at 180 degrees, constantly vigilant. A third moves towards the door with bolt cutters.

I flick screens and watch as the M25 teams start to move. I can see that at least three of the gunmen are already down. I'm guessing dead. There are screams from every direction. Men, women and children dropping to the ground, trying to get cover. Mitford's teams are relentless, moving in, getting closer, taking down the enemy.

The terrorists are shooting, but randomly, in a panic.

Nusayabah stands stock still. She stares straight ahead. She moves to take off her veil, so her son can see her.

Her son is jumping up and down. 'Mama, mama, look.' He holds up the pink rabbit.

Nusayabah moves forward and raises her hand to the screen.

I watch her every move, see her face for the first time. She speaks in a soft voice, 'Hey, Omar. Hey.'

Millie, Mark and Neil are still beside me. We're clinging to each other. The Robsons are beside us, they've been told that they may be needed to appeal to their daughter again.

Millie says, 'Get Ella back. Get her out of the vest. The M25 is all over. Your people are dead. Come on, Clementine. Nusayabah. Stop this now. Stop it or you will never see Omar again. It's all over. Faiza's in Paddington Green. It's over. Do the right thing.'

Just then Omar, says. 'Mama, please come, please come. I want to play Rabbit Hop.'

'Wait there, my lovely boy. Wait there.'

Behind her someone is dragging Ella in.

I hear David White say, 'Tango Alpha Team. You are Green. I repeat. Green.'

The camera angle changes as the front officer moves into a long dark hallway. The view from her helmet giving a terrifyingly jerking motion. Four officers make their way into the house. Two others are in position at the back.

I jump as the shattering repeated rapid noise of a semi-automatic H & K G36 is met by the chaotic applause of an AK47. The camera jumps wildly and for several seconds it is impossible to see anything. As the noise abates for a second, the voice of Sara Martin, comes over the static. 'Armed police, drop your weapons.

Armed police, drop your weapons.'

The camera frame is absolutely still. Nusayabah is holding the detonator as Ella sits rigid. I hear a low moan from Neil.

Supernaturally calm, Sara Martin says, 'Put down the detonator. Move away and no one will be hurt. Don't do this. Drop the detonator. Drop it gently.'

Nusayabah leans across to Ella and pulls her closer. Looking at Sara Martin she says, equally calmly. 'I want to talk to Simon Thompson.'

Nusayabah turns from Sara Martin. She staggers slightly as she looks back at her son. She moves her hand to touch the screen. The child's face lights up. 'Mama.'

Seeing her opportunity, Sara Martin leans forward to take the switch. Everything moves with deathly slowness. In complete technicolour with astonishing clarity.

Sara's hand moves to the detonator. Clementine Robson stares at her son, her hands move back towards Ella. Sara Martin takes her chance and reaches out further.

Ella flinches but with no time to react. The screen goes black.

Tuesday 25th May 17.44

MILLIE

For a moment there is cathedral silence. We stare at the black screen. David White moves first, contacting his ATF50 back-up team on the ground.

'Bravo Lima Team, come in, come in.'

'Sir, Inspector Chalmers. Bravo Lima. We are on the scene at 19 Harman Road. A serious explosion has occurred, we are holding back protestors at either end of the street. Sir, damage is severe. Switching on head camera.'

He clears his throat, 'No sign of Tango Alpha, sir.'

The screen crackles and shows a fire still burning. Rubble across three or four houses.

Neil is weeping, his head in his hands. I move dreamlike to hold him. I have no words, no tears. I can't make sense of anything.

My ears are ringing from the blast.

Somewhere miles away at the back of the room I hear Mitford's voice.

'Sir, situation secured. Hostage-takers dead or in custody. Medical teams on the scene.'

Thompson, too, has his head in his hands. Norton is staring into space.

Alex Dalgleish responds, 'Thank you, Commander Mitford. Are you heading back?'

I switch focus. Neil is trying to call Ella, knowing it's futile but listening to her voice. Over and over. 'This is Gabriella Russell, please leave a message.'

'This is Gabriella Russell, please leave a message.'

I take it from him and hold his head in my hands. Amala moves beside us and we just hold on. Our hearts aching.

8 DAYS AFTER

Tuesday 2nd June

AMALA

They say a week is a long time in politics. It is for Thompson. The front pages of the newspapers are repetitive but no less horrific.

'8 dead in motorway horror'

'Har majiddoon strike terror in holidaymakers near Heathrow'

'8 dead and many injured in motorway carnage'

The shock and horror, the personal tragedies and the cries for retribution give way to pages and pages devoted to mistakes and mishaps. The fact that Thompson and Norton had been looking in the wrong direction for most of the time saturated every piece of news. There were calls to increase security levels again. Demands to up the pressure on immigration. To increase the PPCs. It was predictable. It was desperately sad.

By Wednesday the story was also out about Touchstone. It proved to be the final straw for Thompson. Once the links between Touchstone, Matthew Robson and Nusayabah had been publicly revealed there was no hope for him.

Kardax shares fell by almost 60%. The short selling and the links to Thompson's downfall had dredged up all the dirty deals. The economic ripples spread far and wide.

Thompson resigned. Norton was seen as damaged goods and the role of prime minister is currently being covered by Thompson's deputy until such time as a leadership election can take place.

Matthew Robson also resigned. His long list of affairs published as part of the story.

ATF50, MI5 and GCHQ were still ploughing through the events of the day. Millie had been right. Clementine Robson had been a romantic. A romantic and a planner. She had planned not one but two diversions and had commanded an all-female mujahedeen. All four of the guards with her and all eighteen of the terrorists at the M25 had been women. White British women all prepared to die.

All dead.

Faiza Siddiqui was at Paddington Green. Giving nothing up.

Aafa had been questioned for several days but no one believed he had been involved. He really had switched to teaching. The Education and Light Programme was a charity looking to build understanding of Islam and its true meaning in schools and colleges. His picture had been photoshopped, he had never attended a rally with Abdul Izz al-Din. He was devastated by the part he had played in that terrible day.

Eight people died on the M25 that day. That didn't include the eight terrorists. Eight families who would never be the same again. Eight families who would be haunted forever by that day. 25th May 2023 seared into our hearts, just as Nusayabah planned.

It was a new step in a long war.

9 DAYS AFTER

Wednesday 3rd June 08.30

MILLIE

I hug Grace close. We are in bed watching the Big Pink Friendly Rabbit, Grace is enthralled. I nuzzle her corkscrew curls and breathe her in. I inhale the smell of tea tree and pear in her hair mixed with toast and jam. My heart is pumping. It feels scalded I love her so much. She wriggles slightly to get a better view of the TV. I hum the theme tune, Rabbit Hop, closing my eyes as I remember the last time I had done that.

'Hey, said daddy bear who's been sleeping in my bed?'

Grace looks up to see Mark carrying two steaming cups of coffee. With a pout she says. 'Mummy and me are watching the Big Pink Friendly Rabbit so no talking.'

'Ok, not a peep, promise,' he says, climbing in beside us and handing the coffee to me.

He looks over Grace's head and mouths, 'You, ok?'

We had talked and talked and agreed some compromises. Agreed to give things another go. Not just for Grace. Not just for the baby. But for us. I put the twelve-week scan picture I had been gazing at, back in the drawer.

I sigh, close my eyes and nod.

Mark says, 'We probably better get going in the next half hour. We don't want to be late.'

I nod again. Not trusting myself to speak.

I heave myself out of bed. Mark holds me for a second. He whispers in my ear, 'Come on, we're a team. Thick and thin.'

Wednesday 3rd June 11.45

MILLIE

Neil looks up from the pulpit. He stares out at the row upon row of friends and family. The bottom has fallen out of his world. I hold my belly. I feel my baby. A tiny flutter. I know she is a girl. I know her name. Ella.

He has aged almost beyond recognition. He speaks from a heart that is crushed. 'I met Ella at an Amala party. It started as a normal day. And became the most extraordinary day. She dropped her wine all over my shoes.' He smiles at the memory. 'She really is the clumsiest person I know.' His voice chokes, stumbling on 'is', she couldn't yet be a 'was'. 'I fell in love with her in that second. I loved her with every fibre of my being. I still do and I always will. She made me a better man. She made me believe the world could be joyous and light and happy.

'Ella, Gabriella. It means warrior and she was a warrior. A warrior for the underdog, the broken and the poor. She believed in tolerance but not silence. She believed in truth but not the kind that hides. Real truth that makes people think. That makes people believe the world is only a good place when we make it so. When we fight intolerance. When we speak up. And she spoke up. She used her words to fight injustice. She was a warrior but the good kind, the loyal kind. She was proud to be a writer.' He looks up, nodding to Amala and me, 'But more than that she was proud to be a friend, she was never happier than when she was with her Nofas.

'Ella taught me many things. Mostly she taught me how to love. She taught me that the love of one person for another can overcome almost anything. She also taught me that when you can find no words to express the greatest emotions, sometimes they are found in other people's words. It was Ella who told me about Abelard and Heloise, she said they were two of the most famous lovers in history. We weren't the most famous, but for me we were the truest. My heart is broken. I refuse to be angry at the people who took her from me. I refuse, for that would be to sully her memory. Instead, I will remember the love we had.'

His voice shaking, he looks at the paper in his hand and begins to read. 'In a letter to Abelard, Heloise wrote: "You know, beloved, as the whole world knows, how much I have lost in you, how at one wretched stroke of fortune that supreme act of flagrant treachery robbed me of my very self in robbing me of you; and how my sorrow for my loss is nothing compared with what I feel for the manner in which I lost you."'

His voice breaks and he looks out at the congregation. A group of people devastated and united in grief, the very personal tragedy of a very public murder.

'She is my life. I cannot begin to think of any life without her. Ella, you are everything to me. I will miss you more than I can ever say.'

As he sits, I rise. The tightness in my chest like a vice. I have no idea how I will get through this. Amala is weeping. Willing me on but I am lost. Bereft. I am filled with an unbearable sadness and an uncontrollable rage. I want revenge for Ella. Most of all I want her back. I want to be the three Nofas, telling jokes, laughing and crying into old age.

I want her back. My sister. My Ella.

Acknowledgements

A thank you to so many people.

I have so many great friends and family to thank for early reading, sound advice, and the spur to keep going. A massive thank you to my big brother, Dave, (and the 'bloody brilliant') to my inspirational and amazing sister in law, Jenny, (may never be enough to get us the place in Barbados but enough for a cocktail or two,) Venetia and Brian (for walks, laughs, traybakes and advice on when it's only a Scottish word not a 'real' word) to Caroline, Hilary and Jen (for keeping the show on the road and being truly great friends), to Ingrid (for cake, hugs and medical advice …and a surprisingly comprehensive knowledge on the impact of torture) and the great friends and family who read it, made it better and kept me going; Coletta, Karen, Mike, Stephen, Nick and Josh. To Michael and Gillian my Castlerock neighbours for the craic and feeding me with true Northern Irish hospitality.

To those who helped me navigate the immense and puzzling world of publishing, Oli, Liz and Joe, Julia and David G. Huge thanks to Katherine and Emmanuel for introducing me to Matthew at Urbane. The straightest and most generous of publishers. Lyndsay and Aine for kindness, support and access to their amazing contacts. To Jo who talked me through life as an academic as well as how it feels to live in Afghanistan under the Taliban, one mesmerising night as we watched the lights of the Gaza strip. To Nik for his amazing way for words on the tagline!

A thank you to those people who really helped me and for obvious reasons cannot be mentioned. You know who you are and help keep us safe in our beds with courage, dedication and, frankly, a plain weird sense of humour.

To my whole family thank you and to so many people who have become great friends along the way.

Massive thanks to Gillian, who doesn't think she is a 'real' agent. You're not! You are so much better than that. And Marian, what can I say? Thank you for getting in the arena with me for four long years. Your insight, passion and huge heart are beyond words. You are 'divine' and I thank you from the bottom of my heart.

A special thanks to my parents, Jean and Deric for always being there. I could ask for no more.

And to the squad, Kathryn and Martha. Kind, smart, generous and really bloody funny! You are the most wonderful part of my life and I love you both utterly, completely and beyond measure.

Last but not least, for David, who is, and always will be, the best thing that ever happened to me.

Bibliography

Books used:

- Abu -Lughood, Lila, Do Muslim Women Need Saving? (USA, Harvard University Press,2015)
- Aslan, Reza, No God But God: The Origins, Evolution and Future of Islam, London, (PenguinRandom House, 2011)
- Curtis, Mark, Secret Affairs: Britain's Collusion with Radical Islam, (London, Serpent's Tail, 2012)
- Hirsi Ali, Ayaan, Heretic; Why Islam Needs Reformation Now,(USA, Harper Collins, 2015)
- Hume, Mick, Trigger Warning: Is the Fear of Being Offensive Killing Free Speech, London, William Collins, 2015)
- Holland, Tom, In the Shadow of the Sword: The Battle for Global Empire and the End of the Ancient World (London, Abacus, 2012)
- Khan, Sara with Tony McMahon, The Battle for British Islam: Reclaiming Muslim Identity from Extremism,(London, Saqi Books, 2016)
- Ledwidge, Frank, Investment in Blood: The True Cost of Britain's Afghan War, USA, Yale University Press, 2014)
- Scahill, Jeremy, Dirty Wars: The World is a Battlefield, (London, Sepent's Tail, 2013)
- Wiktorowicz, Quintan, Radical Islam Rising: Muslim Extremism in the West, (USA, Rowman and Littlefield Publishers, 2005)

K.H. Irvine grew up in Scotland and now lives near London.

The book was her 50th birthday gift to herself, believing you are never too old to try something new.

Her work has taken her to board rooms, universities and governments all over the world and has included up close and personal access to special forces.

A Killing Sin is her first book. K.H.Irvine is currently writing her second novel, which follows on a few years later as Britain moves to civil unrest with the rise of the far right as the personal and political become intertwined.